In THE BY-PASS CONTROL Tiger Mann is faced with one of his most frightening challenges: to avert the imminent destruction of the defence system of the United States.

An engineer has disappeared, taking with him the secret of the device he created: a method to by-pass the pushbuttons which activate America's most deadly missiles – and render the regular system inoperative.

The Communists want more than anything else to discover the workings of the by-pass control, and Tiger is equally determined to see that they don't. But to prevent them, Tiger has to discover the missing man first – and that's a job in itself. . . .

Also by Mickey Spillane

VENGEANCE IS MINE
MY GUN IS QUICK
THE BIG KILL
ONE LONELY NIGHT
THE SNAKE
KISS ME, DEADLY
THE GIRL HUNTERS
I, THE JURY
THE LONG WAIT
KILLER MINE
THE FLIER
ME, HOOD!
RETURN OF THE HOOD
DAY OF THE GUNS
BLOODY SUNRISE
THE DEATH DEALERS
THE TWISTED THING

and published by Corgi Books

MICKEY SPILLANE

THE BY-PASS CONTROL

CORGI BOOKS
A DIVISION OF TRANSWORLD PUBLISHERS

THE BY-PASS CONTROL

A CORGI BOOK

Originally published in Great Britain
by Arthur Barker Ltd.

PRINTING HISTORY
Arthur Barker Edition published 1967
Corgi Edition published 1968

This book is set in Baskerville.

Corgi Books are published by Transworld Publishers Ltd.,
Bashley Road, London, N.W.10

Printed Web Offset in England
by Petty and Sons Limited, Leeds

To Vernie Jones,
the Man with the Badge

THE BY-PASS CONTROL

CHAPTER ONE

THE GUY WAS as good as dead and knew it. Crouched there on the floor he looked like a shapeless bundle and only a bloodied face with still-hard bright eyes marked him as a man. His breath came in short, sobbing gasps and he tried to keep his guts in with both hands pressed to his stomach. The knife he had used on me was still within reach in front of him, but he wasn't thinking of making a try for it. All he could hope for was that I would bleed to death before he would, yet he knew that wouldn't happen.

And I was on my feet with the cocked .45 in my fist grinning down at him.

I let my eyes leave his for an instant and drift to the partially closed door behind him where there were three dead men strapped to tables in a soundproofed room whose deaths had been horrible things because they wouldn't talk easily and when they did, died anyway for the pleasure of a butcher.

Two were from a Washington agency. One was my project partner.

Oh, they had talked all right. Vito Salvi knew his work well. Besides a natural aptitude, he had been well trained in Moscow and provided with all the modern luxuries chemical and electronic development could offer torture-induced conversation and he had used them to the ultimate end.

But when it comes his turn to face the big, black thing that lies beyond life, when the butcher is suddenly caught in his own grinder, the maggots show in his eyes and he gives off a livid smell as they crawl out his skin in one last attempt to escape an absolute certainty.

"You've had it, buddy," I said.

He choked a little and blinked away the blood that was streaming into his eyes from the massive slash across his forehead. "No. No . . . it is your own law. . . ."

I never stopped grinning and knew what I must look like to him. "I don't choose to recognize it."

"You will be . . ."

"Prosecuted?" My grin went wider and I leveled the rod, enjoying the moment. "Somebody screwed up your thinking, Vito. An inquiry, that's all. Three men killed by an enemy agent who has a cash reward on his head from two countries . . . and I'm just a bystander who happened to bust up the party and caught a little hell of my own. These things don't get to court and you damn well know it. You found out what two of those men knew and it won't do you a bit of good and even though the Washington boys hate my guts I'll walk out with clean hands for being an enterprising and courageous citizen when they hear the story. Your headquarters won't even know you're gone until time gets the message across. Then you simply get checked off the rolls."

"They said . . ."

"I know. They spilled. You got the works from them and you know it, only you took too long killing them to transmit the information and now it's too late."

He still tried. They all try. They have to. "You could . . . arrest me," he said.

"Uh-uh. It's better this way. Then there's no trouble. It's all over and done with. The slate is clean, another Red is out of the way and our Kremlin counterparts are as ignorant as before. We'll be a little more careful the next time too."

I had the .45 centered right in the middle of his forehead.

Vito Salvi, who was credited with fourteen confirmed kills of our people, didn't even seem to notice it. The recesses of his mind had dredged up a last possible out and his eyes were fiery marbles tainted with cunning as he said, "I could give you valuable . . . knowledge. A doctor . . . put me in the hands of your police. I can tell them many things. My purpose here was . . . twofold. It was not only to extract from those two men. . . . There was another reason . . . more urgent. Your police would want to know. . . ."

"So talk. Vito, I'll judge its importance."

The last hope was there, glowing strongly in the agonized contortions of his face. He talked for two minutes and what he said was like another blade, still wet from my own blood, going into my flesh again.

He talked and when he said all there was to be said, I shot him flat between the eyes that slammed his body over in a full roll against the wall where he jerked once before he was still.

Then I picked up the phone and dialed the downtown number of the New York bureau of I.A.T.S. and told them where I was.

They interrogated me on the scene—two quietly outraged men who headed the newest and tightest security branch of all the Washington agencies and two hard-looking field men who were curiously expressionless until I described the final killing of Vito Salvi without mentioning his last statement. Only then did they register the slightest sign of satisfaction, knowing damn well that the one who had killed their associates hadn't died easily. They knew my reputation and it was too big and too real to let someone like Salvi take the big fall the quick way.

They let me finish, then Hal Randolph said, "Typical Tiger Mann trademark."

I shrugged. "How would you like me to have done it?"

He looked at me closely, following the pattern the way I knew he would, then walked over to the body by the wall and stared at it a few seconds. "Let's start from the beginning, Mann. Like from where you came into this."

The others were watching me now and the two field men had black notebooks in their hands. When I spoke they took everything down verbatim in shorthand. "Sure," I said. "The other dead guy is Doug Hamilton, one of ours. He runs a legitimate private investigation agency out of New York here. . . ."

"Legitimate?"

"You can check it fast enough," I told him. "Martin Grady had him on retainer for three years doing routine security work for Belt-Aire Electronics, a company he owns. Under his government contracts it was required, so . . ."

"We're familiar with Belt-Aire. Where do you come in, Tiger?"

"A week ago Hamilton disappeared. I was on hand, so I got orders to look into it." I nodded toward the room on the side. "I tracked him here."

"How?"

"His car was missing. I reported it to the police and they recovered it. Inside was a notebook that had this address listed, among others. It was as simple as that."

"What others?"

"Simple business addresses. I checked them all out."

"I see," Randolph finally mused. "So you came here and walked into—" he waved his hand around the room—"this. Just like that."

"Not quite. I don't stick my head into holes. Hamilton could have been involved in anything and I'm too old a pro in this business to take chances. I cased the place from all sides and came down from the roof."

"Then how did you know what apartment to hit?"

"Somebody spent a lot of time and trouble sealing up one window on the side with brick. They weren't very neat and left some pieces of material used in soundproofing rooms in the courtyard outside. This place is totally unoccupied like the ones beside it and no bum or scrounger holing up in here is throwing money into renovations like that."

Both the young guys looked up from their notebooks with a small touch of respect in their faces. One said, "You could have called the police."

"I didn't think there was that much time. There weren't more than a half dozen lights showing along the entire block and it was doubtful any of those places had phones."

"Wasn't it foolish coming in alone?"

I grinned at him then and my mouth hurt from where the cut opened in the corner. "I wasn't alone," I told him and pointed to the .45 where they had laid it on the table under a handkerchief.

Hal Randolph turned abruptly, his hands clasped behind his back. He was a big guy, heavy-set, with a florid face that never seemed to lose its mad. He didn't like me and his pet hate was Martin Grady, but now he was caught in the trap his own bureaucratic secrecy demanded of him. "You recognized Vito Salvi, then, didn't you?"

I nodded and leaned back in the chair, trying to wipe the taste of blood out of my mouth. "We had met before," I said, not committing myself any further.

"You knew who he was," he insisted.

"Sure. So do you. That's why I killed him. And don't ask why I didn't hold him. I was lucky as it was. I had just picked the lock and got into this room when he came out of the other and if you take a good look at that door you'd see it wasn't going to be forced easily. Inside there was another exit he could have gotten through if he knew I was here. That bastard knew all the tricks of infighting with knives and guns. . . ."

"Except one," the field man said.

"What?"

"You nailed him," he told me.

Randolph's smile was tight around the edges. "I'm afraid you don't know our friend very well, Courtney. This is Tiger Mann and when you see his package in the department files it will surprise you. Moscow has him on their 'A' list, which makes him a dead boy almost any time at all. He was with the O.S.S. during the war and likes to play spy so much he couldn't leave well enough alone, so now with the backing of millionaire industrialists who don't seem to trust their government's authorized agencies to do a satisfactory job, he gets entangled in everything from espionage to two-bit street brawls for the sake of a buck. I don't know what he calls himself, but he's a professional killer with enough power behind him to clean his hands for him but someday he's going to fall and when he does it will be heard on two continents."

"Three," I said. "And don't hold your breath waiting for it to happen." I pushed myself out of the chair and got to my feet, the pain in my side giving me hell. "You're talking too much, Randolph. I'll be down in the morning to give you a detailed statement."

"Where do you think you're going?"

I found my hat and picked up my gun. "To see a doctor," I said. "One who won't report bullet wounds or knife slashes. Any objections?"

There was just a long moment of silence and Randolph shook his head. He knew I'd be in. I wanted some questions answered too. I got out, went down to the street and walked two blocks before a cab came by. I gave him the number of Rondine's apartment and settled back against the cushions.

No matter how often I'd see her, this woman I loved so much, she was always a startling surprise, not because of the classic British beauty that radiated from the loveliness of a face framed by shoulder-length auburn hair or a contoured body so magnificent as to be almost unbelievable, but simply because *she was there*.

For twenty years she had been dead to me. Twenty years ago she had tried to kill me and had, in turn, died herself. Yet here she was. Rondine? No, it's not really so confusing at all. The first Rondine was her oldest sister who had gone to the Nazis and later to the Soviets. To the Caine family she had never even been born now, and long forgotten except when the memory was dredged up. With me the memory never had died at all. For twenty years I had wanted to kill her and almost did when I found her again. But it wasn't her at all. It was the youngest sister who had inherited the same peculiar combination of genes and chromosomes to grow into the physical identity of the one forgotten.

To me, though, she was still Rondine. The cover name she had used could never be forgotten, only now it was Edith who used it because I had endowed it in the beginning and this one wore it with all the meaning it was intended to have.

She opened the door, stood there a few seconds and when I said, "Hello, Rondine," she smiled and held out her hand, throwing the door wide.

Before I walked in she realized something had happened and the smile faded to sudden concern. "Again, Tiger?"

I knew my grin seemed foolish, but it was all I could manage. "Like the ball took a bad hop, kid."

She tried to make sense out of the slang, got it, and the soft curve of her mouth went grim. "Bad?" With a hand under mine she steered me into the spacious living room and half pushed me into the corner of a sofa.

"I'll live. You remember Dr. Kirkland?"

"The same one?"

I nodded. "Get him over."

Without asking more questions she thumbed through the phone book, found a number and dialed it. The conversation was brief, then she hung up and went to the bar, mixing a drink with the unusual efficiency of women handling bottles at three A.M. When she handed me the glass I took a long pull of the whiskey and ginger, then leaned my head back and closed my eyes.

"Can I do anything?"

"No first aid, kid. Kirkland will be here fast enough and I've had too many of these things in me to know I'm okay until he comes."

"Hurt to talk?"

"No."

"Want to tell me what happened?"

I looked up at her face and saw the serious set to it. There was more in her expression than concern for me. We didn't have to play games with each other any more at all. She wasn't the simple U.N. translator she seemed to be, but a well trained operative with a good cover assigned to work under her embassy's orders. She knew my business too, more than she had a right to know, but there are times when you can't hide things and have to trust to integrity and understanding and the knowledge that other people can have the same ideals as your own.

I said, "Call Charlie Corbinet and get him here too."

There was a slight narrowing of her eyes and she knew, all

right. This one wasn't just a street brawl or an accident. It was in the international realm again and it was far from over. Again, without a word, she went to the phone and did as I told her, then picked up my drink and built a new one. When she handed it to me there were tears showing on her cheeks and her lips brushed the back of my hand.

"Why?" she asked.

"Because I have to," I told her.

Dr. Kirkland was painlessly adept at his profession. The bullet had gone through two thicknesses of tough leather of the gun belt, its force slackened, then had sliced sideways into the flesh along my ribs and come to a halt in a bluish welt just under the skin. Both cuts from the knife were more like surgical incisions, the deliberate thrusts having been lost when I twisted out of their way. He finished, gave me a small bottle of capsules to take if things got rough, told me to stop by at the proper intervals and didn't ask for payment. Martin Grady would foot the bill.

Rondine let me finish dressing before she came out of the bedroom, shaking her head like I was a little kid who didn't know any better. "You don't suppose you're leaving here tonight," she said.

"Some things won't wait, doll."

"Nothing is that important."

"No?"

"Tiger . . ."

I reached my hand out and her fingers closed around mine. I said, "All the other things I've done . . . or you've been in on . . . are nothing like this one. If it checks out all of us can be in trouble." I looked at my watch. Charlie Corbinet was due any second now. "Make like a good secretary and get me one more call in." I gave her the number and felt the sudden shock run through her hand in a spasm of tension. She had heard me call that number before and knew its implications. Only for a second did she stand there, then reached for the phone. When she dialed it she handed me the instrument silently and started to walk out of the room. "Stay," I told her.

"You sure you want me to?"

"I've seen you kill too," I reminded her. "This one will take more than me alone." She nodded, then moved to an armchair and sat down.

On the third ring the phone was picked up, but as was usual, no voice answered. I gave the signal words and the other person said, "Go ahead, Tiger."

Martin Grady was as casual as if he were discussing a simple stock merger, knowing I would never make this call unless it was a total emergency.

"Who's in this area?" I asked.

"Don Lavois and Tony Williams."

"Scrub Williams and send Don in."

"Can you talk?"

"Ears only. We're sitting on a big one. Take any of our top men out of projects you can shelve for the time being and have them on alert. Have them stand by at the usual place until I make contact. We'll need one liaison man and a fast plane handy. You'll be directly involved in this and will have to be ready to move fast."

"The F-51 Mustang will be in from Sarasota tonight then. It will land at Newark." There was a slight edge to his voice now, anticipation rather than nervousness. "You all right?"

"I'll live."

"Serious?"

"Doc Kirkland will send the bill and the details. Meanwhile scratch Vito Salvi. He's had it."

Grady hesitated, his voice cautious. "You *sure*?"

"Positive ID."

"This will get you very special attention in certain quarters, Tiger. They won't like their best trigger man being rubbed out."

"What choice have they got?"

"But *you* have a choice," he said.

"Like a nice vacation in the Andes or that sleepy village in Baja California?"

"I'm thinking along those lines. We can't afford to lose you."

"You can't afford to hold me off this one either. I'm the one

Vito talked to before I killed him and a vacation will get you nothing but silence, so now the choice is back to you."

I could almost hear the silent evaluation he was giving my statement, then he said, "You're asking for it. Take it."

"I got it."

"Need anything?"

"So far, no. Be ready for anything though. This is bigger than anything we ever touched."

"I'll wait for the report. Tonight?"

"As soon as the plane gets in. Others will have to know about it too."

"Use your own discretion. Will they cooperate?"

"They'll have to," I told him and grinned a little. They had no choice either. I hung up, waited until Rondine took the phone away and sipped at the last of my drink. Just as I finished it the doorbell rang, two short, impatient notes on the buzzer.

Charlie Corbinet was our old C.O. in the O.S.S. He was still the raunchy, hard-bitten type he had been when he was our colonel and twenty years hadn't softened him any. Ostensibly, he headed up a small but important industry, but I.A.T.S. had recruited him back into their new organization for the simple reason that they needed his type, his brains and his foresight.

A few of his superiors knew about his connection with me and hated his guts for it but they couldn't do without his guts either and they let our association alone.

Now he stood there in the middle of the room, tall and rangy, the hard planes of his face still an indication of his true profession, his eyes scrutinizing me while his mouth twisted into a wry smile, knowing the yeast had started bubbling in the batter again.

I said, "Hi, Colonel."

"Someday you'll remember they made me a General on my retirement."

"Habit. Sorry." I smiled back at him. "What kind of pay you pulling?"

"I do all right."

"A hundred says I make five times as much."

"You're just greedy."

"Damn right. I work for it too. It isn't enough."

"Ever think one of the right agencies might take you on in spite of your record?"

"Screw them. They don't pay enough. This way I do the same work and make a lot more bucks. I like compensation for the chances I take."

"There's a chance you can wind up in the pokey, too."

"Not as long as I know where the bodies are buried . . . and Martin Grady can bail me out."

Rondine handed Charlie Corbinet a drink, reserving a small one for herself. "Don't bother arguing with him," she said quietly.

Charlie nodded. "I coudn't be bothered." He took a quick taste of his drink, nodded with satisfaction and looked at me again. "I had a phoned report on the Vito Salvi fracas. You sure can stir things up."

"Randolph?"

"Yes. They had been after him for two years."

"When was their last contact?"

"Eighteen months ago."

"Then they're lucky. They had their work done for them." I let it go through his mind, then added, "He had two of your men in that back room. How he nailed them I won't worry about, but what was he after?"

"Classified, Tiger."

I shrugged, making a real production out of it. "It doesn't matter. Whatever they told him won't go any further. It's over with."

"Is it?"

He could see the edges of my teeth in the grin. "Not quite. You see, we had a little talk too . . . before I killed him."

"That's what I thought." Charlie turned, walked to a chair and sat down with a sigh of relief. "Want to come out with it?"

"Sure, Charlie. Tell me why Salvi wanted those men and I'll tell you what he told me. Maybe."

"One of your men was dead too."

"Nobody that counted."

"He was in Martin Grady's employ."

I nodded. "In a minor capacity by government directive. Grady owns pieces of many essential industries that come under the identical setup.

Slowly, Charlie Corbinet turned the glass around in his hand, studied it before he took a drink, then decided. "You really want me to get my head chopped off," he said.

"Not really. I'd just like to see you draw a full General's pay with bonus for the work you do . . . and some real authority to back you up instead of handing it to guys like Randolph."

"Tell me, Tiger . . . why don't you like the way Washington runs things?"

"Because I don't like to be classified with the patsies. I don't like the stupidity that went behind the Bay of Pigs invasion . . . or the Panama crap . . . or the way they can knock us off in Viet Nam while we sit on our thumbs and get laughed at by the real pigs on the other side of the Berlin Wall. Someday they're going to find out a few people in this country got the message a long time ago and are doing something about it—using their time, money and talent to protect what they have. Funny, but it's fun too. It's a real pleasure to shove it up and break it off in Moscow's tail. We're not any better than the Washington boys. We just have more latitude to operate in and can buy what they can't, and have that nice, juicy knowledge that we can't be pushed too far because whatever we do, we're protected, and in that respect we can use the Soviet's own cute techniques to slam back at them."

"I've heard that speech before."

"And I never get tired of giving it, buddy."

"So what did Vito Salvi tell you?"

"Let's start from the beginning. You first," I said.

As usual, he waited, digesting his thoughts, but as usual, he came across. He had to and I knew it so I just sat there until he was ready. "Tiger . . . those two men . . ."

"Go on."

"One came from Poland. He brought the story in."

"What story?"

"There was a man named Louis Agrounsky, an engineer."

He looked at me carefully, but I shook my head. "Never heard of him."

"Very few ever did. He was an electronics engineer employed on our ICBM projects. In fact, the chief technician, in charge of the project. Somehow or other he has disappeared."

"When?"

"About a year ago."

"What makes him important?"

"Only one thing."

I waited. Charlie Corbinet was watching me carefully, the drink in his hand forgotten.

"What?"

"The simple fact that Moscow's top agent was assigned to locate him."

"So?"

"Those two men were assigned to find him too, just to uncover why the Soviets wanted him so badly. They were narrowing down the search when they disappeared and you showed up in time to really scramble things."

Rondine came up with another drink and shook one of the capsules from the bottle and handed them both to me silently. I didn't really notice it, but my side was hurting like hell.

"Now you tell me," Charlie said and I knew he had spilled all he knew.

When I swallowed the capsule and washed it down with the Four Roses and ginger ale I said, "Vito Salvi was ready to do anything to stay alive. He tried to make a deal."

"Oh?"

"I'll give you something to feed on, Charlie. I want you to go home and think on it hard and you'll know what I have to do. There can't be any cross purposes or interference because on this one we'll need everybody we can get our hands on and have to pull out all the stops."

"I'm waiting, Tiger."

"You know how the hot line works?"

Charlie Corbinet nodded, waiting.

"You know about the other one?"

"Suppose you detail it for me," he said.

"Sure." I leaned back and closed my eyes, feeling the capsule beginning to take hold. "Moscow has one like it too. All over the country we have ICBM's buried and waiting to fly off to pre-designated enemy targets. All we need is a blip on a radar screen or early warning to alert the right person who is the only one who can push the button and start the retaliation in motion. Of course, we'll all be dead, but revenge will be sweet and before the enemy birds can hit, our own will be on the way."

He didn't argue, he only murmured, "True," and listened.

"All the birds are tied into an electronic system activated by one push of a single button after the emergencies and fail-safes are off. When they're gone they're gone and an enemy is totally washed out."

"But so are we by then."

"One man installed the system, or was responsible for it, at least. Let's take a premise now. Supposing the one man who installed the system wasn't as clean as you thought he was. Supposing that somewhere along the line his thinking got screwed up and he didn't want to see all that power and control go into the hands of someone who in his opinion shouldn't have that control. Supposing that one man, to satisfy his own desires and warped judgment, installed a system that could by-pass the original pushbutton device and could activate the ICBM system any time he chose to."

The room was so still you could hear the breathing from all three of us. "A by-pass control," Charlie said quietly. "Louis Agrounsky?"

"That's your boy."

"If he touches it the Reds will detect the ICBM's in flight and let their own birds go. Everybody's had it."

"That's not the worst part," I told him. I opened my eyes and saw his hands tighten on his glass until the knuckles showed white. "In his circuits he installed a device that can negate our own original system. If the Reds fire first with our system out then we have no comeback at all. And there isn't time to run down the by-pass control."

"That leaves them sitting on all the eggs. If they find the by-pass first they can deactivate us in a second and leave them calling all the shots in a hurry . . . or else."

"Or else," I repeated sleepily.

I heard him come out of the chair and knew he was standing close to me now. He said, "Do you know where Louis Agrounsky is?"

After a long while I squeezed my eyes open just a little. Even the dim yellow light from the lamp hurt them. "No."

Charlie's soft, "Damn!" was like an explosion.

I knew I was grinning and couldn't help it. I knew that if I opened my eyes both he and Rondine would be standing there in stunned silence, realizing the wild import of what they had just been told, knowing how close we all stood to the edge of sudden annihilation that would be triggered the minute *they* knew they had the edge.

Slowly, I pulled myself back from the limbo the capsule was sending me into and said, "But I think I know how I can find him."

CHAPTER TWO

THE SHADE WAS drawn, but it was a bright yellow patch in the room with the sun beating down on it from a high angle and I knew I had been sleeping a long time. I looked at my wrist, but the watch was gone and the rest of me was naked under a single sheet in Rondine's bed. I glanced around quickly, saw the watch on the nightstand, stopped at five forty-five because it hadn't been wound. I picked up the extension phone, dialed the time-check number and found out that it was almost four-thirty in the afternoon, then hung up and started to push the covers off me.

Rondine came in then, having heard the sound of my dialing. "Why didn't you get me up, kid?" My voice sounded hard and cracked.

"Whatever the doctor gave you was supposed to keep you that way."

"Who put me to bed?"

She gave me a funny smile.

"You could have left my shorts on," I said.

"That wouldn't have been any fun." She sat on the edge of the bed looking at me. "You moan even when you're unconscious."

"Oh, shut up." I grinned at her. "You wouldn't dare."

"No? Why not?"

"You're too prim and proper."

"But you've trained me well."

I didn't know whether to believe her or not. "Get my clothes," I finally said.

"No. I checked with the doctor and you're to stay in bed."

"Who else told you that too? Charlie? Hal Randolph?"

Her eyes gave me the answer fast enough and she nodded. "They went through my own superiors. I guess they know what you'd want to do so they put the pressure on me. I had to let you stay there. Tiger . . . it was for the best."

"Damn it, they were thinking of themselves."

"But I was thinking of you." She wasn't trying to be cagey about it.

"One day, when we're married, you'll get your orders directly from me. Nobody will supersede me and if they try they get clipped, and if you listen, you get your tail burned."

"When will that be?" she probed.

"I'll tell you when."

"You seem to like long engagements, Tiger." She wasn't smiling now.

I said, "When it's over. When we can walk and breathe without smelling death all the time or knowing the world is sitting on the lip of disaster. I don't want you a widow before you're married."

"How do you know what *I* want, darling?"

"Oh sure, you'll take me now because you're a broad and all broads want it now regardless of the consequences, but I'm not letting you stick your neck out in the middle of a mess like this. Crazy broad."

"I despise that word."

"You do? Well wear it well, baby. It's a sign that you're more than a woman. You're a doll with everything going for her from a beautiful face to a wild body with a mind to match and I love you like hell. You have capabilities only I can appreciate and I want them all."

"So I'm a broad," she said, losing the British accent momentarily and dropping into pure Brooklynese.

"Damn, where'd you pick that up?"

"From you." She walked to the closet, took my clothes out and laid them down beside me, the gun to one side. "Now get dressed. Want me to watch?"

I gave her a small push. "Get out of here. Some things I can do by myself."

"But in some things you need help, right?"

I gave her a nasty grin. "Right. Now scram."

With a slow unwinding motion she eased off the bed, stood there looking at me, then started for the door. Her hesitation was deliberate and she didn't mind me knowing it. She turned around slowly, her hand on the knob, and asked, "Do you really know where he is?"

"Who?"

"Louis Agrounsky?"

I had my pants on and the holster hooked up, then I shoved the .45 into the speed rig before I even reached for my shirt. "No, but like I said, I think I know how to find him."

"Can I help?"

"Maybe, but not at this point."

"The other agencies . . . ?" she started hopefully.

"Screw them, I told you. Later I'll tell you why."

"Can you tell me where you're going now?"

"Sure. Downtown to the New York offices of I.A.T.S. and tender Hal Randolph and Company a report, after which they'll either put up or shut up."

"Do you always have to be like this?"

I paused in the middle of tucking my shirttail in. "You want me any other way?"

"Sometimes I think so."

"Then screw you too, baby."

Her face went flat, the pain of my words knocking the expression from it. "You didn't have to say that."

"No? Then keep out of my business. Otherwise you stop being a broad and become a dame. I'll do what I want to do and sometimes what I have to do. One thing I won't do is succumb to sentimentality or the wishful thinking of a woman. When I'm working, stay off my back. You know my business so don't try to steer me clear. The woman isn't born and her mother's already

dead who can do that trick. I'll run things my own way and if you
don't give me credit for being an old soldier type with twenty
years over your fair head, then regroup your forces, kid, and find
another guy who will bow and scrape and do it when you tell
him to go potty. Clear, doll?"

Rondine studied me a moment, smiled, and her shoulders
moved in a gesture of resignation. But her eyes were hard. In her
own way she was a pro too—a young pro, but she had kills behind her and they had to start somewhere. "Clear, Tiger." She
turned the knob, opened the door and glanced over her shoulder.
"Still love me?"

"Stick around and you'll find out the hard way."

"You and your play on words," she said.

Hal Randolph had arranged the inquisition very neatly. I had
gone this route too many times before with him to try intimida-
tion. Now the props were staged to impress me. The head men
from three agencies were there, faces I knew well, a pair of
immaculately groomed court-reporter types perched behind their
machines ready to note every word spoken so that they could be
analyzed in detail later, and Randolph at the head of the conference table forcing an amiable smile designed to put me at ease. I
caught Charlie Corbinet's eyes from his corner position at the far
end, the half-smile in them and winked in his direction.

I took the only empty chair at the table, pulled it out and sat
down crookedly, feeling the bite in my side again. "Well, gentlemen?" I said.

Both stenographers took it down immediately.

Randolph cleared his throat and nodded absently before he
gave me a second glance, and this time the almost amiable expression was gone. "I'll come directly to the point. Mr. Corbinet
has repeated your conversation to us. In view of the recent . . .
situation, we would like to hear it firsthand."

"Sure," I told him. "In detail?"

"From the beginning."

It didn't take more than three minutes to lay it out. In three
minutes something heavy seemed to hang over the room like a

death shroud and the faces of the assembly were drawn tight. The stenographers had taken it down verbatim and were the only ones who didn't seem to make much out of it. Maybe they had done it too often or heard too much and the lines were just another paragraph in the book of the fall of mankind.

When I finished Randolph sat there a moment, his breathing audible in the silence, then: "There was one thing you left out, Tiger."

"Oh?"

"You indicated to Mr Corbinet that you knew how to locate Louis Agrounsky."

"Not quite, Randolph," I said.

"What did you say then?"

"I said I *thought* I knew how to find him."

"Perhaps you'd better be more explicit."

"Not just yet buddy." I twisted around in the chair and leaned back, grinning at him a little. "Like you told me some time ago, I'm walking a thin little line and one slip and over I go. If you can give me a push you'll even help a little and the end results would be pleasing to a lot of people here and there. You'd like to see Martin Grady fall along with the rest of us and if that ever happens the political stock of a lot of boobs would soar. Right?"

I had all the eyes on me now and Randolph didn't say a word. "Let me lay it on the line, gentlemen. My neck's out as far as yours and probably a lot further. We're in this together whether you like it or not and until this picture is cleared up we'd better start sleeping in the same bed or take the chance of being splashed all over what's left of the U.S.A."

The few coughs and quick looks that passed around the table meant that they got the point. The one closest to me, whose seemingly unimportant job in Washington was a cover for his internal security position, held up his hand for attention. "Mr. Mann . . . you're suggesting a merger of forces in this case . . . or a hands-off attitude regarding your rather unique operation?"

"A merger, Mr. Delaney. We can't afford to be at odds on this."

"What makes you think we need your organization?"

"Because we can operate at levels you either can't or won't," I told him bluntly. "You know damn well Martin Grady operates on an international basis and isn't forced to work on a limited budget. Before you can get an appropriation to purchase certain necessities . . . like information . . . we can have it bought. We already have men inside legations and embassies and whatever news flows out of an enemy country filters through our hands as fast as it does yours. But that isn't the end of it. We're talking about Louis Agrounsky. He must be found. I think I can find him."

"I see."

"Do you?"

Delaney stared at me hard, his forefinger tapping the edge of the table silently. "You can give us the benefit of your thought, Mr. Mann."

"No. You'll get the benefit of what I find out, but I'm keeping the edge. I want the heat off our group and the advantage of being able to draw from your man power and resources if necessary."

"Where does that leave us?" Delaney asked softly.

"Stranded," I said, "unless you do it my way."

Hal Randolph had that florid look back again, the strain of what he was thinking making the muscles in his neck bulge. I was pushing them all the way and not leaving them open for a lot of empty discussion.

It was Charlie Corbinet who quieted the hum down when he said, "I would like to make a suggestion."

Heads swiveled toward him and waited. Unlike most of them, Charlie was more than a desk supervisor. He worked in the field when he had to and had never lost his touch. He had been on the big hot ones with the best of them and was rarely outguessed.

Randolph said, "Well?"

"This won't be the first . . . or last . . . time strange bed partners have come together. My association with Mr. Mann is nothing new to anybody present and the results have justified the arrangement. Whether we like it or not, we'll have to go along with him or go without his services. If his capabilities are lost to us through lack of cooperation on our part it will be to our disadvantage."

"If I get knocked off," I interrupted.

"Exactly," he replied. "I realize that if we do agree to a union with the Martin Grady forces certain political powers will lose their ability to censure or eliminate the Grady machine in the face of public opinion . . . if this ever reaches that stage. In effect, it's a stalemate. I suggest we go along with Tiger here, on the agreement that no word of this merger leaks out. It won't hurt to save face if we have to."

Hal Randolph snorted at that, but lost the silent vote. It was over as quickly as it started. I had made my point the hard way. I stood up, wincing a little. "One more thing," I told them. "I'd like two signed copies of this informal agreement. One to be delivered to Martin Grady himself. I'll keep the other copy."

Delaney smiled a little, his eyes sparkling. "Yes, I imagine you would. And we would like some protection too."

"Name it."

"On a previous occasion you operated in a reserve officer capacity for a short time. I suggest we renew that arrangement for a specified period in the event we want to pull the stops out on you. It might keep you on your toes to realize that a court-martial can always hang over your head if you get too far out of line."

I put my hat on and shoved the chair back. "No trouble, gentlemen," I said. "I was just going to make the same suggestion myself."

I met Charlie Corbinet in the Blue Ribbon Restaurant on Forty-fourth just off Seventh Avenue at five in the afternoon. The afteroffice crowd had just started to filter in, but I had a corner table in the bar by myself and a cold beer to keep me company while I waited.

He slid in, ordered the same and said, "You're a cagey bastard, Tiger."

"Yeah, I know. How'd it come out?"

"All your way. I'm appointed the official baby sitter and you're to report through me." He gave me a dubious grin and added, "You're getting closer all the time. You're practically an agency man."

"Screw that stuff."

"Well, you're in the Army now. They've expedited your papers. You'd better behave. Delaney wasn't kidding about a court-martial. Don't slip up."

"I haven't in twenty years."

"You almost did a few months ago."

Rondine again. He meant the thing with her.

"But I didn't."

"Let's say you were lucky."

"That's why I'm still alive."

Charlie nodded and took a sip of his beer. "What's your first step?"

"Trying to get your department to give me all the details on Louis Agrounsky."

"You'll get that tomorrow. That wasn't what I meant."

"How long can I have before you file a report on my activities?"

"At your discretion. I know you can play the game. Maybe the others don't but we're the same breed, or have you forgotten?"

I laughed and finished my beer. The waiter asked if I wanted another but I waved him off. I said, "I haven't forgotten anything."

"Then?"

"There's a funny little guy who doesn't belong in the picture, yet he's there."

Charlie saw the point immediately. "Doug Hamilton?"

"Vito Salvi killed him along with the other two. His abduction was deliberate and that torture murder had a purpose. I want to know why."

"You could have asked Salvi," Charlie said quietly.

"Not when I was shot to hell and bleeding all over the floor. I wasn't taking any chances on Salvi getting me after I dropped in a faint, old friend. I wasn't thinking fast at that point or I might have sweated it out a little, but what's done is done."

"Sure," Charlie nodded. "Incidentally, you're off the hook on that one. They dreamed up a cutie to cover those kills."

"I'll read about it in the papers."

"All part of the terms of the agreement you made."

"Great." My voice sounded sour. I wasn't very happy about the bed I had made or the others who were going to sleep in it with me. I laid a couple of bucks on the table and got up. "I'll call you, Charlie," I said.

"I'll be waiting."

I had scheduled Don Lavois to meet me at Ernie Bentley's lab at nine with the information I requested. I got there a little early and caught Ernie with a fresh pot of coffee and let him pour me one in a beaker. It was black and thick, almost a distant cousin of some of the explosives he was expert at concocting.

He handed me a bag of doughnuts and perched on the edge of a work table. "Hear you have a big priority job going."

"Grady set any limitations on you?"

"None. Fullest cooperation. I passed on the authorization to London and Paris and they're set to roll if they have to. Martin sent a draft through to the bank to cover any emergency." He took half a doughnut, dunked it and stuffed it in his mouth. "What's the procedure?"

"Right now, I haven't any. When Don gets in I'll probably know the direction it'll take." I checked my watch, found it almost nine when the buzzer flashed from downstairs and Ernie touched the unlock button beside his desk.

Don Lavois was a big guy, wide in the shoulders with one of those pleasant faces that had seen a lot of action. There was a slight twist to his nose and a little scar tissue gave a lift to one eyebrow. A fine white line, nearly unnoticeable, traced a curve down his cheek where he had taken a razor slash when we were on the same job below the border. He was a good guy to have around . . . one of the original bunch of whom so few were left any more.

He grinned and stuck out his hand. "Hi, buddy," he said. "Nice to be back."

I wrapped my hand around his and squeezed hard, my mouth splitting in a smile. "Let's hope you think so when you hear the poop."

Don's shrug was a masterpiece of understatement. "After that last bash anything will come easy. How many we have going on this one?"

"We'll do the initial fieldwork," I told him. "Sit down while I fill you in. Want some coffee?"

"Sure."

While he sipped the scalding brew, I gave him the situation to date, watching his face for any reaction. He was as good as ever, never changing expression, simply absorbing the details without question until I had finished, then giving a slight nod of understanding. But behind his eyes was that touch of ice that meant he recognized the greater implications and the possibilities that would result if we missed the target.

He put down the graduated jar he had been drinking out of and stuck a cigarette in his mouth. "A rough one, Tiger."

"Damn rough."

"Where do you want me to start?"

"Backtrack Vito Salvi. He would have done all the groundwork on Louis Agrounsky and if he had any leads, we'll need them."

Don looked up from the match he had cupped in his hand. "If he had to chop up Doug Hamilton and those other two then he didn't have much, did he?"

"Maybe he was just insuring his information. Salvi was an old pro, buddy. I can't see him giving me the entire story no matter how far the chips were down. He still would have held something back. He knew I was in the same league so he gave me more than he would have tossed to anybody else, but he was still on the other side and there are a few rules you'll stick to no matter what."

"Okay, Tiger, so I'll run it out. Then what?"

"Play it by ear. I'm going after Hamilton. He's the sour note in the concert. If you cross swords with I.A.T.S. or the locals, get right to me. We'll get cooperation from the police and the Washington agencies up to a point, but don't push the issue if you don't have to."

Don grinned at me again. "Do I get to meet any beautiful blondes?"

c

"Knock it off."

"I was just thinking about Panama."

"So I was lucky."

"Brother!" he said with a short laugh.

Ernie Bentley gave us both a disgusted snort and shook his head. "You let Martin Grady hear that kind of talk and you'll wind up behind a filing cabinet. For two guys with all the field experience you've had you still play kid games."

Don glanced at him, smiling. "You know what they say about all work and no play, Ernie."

"How many times has a woman ever shot you?" Ernie asked him.

"Once."

"I heard different."

"The other wasn't in the line of duty." Don grinned again. He nodded toward me and said, "Ask him the same question now."

"Shut up," I said. I looked at my watch. "Let's get things rolling."

Doug Hamilton had lived in Manhattan in a four-room apartment that was one of the newer eyesores in a rebuilt city. Five years ago the site had been a row of great restaurants frequented by those who had loved the city and made it a modern wonder of the world. Now it was an index system of people in a massive complex of commercialism whose character had gone from blood and flesh to concrete and steel.

The personnel folder Don had delivered to me on Hamilton listed his salary from Belt-Aire Electronics at two hundred dollars a week and estimated another one-fifty from other contracts he handled through his office. His agency was small but efficient and in business since the end of 1946. Recommendations had come from five other major companies who had used his service with satisfaction and all the checks Belt-Aire had put through gave him a clean bill.

The only thing wrong was that the cheapest one-and-a-half-room apartment in the building went for three-fifty a month and

Doug Hamilton had one of the most expensive layouts in the place whose advertised rental was almost ten thousand dollars a year.

Six months before he had lived in a fifty-dollar flat in Brooklyn.

When the doorman called the superintendent into the lobby for me I got one knowing look and didn't have to bother with explanations. He was old and wise and had seen too many people like me and judged accordingly, except that this time he mistook me for a cop. "Aren't you people ever going to call it quits?"

"Shortly."

"They've photographed the place, they've dusted it, I've talked to a couple dozen other cops and I can't think of a thing to tell you I haven't told them." He waved his hand aimlessly toward the street outside.

"Well, you know how it is. Just a job," I said.

He nodded, hunching his shoulders in a shrug. "Sure, but what's to see? No other tenants on that floor yet. He paid rent in advance, never bothered anybody, no parties or stuff like that. I liked him."

"Somebody didn't."

The super motioned with his head for the doorman to go back to his post, then said softly, "What's it all about? All I get is that he died."

"He was killed."

"I figured that. He was a private dick too. I saw a lot of his outgoing mail with the agency name on the envelopes. What happened?"

"Nobody knows just yet. He got involved with something too big for him."

"So what do I do with the apartment? He was paid up for a year, in cash yet."

"Check with your lawyer. How about letting me see the place?"

He pointed to the elevator. "Be my guest. It's still open. Top floor."

"Thanks."

The elevator opened into a small private lobby with the floor

blanketed in a thick nylon pile rug, the walls boasting finely
framed oils by some good but obscure artist. The door to the
apartment swung open all the way and the smell of cigar smoke
still hung in the air.

I walked in, stood in the doorway a moment and looked
around. Nobody had bothered to shut the lights off. Doug
Hamilton had rented the apartment unfurnished, but wasn't
responsible for selecting his accouterments. All the earmarks of
a decorator were there—one who had unlimited funds to work
with.

Somewhere along the way Hamilton had made it. Then he had
to pay for it. The hard way

I knew I wouldn't find anything there. In a way I wasn't looking for anything either. All I wanted was an insight into the man
I had never seen until he was dead, strapped out on a torture
table with the handiwork of an expert etched into his flesh.

For ten minutes I walked around the place, opening cabinets
and drawers, seeing the accumulation of a person taking on a
new life. He had had everything a man could ask for except living and even that wasn't much. All the information Don Lavois
had dug up showed Hamilton to have been a frugal liver and it
still showed here. Two quarts of scotch, one opened, two suits, a
half dozen shirts and shorts with socks to go with them, a few
odds and ends and that was all. It was as if he had just moved in,
yet he had been there several months.

Over all lay the powder smudges the police had spread and the
evidence of their search. Methodical and thorough. The kill
hadn't taken place here so there wasn't much to look for. Routine,
with everything they found held in check until it matched something else.

Some of his work Hamilton had done at home and one corner
of the living room was taken up with a mahogany desk and a
small filing cabinet, but the files held nothing more than carbons
already filed with his employers, receipted bills and notes on
planned activities.

Out of curiosity I fingered through the top drawer looking for
the folder on Belt-Aire Electronics. It was there, all right. Just the

folder. I pulled it out of the alphabetical sequence and looked at it. Not too long ago it had been well filled. The gauge lines at the bottom of it had been creased on the last one to accommodate a good half inch of papers. I stuck it back where it came from and pushed the drawer shut. Either Doug Hamilton had kept his present employer's information more confidential than the others or someone else was interested in what went on in Belt-Aire Electronics.

On the way out I stopped at the desk where the super was thumbing through some papers, waited until two women passed by us and said, "Did anyone make arrangements to forward his mail?"

"No . . . no one mentioned it."

"Anything come in for him yet?"

"Not today."

"Hold whatever shows up. You'll be notified what to do with it."

"Sure thing," he said, then added, "Think I should button up the apartment?"

I gave a small shrug. "There will be a court action in a few days and you'll be notified. Meanwhile you might as well keep the place locked. I don't know who would be interested in seeing the place anyway."

"Well, I could rent . . ."

"Take it easy. He paid in advance, didn't he?"

The guy looked a little sheepish, passed it off and went back to his papers.

I went outside and waved down a cab and gave him the address of Belt-Aire Electronics.

CHAPTER THREE

THE FACTORY WAS a new one, erected on reclaimed land between La Guardia and Kennedy Airport, completely surrounded by heavy wire fencing and patrolled by armed guards. There was a good reason for all the security checks. Inside, this single Martin Grady firm was engaged in a top priority project of a missile guidance system that could pick a flea out of the stratosphere, and when the system was completed it would put us hands-down ahead of any potential enemy.

I had to wait twelve minutes at the gate before I was cleared through to the main office where the plant manager introduced himself as Henry Stanton and gave me a nervous wave toward a leather chair facing his desk.

"Mr. Grady seems to have the utmost confidence in you, Mr. Mann," he told me.

I nodded while he offered me a smoke and held a lighter out to me.

"We don't often get visitors. That is, those not in an official capacity."

"Oh?"

"You understand our operation here?"

"Completely," I said.

"Yes." He licked his lips, then walked behind the desk and sat down with a resigned sigh. "Now, what can I do for you?"

"How much did you hear about Doug Hamilton?"

"I was notified immediately that he had died. Nothing more. Mr. Grady said that there would be an investigation including one by his own, ah . . . people. I was to cooperate fully."

"Has anyone else been here?"

"You are the first. Now . . ."

"Hamilton filed reports on the personnel employed here. Where are they?"

"Locked in our vaults. However, another copy of each report was submitted to the proper authorities in Washington. Those people engaged in any portion of the project considered secret have been given a separate security clearance by the proper agency while those in lesser categories were investigated by us and approved by Washington."

"I'd like to see the files."

"They're quite extensive."

"Only the ones Hamilton processed."

"Well, that's comparatively simple then." Stanton flipped a button on the desk intercom and said, "Miss Hays, will you come in please."

His secretary was one out of the old school, in her mid-fifties, starched and stiff with gray hair wound in a bun on the top of her head. She didn't even glance my way until Stanton acknowledged me with a nod. "Miss Hays, this is Mr. Mann, a representative of Martin Grady's. Will you show him to Miss Hunt's office and instruct her to let him go through our personnel files."

"Certainly, sir. This way, Mr. Mann."

"Will there be anything else?" Stanton asked me.

"I'll let you know if there is. Meanwhile you'd better get me cleared to get around this place on my own. Do you know Hal Randolph of I.A.T.S.?"

His eyebrows went up a little at that. "Quite well."

"He can expedite matters if there's any trouble," I said. "Let's go, Miss Hays."

I followed her into the outer office where we picked up another security guard who trailed us from five feet back, down a good hundred yards of softly lit, air-conditioned corridor to a door

marked CAMILLE HUNT, PERSONNEL. My guide touched a
button on the wall and when the buzzer sounded, pushed the
door open and led me in while the guard waited outside.

Miss Hays' instructions went to the secretary at the desk,
passed through the desk phone to someone behind a door marked
Private and I was told to wait. Miss Hays' curt nod told me she
didn't like me a bit, but she was at my command. She swept out
like a dowager queen, her nose sniffing the delicately perfumed
air of the office with obvious distaste.

I didn't have long to wait. The desk phone rang, the chubby
little secretary in the thick-framed glasses listened briefly, then
crooked a finger my way. "You may go in now," she said.

Camille Hunt was a strategist. She was the personnel director
and was there to see what people were made of before they were
hired. It wasn't just an office she had; it was a camouflaged command post and she was the acting C.O. Come in smiling and
you'd stop; come in grim and you'd smile. Somehow you could
drop your guard and any stories you had ready would bobble out
and if they were off-beat she'd have you.

The walls were a dark green, decorated with large color plates
of every plane our Air Force had ever operated, interspersed with
violent, surrealistic oils and an oversized recumbent nude done
with such detail it seemed to dominate the entire room, Air Force
and all. The desk was placed in front of curtained false windows
and was so skillfully lit and shadowed by a pair of lamps that you
couldn't quite tell if anyone was sitting there behind them or not.

She wasn't. She was sitting far to the left scrutinizing me carefully, ready to catch any reaction, but making the mistake of letting enough light bounce off the sheen of her nylons so that I saw
her without letting her know it. I could have told her I had seen
the act pulled before and could play it as well as she could, but
that would have spoiled the fun. Instead, I walked up to the
nude, looked over all its good points without ever turning around
and said, "Remarkable likeness. A little on the fat side though."

Then I went around, sat in her chair behind the desk, swung
both lamps around to catch her squarely in their beams and felt
my grin stop before it started.

Camille Hunt *was* the nude in the picture. And she wasn't on the fat side either. That part was just uncalled-for license on the part of the artist.

She sat there with one leg crossed over the other, the idle motion of one foot the only part of her that seemed alive for the moment. Her chin rested in the fingers of one arm propped on the chair, the scarlet of her nails matching that of her mouth. Eyes black as midnight only reflected the denser black of her hair that seemed to flow and meld with a dress of the same space-night color. But even in that colorless void there was no mistaking the exquisite shape of her body or the beauty of her face.

Yes, she could make quite an interrogator. If you fell into her trap.

"Hello, spider," I said.

"Hello, fly," she smiled.

"This one got away."

"I expected it to. Mr. Grady had already briefed me on you. I'm glad you didn't disappoint me."

"Never let it be said."

"Do you mind turning the lights off?"

"I like to look at you."

"You'll get more out of the picture."

"Vicarious pleasures don't interest me that much. Walk over here."

Watching her move was like seeing a ballet. Every movement was fluid, purely feminine, as deliberately provocative as a woman could make it. The game was over, but she was still insisting on playing it.

I followed her with the lights, then bent the goosenecks down so we could both see each other in the reflected rays and when she let her eyes meet mine she stopped with a sudden filling motion of her chest. "So you're the great one."

"How much did Martin Grady tell you?"

"Now I rather think he was warning me." Very casually she pulled out a straight-backed chair and sat down beside the desk. "Would you ever hire me?"

"What for . . . stud services?"

"Hell," I grinned at her, "Grady never mentioned that department.

"But I can see it," she teased. "It's my job, reading people. I'm expert at it. You'd probably perform very well."

"I come with the best references."

"No doubt, but that isn't getting to why you *are* here. Do you mind?"

I leaned back in the chair, hooking a drawer out with a toe to prop my feet on. "Doug Hamilton submitted reports on personnel he checked out. Did they clear through you?"

"Yes, all of them. He investigated their backgrounds, former employers, associates, credit arrangements—the usual thing where top security wasn't involved. I had the final say as to their ability or personality requirements."

"What about top security?"

"All handled directly by Washington through Mr. Grady. I only handle the lower echelon of employees, but even then it is necessary to look for people absolutely qualified. I don't think there is any need to brief you on the nature of the project here."

"There isn't. Can I see his files?"

"If I may have my phone," she smiled again. I pushed the instrument to the edge of the desk and watched the graceful sweep of her body as she leaned forward to pick it up. "Linda," she said, "please bring in all the A-20's from the vault."

"Who else ever got to see those files, Camille?"

She cocked her head, her grin impish. "No one. . . ."

"Tiger. It's my name. My old man gave it to me."

". . . Tiger. Another copy went to Washington and if there was no protest and I was satisfied, the person was eligible for employment here. It was simply background material. Any advancement was predicated upon results shown us and not upon previous achievement . . . or lack of it. There were specific clearance requirements for everyone from janitorial to shop positions and they all followed the same form."

The secretary came in then, laid down a single folder on the desk and left. I picked it up, hefted it and scanned the contents. It was thicker than the one in Hamilton's private file, but probably because his copies were on onionskin while these had been submitted on printed bonded forms. Each one was numbered and there were eighty-four persons involved.

"How long a period of time does this represent?" I asked her.

"Three years. Those are only reports from Hamilton himself."

"Not much of a turnover, is there?"

"Very little. Mr. Grady pays top salaries in every department with greater benefits than anyone else. It's his policy."

"Yeah, I know."

"The Hamilton reports came in during the time of expansion. If you note the dates you'll see that we reached peak employment about four months ago and have been static since, having fulfilled our needs. However, we never know what our complete capabilities really are. Further expansion may be necessary."

I was going through the file, looking at names and places, scanning the reports without seeing anything that looked familiar. "Hamilton ever come up with any negative endorsements?"

"Generally about one out of three. Copies were sent on to Washington in the event those persons tried for positions that required security. Most of it was information of criminal records or subversive activities or associations."

"How many have been fired?"

"None. Several were transferred to other projects at Mr. Grady's request and subsequently replaced, but our system has been very efficient in enabling us to choose dependable employees."

I looked up at her and gave her a crooked smile. "No doubt. How about rejects after they were cleared by Hamilton?"

"A few, but all were unsatisfactory because of not being technically qualified. Are you thinking they might have held some sort of . . . animosity for Mr. Hamilton?"

I laid the folder down and leaned back in the chair. "In that case they would have taken it out on you, wouldn't they? Hamilton cleared them . . . you didn't."

"True," she nodded, "but unlikely. You see, the ones I'm referring to were machine-shop technicians who realized they didn't have the necessary skills and more or less disqualified themselves.

They were all readily employable by other firms who demanded less than we."

I nodded, then, "I'll take these along and get some stats made, okay?"

"Certainly. Just take care of them."

"You have an alphabetical list of all employees?"

"Naturally."

"Can I see it?"

"Top drawer on your right. Directly above your feet. You'll have to put them down to open it." Her lips were parted and I could see the white even edges of her teeth. This time it was her eyes that were laughing at me.

I opened the drawer, flipped through the "A" file looking for Louis Agrounsky and found nothing even close.

"Can I help you with something?"

"Nope, just curious." I pushed the drawer shut and stood up. "You don't mind, then, if I take this file along with me?"

Camille Hunt tossed her hair in a vague gesture. "No . . . but remember that it *is* confidential information."

"We're both working for the same person, remember? I'll get it back to you."

Both of us stood up together. I hadn't realized how tall she was until she faced me, a peculiar expression playing across her face. Her tantalizing little game was still going on, still trying to find a chink in my armor plate. I got a good picture of what everybody else had to go through, and if she couldn't make a man sweat nobody could.

I turned my head and looked at the picture on the wall. The likeness was amazing. "I'd like to paint you," I told her.

She followed my glance. "Oh? Do you have the talent?"

"No. None at all. I'd just like to paint *you*."

"But why?"

I let out a short laugh. "Because it would be fun, kitten. I'd do it with an oiled feather."

The corners of her eyes crinkled. "It might be an experience at that."

"They say it can be very exhilarating."

"I doubt it."

"Don't knock it if you haven't tried it." I walked to the door and opened it. My armed guard was still waiting in the outside office.

"So long, spider," I said.

"So long, fly," she told me. "Come back to the web any time."

Doug Hamilton had his office on Lexington Avenue, an efficient place staffed by a junior partner named James Miller, two secretaries and a receptionist. An earlier call to Virgil Adams at Newark Control cleared me to see the Belt-Aire employee files as a Martin Grady representative, and although Hamilton's own secretary was still shaken by what had happened and a little apprehensive about the whole thing, she showed me into his office and pulled out the cabinet drawer and extracted the folder on the company.

I leafed through it, scanning the data quickly, but as far as I could see it was an identical set to the one I already had. "Has anyone else been here yet?" I asked her.

"Yes . . . the police, naturally, and a Mr. Randolph from a Federal bureau. They saw this file too."

"Anything removed from it?"

"Nothing. You can see each sheet is numbered and they're all in sequence. I really don't know what they were looking for and there was nothing I could tell them."

I closed the folder and handed it back. "Been here long?"

"Five years, Mr. Mann."

"Then you remember when Hamilton took on the Belt-Aire assignment."

"I drew up all the contracts."

"You type the reports too?"

"Yes, all of them."

"Then Hamilton kept notes of his research?"

"Of course, but as in all confidential matters of this sort, they were destroyed after the reports were typed. There are none left at all."

"He never did any of his own at all?"

"Well . . . a few, I believe. There was a time when we were rushed with other things and he did some personally to get the job done."

"Remember which ones?"

"I . . . I'm afraid not. I wish I could help . . . but typing reports are such daily routine . . . and after hundreds . . ."

"I understand. Just one more thing. . . . Hamilton moved into a pretty expensive apartment not too long ago. Know where he got the money?"

For a moment she hesitated, then: "Mr. Hamilton was a bachelor. He really never had a need for anything pretentious and consequently saved his money. I know his bank account was substantial. I . . . rather think he . . . simply wanted a change."

"It was a pretty drastic one. Did he have a woman in mind?"

She blushed, dropping her eyes. "No. I'm afraid not. He wasn't much . . . for marriage."

When she glanced up again I caught that old, old look in her eyes. Office secretary in love with her boss. It was happening all over the city and most of it earmarked ahead of time with tragedy.

"Tough," I said.

She knew what I was thinking and shrugged. "Life."

"The office still goes on?"

"Mr. Miller will handle things. The arrangement was provided for when he became a junior partner. Mr. Hamilton has a sister somewhere in the Midwest and she will inherit according to the terms of his will. She's already been notified by Mr. Hamilton's lawyer."

"Well, thanks for the help. If I need anything I'll contact you."

"Very well."

"If you get the time see if you can locate the reports Hamilton did himself."

"I'll try. I can't promise anything."

"Good enough."

Dead ends. The big nothing. Four men dead, one missing who held the secret of world calamity and no place to scratch the surface. There was still the probability that Doug Hamilton's death was an accident that never should have happened, a coincidence that occurred because he inadvertently blundered into Vito Salvi's world. It was probable too that the empty folder in his apartment had no real meaning at all, and was simply a place to file notes he later had retyped at his office.

I picked up my hat and let myself out of the office into the screaming roar of New York going home. It took ten minutes to find an unoccupied cab and a half hour to cross town to Charlie Corbinet's apartment. He had the door open for me when the elevator reached his floor and waved me in.

"Drink?"

"A short one," I said. "The night's just started."

He mixed a couple, handed me one and sat down opposite me. "Come up with anything?"

I ran down what I had for him and let him sift the facts for himself. I could see him arrive at the same probabilities I had, then he got up with the nervous impatience he never lost and paced the room deep in thought. Finally he said, "We've been backtracking Louis Agrounsky from the time he worked on the ICBM hot-line system. One team's been going forward, the other back. Since Agrounsky originally had a security check run on him, going back wasn't difficult. We merely repeated the process looking for flaws in the first investigation."

"And?"

"Clean as a whistle. No criminal record, no unsavory associations, the best references . . . not a thing out of the way. Not even a political angle. He registered but didn't bother voting. The only new fact added was an afterthought by his former college dean who mentioned that in his senior year Agrounsky came near a nervous breakdown that was attributed to overwork. The attending physician had died but his records were still available and showed Agrounsky to have been under his care two weeks before returning to school. Complete rest was prescribed and there were no aftereffects."

"It could have been the beginning of something," I suggested.

"Possibly. Had this ever been uncovered earlier it's doubtful if he would have been put in charge of the project."

"Any evidence that he covered it up?"

"None. Since it wasn't a mental illness the dean never thought it important enough to mention. It seemed to be a common complaint of his best hard-working students who get overly dedicated."

"Where do you lose him then?"

"After the hot-line installation he went into the second space project. If you remember, there were two failures before the technical difficulties were overcome and the shot successful. He was scheduled to begin work on the new booster engine the following week but had to be called off it when he had a minor car accident. The hospital reports stated minor lacerations, a broken thumb and a slight back injury. At that time he was living in a house he had bought in Eau Gallie, Florida, with about twenty thousand dollars in the bank. Apparently the back injury bothered him and he canceled out any future work and lived off his savings. It was here that contact was lost.

"Agrounsky had few friends. He was pretty much of a loner. He was seen occasionally in town making small purchases but it was the bank teller who saw him most often. He made steady and increasingly large withdrawals that were not commensurate with his usual spending habits. However, nobody questioned it. Later he closed out his account entirely, sold his house to an engineer working on the project, and hasn't been seen since."

"Woman involved?" I asked him.

"No. We checked that angle out thoroughly. He didn't gamble or drink, either."

"Everybody has one bad habit."

"Agrounsky didn't. None that we could find."

"People like him just don't disappear."

Charlie turned, stared into his drink, and gulped it down with a quick motion. "He sold his house furnished, packed two suitcases in a five-year-old Ford and drove away. A month later he sold the car to a dealer in Myrtle Beach, South Carolina for a hundred bucks and nothing more is known of him."

"If he was broke he'd have to work or go on relief."

"No Social Security has been paid. We've gone over all the relief rolls, queried every jail and hospital in the country . . .

and still nothing. No passport was issued him and there's no record of his having gone into Canada or Mexico." He paused, mixed himself another drink, and shook his head. "Hal Randolph thinks he's dead."

"If he were, Vito Salvi wouldn't have been looking for him," I said.

"I know. I don't think he's dead either." Charlie swirled the drink around letting the ice chink against the glass. "What do you think, Tiger?"

"The same thing you do," I told him. "Someplace he's holed up trying to make a decision and if we don't get to him before he does, we've had it."

"And you still think you know how to find him?"

"I have to, old buddy," I said. "If the Soviets had their best man looking for him they'll throw in their next best. We can't cut it off. Vito Salvi had a big jump on us and could have been closing in when he found himself being tracked by your two men and nailed them. How Hamilton got into the act, I don't know yet. Now . . . how far did those two agents get in locating Agrounsky?"

"Absolutely nowhere. That's why they concentrated on finding Salvi . . . hoping he'd lead them to him. Their last report was that an unusual contact was made by a minor Soviet attaché they had been covering who was suspected of passing funds to their agents here. The general physical description matched that of Salvi except for facial characteristics which could easily have been part of a disguise. They followed him and nothing more was heard about them until you pulled the cork."

"I suppose Randolph has a team going back on Salvi too."

Charlie nodded. "They're getting a big zero there too. Salvi was too much of a pro to leave trails. They'll get to him eventually, detail by detail, but it will probably take weeks."

"We haven't got that long," I reminded him.

"Come up with something then."

I put my glass down and lit up a cigarette. "There's a little hook in that picture of Agrounsky I can't quite put my finger on."

"Tiger, we haven't missed a bet on him."

D

"Just the same, I have that funny feeling."

"Play it then . . . you're on a fat salary. I don't think you'll get anywhere thinking he was employed by Belt-Aire though. He had no reason for falsifying his name or background and if he needed money he could have gone right into any one of the current government projects and made out a lot better."

"So I'll work on it until I'm satisfied."

"Remember the time element."

"How can I forget it?" I pushed myself out of the chair and reached for my hat. "Reach me at the Salem if you need me. The name is T. Martin. I want the latest photo of Agrounsky you can find."

"You'll get it. Good luck, Tiger."

"Thanks," I said, "we can all use some."

Ernie Bentley had left an envelope of photostats at the desk for me with a note to contact Newark Control as soon as possible. I picked up my key, found a pay booth in the lobby and gave the operator the Newark number.

Virgil Adams answered and as soon as I coded my ID he said, "London just called, Tiger. Moscow's assigned a replacement for Vito Salvi."

"They're working fast. Who is it?"

"No positive identification yet. Our sources picked it up from the embassy in Paris and passed it on. We'll keep trying to get a make on him but since they reorganized their operation it may take a while. One thing we know—he isn't being sent . . . he's already here. They've surrounded this deal with the utmost security and it won't be easy to break. Getting that much was just luck."

"Grady's money can buy almost anything."

"If it's available," Virgil said. "We do know they've been holding a couple of top operatives somewhere in the country for any emergency ever since the Sokolov and Butenko spy trial bit in '64. Right now there are some interesting developments overseas. The Kremlin's big strategic planners who were in Bonn were recalled to Moscow for an emergency session with the brass and it had to do with the situation here."

"You set the feed lines yet?"

"Grady's authorized twenty-five thousand for a definite lead. He'll go higher if he has to. We've spread the word so anything can break, but we're not counting on it. Frankly, my friend, it's up to you."

"Thanks a bunch."

"Do you want anybody else in the field with you?"

"Don Lavois is enough right now. Everybody is cooperating at this point and as long as it lasts we'll be enough."

"It's your game, Tiger," he said, then added, "Oh, one more thing . . . you might find it interesting."

"What?"

"Our informant in Prague mentioned that the price on your head has now gone up. You not only top the 'A' list, but are a project in itself."

"How much am I worth?"

Virgil chuckled humorlessly and said, "Enough to buy a villa on the Black Sea, a new Ziv, a dozen servants, endless ration cards and political recognition."

"How about that? Why don't you collect?"

"I like my vacations in Florida," he said before he hung up.

When I put the phone back I was grinning. Someday I'd have to show him the four pages from the book I had taken from Marcus Pietri's pocket after I killed him. Virgil didn't know it, but he was on the "A" list too. Down near the bottom, but on it nevertheless.

Up in the room I dropped the stats in my bag, sealed the originals in the envelope for mailing back to Belt-Aire and put in the call to Don Lavois. He picked up the phone, took my recognition signal, answered it, and said, "Something a little odd on Salvi, Tiger."

"Like what?"

"The Feds swarmed over the neighborhood where he was holed up and took that building apart. They got nothing at all out of it but a lot of trouble. I dogged them for a while, but as long as they were doing the work there was no use butting in. I went in after they left just for a look around but didn't turn anything up until I reached the bathroom. One of the cops must have used the john and didn't check it after he flushed. It had backed up a little."

"Lousy toilet training."

"Habit," he said. "Whoever looks back? Anyway, I got a coat hanger and probed down the well. There was a cute little gimmick there—a thin spring wire across the toilet trap out of sight under the water level with a six-foot length of nylon cord tied to its middle and on the other end, flushed partly down the drain, a rubber prophylactic with a quarter pound of heroin in it. A neat trick, but not exactly an old one. It never would have been noticed if somebody hadn't been pretty constipated."

"Hell, Salvi couldn't have been a hophead."

"It was there, buddy. It adds some interesting sidelines."

"Good enough. I'll get a look at the autopsy report on his body. Think it could have been left there by an earlier tenant?"

"Nope. The spring was simple steel and the surface rust indicated recent installation."

"What did you do with it?"

"Left it right where it was."

"Good enough. How you going to play it from here?"

"As far as anyone knows in the neighborhood, Salvi never even existed. His cover was beautiful. He rented that place by phone, paid by cash in advance, probably bought everything in scattered places and transported it himself. But he did have to buy that H from some source. It's the only lead we have."

I said, "Then get Ernie to give you the latest list on narcotics suppliers he has. Keep in touch through Newark Control."

"Roger. Any direct contact with you?"

"As little as possible. And watch yourself. The Reds have a new man in on the play."

"So I heard . . . only it's not me they're after."

When I cradled the receiver I walked over and sat on the window sill and looked at the city at night. There was a funny light feeling in my stomach that I never had before. I had been in on the chase and been in on the kill. Often, I had been the rabbit and felt the hot breath of the dogs on my back and smelled the saliva they oozed in the fury of the pursuit, but this rabbit had gotten away every time.

So far.

It wasn't the dogs that gave me the feeling. It was the thought of the lights of the city going out all at once in the wild terror of an even greater light that would hang in the air like a gigantic mushroom in a field of mushrooms that would all blossom simultaneously if given the opportunity.

I double-locked the door, chained it, stretched out on the bed with the Belt-Aire employee list and ran over each page, detail by detail. Most of the information was a one-or-two-word answer to specific questions, but the end of each page contained a short summary, a personal observation that included notations of "occasional drinker" and "periodic low stake card games." One even suggested a rather full sex life. Apparently none of these affected the employable qualities of the person because they were all on the payroll now. Evidently Hamilton had done most of his investigative work during the first half of the year because each page had a month typed in the lower left-hand corner. Except for one, it didn't match the date of the report, so probably marked the date the investigation began.

After an hour of it I put the sheets down, the .45 on half cock beside my hand and fell asleep.

CHAPTER FOUR

THE FACES BEHIND I.A.T.S. HAD done their work well. They were far from inefficient. Hamstrung by directives and stymied by bureaucratic precedents perhaps, but not inefficient. Hal Randolph and his retinue were there personally a half hour after I requested a look at the autopsy report on Vito Salvi, their expressions bland . . . waiting.

They had come in shortly after I entered the request and had a mild little man tell me I would have to wait a few minutes. The mild little man had gotten to a phone as he had been told to while I cooled my heels in a drab office that had the antiseptic smell of a dead room and when Randolph saw me he said, "Let's have it, Tiger." The other two were the same ones who had come with him when I shot Salvi and they waited with the same professional interest they had shown before.

I said, "Routine check. I killed the guy, didn't I?"

"No comedy. Just say it."

"There's nothing to say until I see the report. Now you quit playing games and clear the air."

Randolph nodded and the mild little man didn't have to go any further than the desk drawer that had been in front of him all the time. He took out two sheets stapled together and handed them to me.

Vito Salvi had died of a gunshot wound from a calibre .45 bullet and at the time of death had multiple lacerations and abrasions not directly responsible for his demise. Three other bullet wounds and several knife scars were found, a small stomach ulcer, a possible cured syphilitic condition and the early stages of a cataract beginning to form in the right eye. His last meal had been chili, creamed corn and bread which matched the garbage remains in his apartment.

I handed the sheets back to the mild little man who took them impassively and stored them back in the drawer. When he shut it he looked at me quizzically and asked, "Is that all?"

"That's all," I told him.

"Come off it, Tiger," Randolph said. "Don't hide one damn thing. This isn't a schoolyard." His face was tight and somehow his eyes seemed buried in the flesh around them. I think for the first time I liked the guy. He was big, mean and nasty, but he was being pushed and knew what it felt like to have a rock hanging over his head. "What are you looking for?"

I shoved my hat back and got up off the edge of the desk where I was sitting. "Evidence of narcotics addiction."

"Why?"

"To see whether a guy who could torture three people to death was doing it for a reason or because it was part of his makeup."

"He didn't use the stuff."

"Now I know."

The one leaning up against the cabinets said too casually, "You get off the hook too easily, Tiger."

"I've had practice."

"Not with us."

"You too. Let's just say I'm exploring every possibility."

"We thought of it too. Earlier than you did. The question is why you came up with it now."

I shook a cigarette out of the pack, lit it and looked across the room at him. "Because drugs are a big item of trade, buddy. The carriers sometimes become the victims and we're all looking for something to start with. I didn't think it possible, but I wanted to be sure. Now . . . if you're not satisfied with my explanation you can stuff it. I don't like being run down like a two-bit private op every time I get a thought. Let me remind you that at your instigation I'm back with an official status, cooperating fully with one of your representatives, and try this stunt again and I'll go it cold and anything I get finds its way to the papers first and you second."

"Don't try it, Mann," Randolph warned.

"Mister," I reminded him, "I did it before and I'll do it again. Quit crowding and don't pull any court-martial crap on me or I'll jam it up your tail."

It sat that way for a good ten seconds, the slight movements of their eyes recording their impressions. I let them sweat it long enough, then I said, "Shove a probe down the toilet of Salvi's bathroom and see what you find. Don't bother pushing on the deal because you had all the time in the world to come up with it. I would have told you only you didn't ask politely."

Randolph's face started to blossom into the familiar florid hue and I grinned at him. He said, "You bastard."

"Any number of people could have told you that."

There wasn't anything more to say. I knew what I wanted to know and walked out. From the corner I watched the three of them scramble into a black sedan and take off out of there in a hurry. Somebody on that Salvi searching party was going to catch hell pretty shortly.

I found a phone booth in a drugstore to call Charlie Corbinet. He still had his fingers on enough direct contacts through the local police and the Treasury Department to come up with some possible new leads in the narcotics situation and I wasn't betting on full cooperation from Hal Randolph at all. He'd play it his own way as long as he could and would call me in only when it was expedient. That was a chance I couldn't take.

Charlie mulled the information over, said he'd get right on it, then added, "I sent over those photographs of Louis Agrounsky to your hotel an hour ago."

"Thanks, Charlie."

"He was a rarely photographed person so there isn't much to go by. One set is the official pictures used on his project admittance badge and the other lifted from a motion picture film the government authorized for a news broadcast when the last space shot was made. It wasn't our policy to let these men be well known and they preferred the anonymity anyway, so it was the best I could do. A detailed physical description is there too in case you need it."

"Good. I'll pick them up right now," I said. "Heard anything on the hot-line circuits yet?"

"Tiger, we have every available technician checking out the entire system, but it's so damn complex it will take a long time to locate the by-pass. One team is concentrating on how it could have been done to start with. There were supposed to be a dozen positive locks that would eliminate any possibility of accidental or deliberate firing except from the final control but there are still ways it could have been done by a man like Agrounsky as long as he was in charge of the system's installation. It's a pretty shaky deal, friend."

"It could be worse."

"Another note's been added."

I waited, saying nothing.

Charlie said, "One of the few people close to Agrounsky told us he had a peculiar off-duty hobby he had been working on for years—miniaturization of electronic components that would make transistors as out of date as the vacuum tube. He had a sub-mini circuit no bigger than a dime that could run a twenty-one-inch TV set an hour before it blew. He never explained his experiments and if he recorded his experiments, we haven't been able to find any notes on it."

"Damn!" I said.

"Yeah, I know what you're thinking of," Charlie told me quietly. "A remote control system that can activate a unit so completely hidden it will be impossible to find."

"The entire hot line will have to be totally disassembled."

"Tiger, we can't afford it. Agrounsky must be found."

"I know. Who was the friend who knew about his hobby?"

"Claude Boster, a technician still assigned to the Cape. He lives in Eau Gallie, Florida, but he has nothing more to say than what

I've told you. We'll still look for Agrounsky's notes, but he probably took them with him."

"Okay, Charlie, thanks, I'll keep in touch."

Twenty minutes later I was at the hotel, picked up the envelope he had delivered and took my first look at Louis Agrounsky. He was a harried little man crowding fifty, thin, partly bald with an intense look to his eyes and a tight, withdrawn set to his mouth. I stuck the photos in my pocket and walked out of the building.

When I spotted the first cruising cab I flagged it down and gave the driver the address of the Belt-Aire Electronics Corporation and settled back to watch the city go by on the way out over the Triborough Bridge.

One man, I thought, one little man who held the world in his hands. Louis Agrounsky. A loner, dedicated. He had worked himself into a nervous breakdown when he was a student and those things always left scars. A genius with scars. Then one of those scars developed adhesions and while he was involved with the mechanical solutions of world problems he took exception to the belief that control of world stability should be in any single person's hands whether it was the President's or the head of NATO. What did they call the hot-line system? Yeah . . . the permissive action link. Nuclear weaponry, whether aggressive or retaliatory, was locked tight under the control system, totally impotent until the safety factors were rendered impotent, until an electronic message communicated by the President, who holds the coded electronic key to the weapons in his sole possession, was delivered by the right push of the right button.

But Agrounsky didn't favor ultimate control. He wanted a say in the matter and that's what comes of being a genius. He could force the matter himself. He installed the system, but gimmicked it quietly, and in the labyrinth of electronics who could say how or where? A reinstallation of the entire system would take years, and to nullify the present system would leave us immediately helpless. And all this while one man was sitting there trying to make up his mind.

Where, damn it, where!

I got out of the cab and walked up to the gate where a guard met me with a nod of recognition, checked my identification, and telephoned into the main office. Henry Stanton came out to meet me, still licking his lips with a nervous gesture, and ushered me inside.

"I . . . hope everything is all right. Drink?"

"No thanks. I want to see Camille Hunt."

"Certainly. I'll have . . ."

"I know where she is."

"But you need a pass and . . ."

"Get me one. I'm tired of chaperones."

Stanton drew himself up, an overworked executive who has to put up with things not in his own domain and was ready to read me off. There were tired lines around his eyes and he was sick of being polite.

"Just do it," I said. "If you really feel like forcing the issue I'll make one call and get you canned. Or I can belt you in the mouth. So scrap all the regulations you've been issued, drop the ideas you have and play along. I'll assume that by now you've contacted Martin Grady and are just trying to protect your own status. Forget it. I'm no efficiency expert or anyone who can jeopardize your job or the project here. All I want is to protect both and I'm as tired as you are of all the manure. Now hop to it or you'll see what I can do if I'm pushed."

Stanton had made the call, all right. It showed in his eyes and in the sudden change of demeanor when I laid it at his feet. It didn't take him long to have a little blue temporary pass issued me that I could wear pinned to my lapel, and when I pinned it on he said, "I trust there will be no interference with this project, Mr. Mann. It's a matter of national importance."

"Not from me," I assured him. "We're all in this thing to-gether."

"What thing?"

"You just take care of your project."

Stanton's face seemed to set itself. In his own way he was dedi-cated too. "I intend to," he said, and his tone was as cold and hard as steel wire.

Patriots, I thought. In '42 they went into factories and drove rivets into the bellies of bombers. They read the signs that said SILENCE SAVES LIVES and TALK SINKS TANKERS and you couldn't pry their mouths apart with a crowbar. Some were big and strong and some were short and weak, but they had one thing in common—they were patriots out of an old school you could hardly find any more in this age of radicalism and super-liberal stupidity.

I winked at him, made sure my badge was on firmly and walked outside past the guard who was ready to be my date if it weren't for the blue badge and found my own way down to the door that read CAMILLE HUNT, PERSONNEL.

The secretary wanted to announce me, but I pushed her hand away from the phone and let her see the Martin Grady ID in the wallet I held in my hand, and to make sure she didn't budge, let her catch a glimpse of the .45 in the speed rig on my belt when I put the wallet back.

Just to ease the tension I patted her cheek and said, "That's a good girl. Now how about making a pit stop in the powder room for a little bit until I finish my business?"

She was glad to get out of there. Interested, but glad. Later she could have something to add to the office gossip.

It was nice to catch her off guard for a second. Nice to see the sudden rise of her head with the desk lamps framing her face with shadows that brought out all the loveliness of every striking feature and accentuated the blossom of a lower lip held between her teeth in concentrated thought. Her hair was still lost in the darkness of the background, but this time there was no concealing the ripe maturity of her body in reflectionless black because now she wore a gossamer thing of yellow that made her breasts fuller and swept in tucks to a waist girded in a broad green belt.

"Hello, spider."

Camille Hunt held one hand up to shield her eyes from the glare of the light, giving me time to cross the room, then she smiled. "Hello, fly. You took your time."

"It's only been a day."

"That's much too long. They usually can't wait to be bitten."

"You're talking about the true *diptra* types."

"And you?"

"More like a mud dauber. I break down webs and eat spiders."

Camille leaned back and smiled gently. "Oh?"

"Don't get dirty," I said.

"You mentioned it."

"But I didn't mean it."

"Then we'll start over without any promises."

"We'd better."

She smiled again and sat back in her chair. "Now . . . about that job . . ."

"I'm unemployable."

"Then . . ."

"I came to see you, understandable?"

She waved me to a chair, still smiling. "Oh, I understand, but I just don't believe it."

I threw the envelope on her desk. "That was my excuse. You can put these files back in the vault again. When I'm done with the copies I made I'll destroy them."

"Were they any use to you?"

"Not specially. Look . . . how familiar are you with the personnel here?"

"I know everyone by sight, Mr. Mann."

"Tiger, kitten . . . remember?"

"I won't forget any more."

"Ever see this man here?" I spread the Agrounsky photos out in front of her and waited while she studied them carefully.

Camille took her time about it, making sure of the details of his face, then she frowned very slightly. "This man doesn't work here, I know that."

"Could he be disguised in any way?"

"No . . . I'm sure I would see through it. Besides, our people are all fingerprinted and filed with Washington. There is no doubt as to their identities." She put the photos down and looked at me across the desk. "Facially, he isn't an impressive-looking person. Rather common, I'd say, the type who could get lost in a crowd of two. However, there is a slight degree of familiarity here."

There was a sudden constriction in my stomach and my hands wrapped tight around each other. "How?"

"When we last expanded we interviewed several hundred people for employment. Those I selected were given to Mr. Hamilton to process in the usual manner and the final selection was made on the basis of his reports and my personal approval. I have the feeling that this man might have been among those interviewed."

I sat back and rubbed my face. "And you don't have the original applications," I stated flatly.

Her expression took on a serious note. "No . . . but often I do record my own personal observations of people as a matter of interest. It isn't part of my job, actually, but character studies *are* important in this work."

"You have the notes?"

"At home. They may not be very helpful because sometimes I use names or numerical identification rather than names."

"It's worth a try."

"Who is he, Tiger?"

"Louis Agrounsky."

"The name isn't at all familiar and names I recall well. Why is he so very important?"

"Because he's holding a death threat over the heads of everyone in this country." I got up and nodded my head toward her. "Let's go, sugar. We need every minute we can get."

Camille Hunt didn't answer. She simply looked at my face and without a word reached for her coat and handbag and followed me out the door. I turned in my badge at the gate, was cleared into the parking lot, got in her car beside her and we drove out to the highway.

Her apartment was on the east side of Central Park in the Seventies, an upper-middle-class section newly renovated to accommodate those who still liked the sprawling octopus of the city enough to live in it. The doorman took care of the car while a black-suited assistant in the lobby ushered us to the elevator with a smile of subservience and made sure we pushed the right button.

Camille lived on the sixth floor, her apartment facing the street with a grandiose spread of glass. She threw her coat carelessly across the back of a chair, pushed a panel open to expose a built-in wall bar and said, "Make a drink while you're waiting."

I built a pair of them, whiskey and ginger ale heavy with ice, and set them on a coffee table. Camille didn't take long. She came back in a few minutes, changed into a black skirt and sweater, with a fistful of papers in her hand and laid them out on the table in front of me. "There they are. I've noted physical characteristics and reactions to the interview along with my personal reflections, and if it can help . . . I'm glad." She picked up her drink and sat down opposite me.

The notes were impersonally objective, recording what her eyes saw and her ears heard. They described the interviewees well right down to the shape of their heads and the tone of their voices. In places that seemed like simple doodles she explained the meaning of the characters there, what might denote intelligence or lack of it, or what might mean to her a personality trait not suitable for a Belt-Aire employee.

Each one I went over in detail, trying to make a description fit Louis Agrounsky, but none came up. If he had ever been face to face with Camille Hunt it wasn't acknowledged there.

It took an hour. She said nothing, merely refilling my glass when it was emptied, occasionally handing me a page when I took one out of sequence, letting me digest every word she had written until I threw the last page down in absolute disgust and leaned back in the couch with my eyes half closed.

"Hell," I said, "it's another blank."

"I'm sorry."

"Not your fault, kid."

"Is it something you can talk about?"

"No."

"Does it involve Belt-Aire?"

"I don't know. It involves Doug Hamilton's death but I don't know how." I looked up at her. "How well did you know him?"

"Very impersonally. He was employed by the head office. We
. . . worked together as part of personnel requirements, but I
knew little about the man. When we got the contract and he was
assigned to investigate our employees, I had lunch with him
twice, helped him with the files and accepted his recommendations. Personally, I found him rather ordinary. He was very efficient in his work though."

"He made one mistake. The big one."

Camille got up from her chair, picked up our glasses, and filled
them again. Then she sat on the arm of the sofa and held one out
to me. "The papers said he was involved in an accident. Two
detectives came to ask me questions and a pair of nice young men
who were polite but determined in finding out all I knew about
Mr. Hamilton."

"And?"

"I answered their questions as directly as they were put. They
didn't seem quite as determined as you. What really happened to
him?"

"Killed, sugar. I know how, but not why."

"And this Louis Agrounsky?"

I shrugged. "A name. Nothing more. It's ended here now."

"I'm sorry," she said.

"Why?"

The fragrance of her perfume was a gentle thing like flowers in
the night. Gently, her fingers touched my face and I felt her lips
touch my hair. "Because I won't see you again."

"Afraid of the fly, spider?"

"I haven't had time to weave him into my web."

My fingers hooked into the soft texture of her hair and I
brought her face down close to my own. "It wouldn't do you any
good, baby. I could always break loose."

"It would be a great fight."

"Would it?"

"Not really," she said. "You'd win in the end."

"I always do, kitten," I told her.

She smiled, her mouth wetly pink and inviting, offering itself to
be taken. I touched her lips with mine, the warmth of her a subtle

radiance I couldn't resist, a quiet ember that flamed into a wild heat stirred by the frantic quest of her tongue.

The glass fell from her hand and tinkled in fragments on the floor. Almost in slow motion, she tumbled from above me into my lap, a tremulous abandon hardening her body into firm complexities of muscular curves that rose and fell under my hands, quivering with each touch.

Her voice was a demanding sob, whispering to me, her breath a sweet thing that was at one with her lips as she reached out for me and when I held her face in my hands and looked at her there was a wetness to her eyes like a beggar's plea and she said, "Tiger . . . now . . . please."

Camille Hunt was an animal in her own right, a wonderful, primitive thing suddenly released from the constraints of civilized bondage and her own hands stripped her naked in her yearning for fulfillment. Her skin had the glossy texture of satin, tanned by the sun and striped with ribbon bands of a bikini. The swell of her breasts and hips, the hollow of her stomach and the luxuriant sweep of her thighs burst upon my sight like the clashing of great cymbals and I reached out and let my fingers bite into the resilient flesh and dragged her down beside me.

And suddenly time seemed to disappear, events jumbled themselves into a kaleidoscopic pattern that had no meaning at all and the only sounds were the short breaths of savage desire, the sigh, the gasp of success and the moaning demand for even greater achievement until it all was finished like a parachute collapsing over inert jumpers who have known the thrill of the free fall and lay in the pleasure of survival.

I looked at my watch, shook her awake and felt the edge of anger gnawing at myself for letting any time out of my grasp at all. Outside the day had turned into night and the lights of cruising cars threw a brief glow against the windows that bore the trickling stains of a light rain.

"Camille . . ."

She turned in my arms, her voice drowsy. "Tiger?" she said softly.

"Have to go, doll."

E

"Don't."

"No choice."

Her eyes came open, the sleep still in them. Very gently she smiled up at me. "My web isn't very strong, is it?"

"Too strong."

The tips of her fingers crossed my mouth. "I know," she told me. "Will you ever come back?"

"Like the moth to the flame." I got dressed quickly, found a blanket in her bedroom and threw it over her and watched while she tucked it under her chin with a contented grin.

"You got the job," she laughed and closed her eyes.

Someday I was going to find out when Ernie Bentley slept. He had a wife at home but he never seemed to make it there. Something going on in his test tubes or under his microscope was always too fascinating for him to leave. Any industry in the world would be glad to give him a top-ranking position in their organization, but he preferred the setup Martin Grady offered him and the freedom of unlimited experimentation every scientist hoped to achieve.

He came out of the darkroom with copies of Louis Agrounsky's pictures and handed me several. "I'll mail copies to Newark and the other centers," he said. "I may even have a few leads myself. A character like this one isn't going after nominal employment with a background like his."

"For instance?"

"Some of the places that deal with subminiaturization components. It's been fairly well developed for the practical purposes of rocketry, but there's no end to the field in sight. Eventually they'll wind up with power units as big as the head of a pin. I know a few people who have put out papers on the subject and there might have been correspondence between them."

"There's only one catch, Ernie . . . Agrounsky deliberately left his field and disappeared. He hasn't shown up."

Ernie shook his head in disagreement. "He still won't take anything small. His mind won't work that way. No matter what he does, he'll have to emerge."

"That first breakdown he had could have been just that—the first," I reminded him.

"Possibly. In that case, all his knowledge, his training would come out in a hobby. He couldn't cover it up."

"Like hell. If he broke completely everything could be shattered."

Ernie gave me a little shrug, not really caring one way or another. That one motion said it was up to those in the field, not to him, to locate the guy and solve the problem. His was more immediate. He shoved his glasses back on his head and said, "Have you contacted Don Lavois yet?"

"No."

"Then you'd better," he told me. "He picked up something about a big buy in the narcotics market."

"Damn," I said and reached for the phone. I dialed his hotel, asked for his room, and let it ring a dozen times before I hung up. "Not there. Look, Ernie, I'm going back to my place and change. If Don calls, have him hop on over, otherwise I'll call him from there."

"Will do, buddy. Take care of yourself."

I stuck the photos he had given me in my pocket and took the stairs down to the street, picked up the first cab and had him take me over to the Salem. It took ten minutes to shower and change and when I was ready I tried another call to Don. The desk said he still hadn't come in and the message I left was to have him call on Mr. Martin as soon as possible.

While I made the call I fingered the employee list Doug Hamilton had checked out, tried to think it through without getting anywhere, then threw the papers back in my suitcase in disgust.

It was time again, all-important time. What was the next step? Which direction? You'd think that there were enough men in the field to come up with something, but so far there was nothing but blanks. Vito Salvi had a good reason for killing those Washington boys, but why Hamilton? Why him?

I kept remembering the bodies the way I had seen them last, remembering something I had almost forgotten. Of all the three, Hamilton had shown the signs of being there the longest. Salvi would never have involved himself with him if he hadn't been important. Hamilton hadn't walked in cold . . . he had been directly involved somehow. If he had stumbled on the deal accidentally he simply would have been killed and his body disposed of. But no . . . he did have that address book. He knew about Salvi and where he was. For some reason he had waded into the situation head first and had gotten trapped in something way over his head.

Doug Hamilton might have been stupid, but not *that* stupid. He wasn't exactly new in investigative work and would have covered himself somehow. I looked at my watch, the time twenty minutes to ten, then slapped my hat on and went back downstairs. At the desk I left a note for Don to wait for me, told the clerk to let him have my key to get in and slipped him a buck for his trouble. I took the first cab in line outside the door and gave him the number of Hamilton's apartment, sweated through the six-minute ride and paid him off in front of the building.

The superintendent wasn't too happy about the intrusion. There was a time and a place for everything, he told me, and the middle of his favorite program wasn't it. But he didn't argue too much. I was still cop to him and he knew the value of staying on the right side when his own skirts were clean.

"Okay," he said, "so now what?"

"Did any mail come in for Hamilton since I saw you last?"

"Few things."

"I'd like to see them."

"Don't they go back to the Post Office Department?"

"Sure," I told him, "after I check the addresses."

"They're at the desk."

I stepped back, let him give me a disgusted look, and followed him back to the lobby. He went through the door in the wall, back around the counter and rummaged around in his shelves. Then he handed me five envelopes and leaned on his elbows while I went through them.

Three were bills, one from Con Ed and two from gasoline companies whose credit services he apparently used. The other two were circulars from merchandising outfits I recognized.

"This all?"

"He never got much here. Had an office, didn't he?"

I tossed the envelopes back on the counter. "Uh-huh. We just have to keep checking, that's all."

"Think I ought to readdress them to there then?"

"Hold them for a few more days. You'll be told what to do with them."

"Okay by me. He's still a paid-up tenant as far as I'm concerned. All part of the service."

"Anybody ever been up to see him since I was here?"

"Nope. He never had many visitors. Besides, we aren't that exclusive. If anybody wanted in they only had to ring the bell. The doorman isn't on except daytime and I'm pretty busy all over the building."

"But they'd have to ring the bell?"

The super shrugged, making another vague gesture. "Unless they come in behind somebody else. Then what good would that do? They all keep their doors locked here."

"Standard equipment?"

"What else?"

"Pick proof?"

"Depends on what racket you're in. The locksmith over on Third that we use when a tenant loses his keys opens them fast enough. He's bonded though. Good man."

"You have a master key?"

"Nope. Nothing except for building entrances, storerooms and like that. You think somebody jimmied his place?"

"Possible."

"Well, he was a funny guy."

I looked at him. "Why?"

"Nothing special," the super chuckled. "He wrote a letter to himself once though, about a week before he died. That's funny. Now what was he going to say in his answer?"

I leaned on the counter, staring down at him, and his face seemed to tighten when he saw my expression. "Where did he send it to?"

"Damned if I know. It was just from himself to himself. He

gave it to me to mail on the way out like he did sometimes. I do it for everybody. Part of the service," he said defensively.

"Well, where was the address?" I demanded, an edge in my voice.

"I told you, I don't know. It wasn't here or I just would of stuck it in his box."

"His office?"

"So who can remember? Look, mister . . ."

"You checked it, didn't you?"

"Sure, I told you, but I just thought it was funny. I didn't look. If that's all you want I got things to do. I . . ."

"Go ahead and do them," I said, and watched him swallow hard and scuttle back into the office. He came out the door, gave me the look too many people reserve for cops, and walked up the lobby indignantly.

A break, at last there was a lousy break in the pattern. I went back to the street, turned north to the first open store that had a pay phone in it and dialed Charlie Corbinet.

He finally lifted the receiver and I got a taciturn "Yeah?"

"Tiger, Charlie."

His tone changed immediately and he said, "Nothing new on this end yet. One team thought they had a lead on Agrounsky in Philly but it turned sour."

"Then try this . . . get the Post Office Department checking all the General Delivery boxes in the area for a letter Doug Hamilton addressed to himself. He might have had something hot and didn't want to keep it where it could be found."

I could hear him scribble on a pad beside the phone. "Where'd you pick it up?"

"By accident from the super at his apartment building. It may not be worth anything but it will have to be run down. He was in this tight, buddy."

"Will do. Shouldn't take long. Call me back in a couple of hours."

"Right."

I hung up impatiently. With luck the Post Office boys wouldn't take that long and we'd be able to move out. It had been morn-

ing since I had eaten so I stopped by the Blue Ribbon Restaurant
on my way back to the hotel, had a welsh rabbit with a cold beer
on the side, then took my time getting back to the Salem.

The desk clerk saw me as I came in, and remembering the
buck, smiled. "Your friend is waiting for you upstairs, Mr. Martin.
He came in a few minutes after you left. He has your key."

"Thanks," I said.

The elevator was on self-service and crept up to my floor, the
door opening as if it were getting tired of the job. I walked down
the carpeted hallway to my room, knocked twice, out of habit
standing back from the door jamb.

Inside a TV was softly reciting the news and sports. I knocked
again, louder this time. Nobody answered.

I didn't like it. There was something there I could smell and
when the feeling started up my spine I knew it was all wrong
somewhere. I yanked the .45 out, cocked it in my fist and tried
the knob. The door opened, all right, and that was all wrong.
Don Lavois never would have sat behind an unlocked door for
anything.

With the nose of the gun I gave the door a shove and it opened
almost soundlessly, swinging inward until a shaft of light flooded
the hallway. I hated to take the chance but I had no choice. I
went in in a crouch, the gun ready to spit if anything I didn't
know moved.

But it wasn't necessary. Nothing was moving. There was nobody in the small bathroom or the closet. There was only Don
Lavois on the floor dead with a small-calibre bullet hole directly
between his eyes, lying on his back where the shot had thrown
him when he had opened the door for a killer, thinking it was me.

CHAPTER FIVE

Don's coat was draped across the back of one chair facing the TV set, the wallet still in the pocket. There were three one hundreds, two fifties and a five there, his expensive diamond-studded wrist watch dropped carelessly on the set.

Robbery wasn't the reason for his murder.

He had uncovered something important he wanted to pass to me. He found out the reason for the narcotics Vito Salvi had hidden in his apartment and possibly the supplier of the stuff. A quarter pound of H at its highest purity factor was worth a hundred thousand dollars and that placed the action in the big league, big enough to make somebody keep his eyes open if someone was around asking the wrong questions.

Don Lavois had plopped himself right in a trap. Damn, I should have called in one of the others who knew their way around the junkman's back yard, someone they would not have suspected of being inquisitive! One question too many in the wrong place and a killer tailed him home. It was plain enough now . . . he stopped at the desk in his own hotel, picked up his message and came to mine. The killer had to have a good break and an easy getaway and I supplied all the avenues of escape. If he overheard the desk clerk's conversation with Don it would have made it even simpler. And Don, expecting me, took it head on.

I looked down at his body. His gun was still in the holster on his belt.

The desk clerk was glad to give me the information. Yes, there were several people at the counter when my friend picked up my key. No, Mr. Martin, he couldn't remember any of them. Oh yes, just one. A nice old lady on the ground floor who had been a resident for ten years. I thanked him and hung up.

Newark Control answered my call on the first ring and after I identified myself, put Virgil Adams right on. I gave it to him quickly and in detail, knowing that everything was being taped for analysis later.

When I finished Virgil said, "Have you inspected the body yet?"

"No. I'll let the police do that. They won't want anything touched."

"Take a chance. See if the bullet penetrated."

"Hang on." I laid the phone down on the table and knelt beside the body, turning the head to get a better look at the wound. There was an exit hole in the back of the skull no bigger than the one of entry. I felt myself grimace, looked up toward the far wall and saw the tiny black ring in the window sill where the slug had buried itself after passing through Don. Automatically, I went to the spot, took the filler out of my ball-point pen and probed into the hole. The filler capsule was a good four inches long, but it never touched the slug deep in that hard wood and plaster.

I picked the phone up, said, "High-velocity slug, probably a .22 and steel tipped. It went through everything."

"Then it fits, Tiger."

"Spell it, Virgil. What the hell are you talking about?"

"Niger Hoppes, the Soviet agent who escaped the Canadian network three years ago and made it back to Russia."

"I remember him."

"He never stayed there. He came back and was planted somewhere in the U.S. and held in abeyance until they needed him. And they need him now. He works with a .22 Magnum silenced pistol and is an expert marksman. He's the one who picked off Daniels and those two consulate employees in Madrid our people had tagged as spies. Got them inside a jail cell from a building too hundred feet away."

"Damn it, Virgil . . ."

"Don't play him down. He's another assassin type. He and Vito Salvi worked as a team right after the war and he knows his business. Product of everything from the C.Y.O. up . . . a party member and damned dangerous."

"What was Don's last report?"

"He had found a contact who was willing, for a price, to point out a person who was reputed to have been involved in an extraordinary narcotics deal. There were no names. He was down on Canal Street at the time but headed someplace else and was supposed to call back. He intended to make contact with you first to see how you wanted it handled."

"It was handled, all right."

"What's your next step?"

"I'll bring in I.A.T.S. Let them shuffle it around."

"You think you can make it work after the Salvi deal?"

"They'll be spooked."

"Then duck out. I've already contacted Martin Grady and this thing is too big for any delays. He'll cover you in anything you'll need. He wants you active, not hamstrung in an inquiry."

"Will do, Virg. I'll check out of here and into another place."

"Better use our own premises. . . . There's a new place on Fifty-sixth off Seventh Avenue, first floor over Shigley's. All utilities and a month's stock of food with some booze on the side if you need it. Grady owns the whole building and the key is with Shigley. The code word is *Hallmark*. Don't let anybody near you. . . . We want to keep this spot in operation."

"Who's replacing Don?"

"I've already dispatched Mason to Detroit to pick up Dave Elroy if it's all right with you."

"Good choice. He knows the narcotics end."

"That's why I asked for him."

"Get him right on Don's assignment then."

"Roger. Got a report?"

I brought him up to date, made sure it was recorded, and

signed off. As quickly as I could I packed up, went downstairs to pay my bill and picked a dime out of my change to use in the phone booth. I dialed Charlie Corbinet's number and said, "We lost another one, Colonel. Don Lavois . . . he's in my room at the Salem. I'd suggest you get over here before they try to clean up the room and get a story ready for the city police."

"You know what Hal Randolph is going to do."

"Damn right, so I'm taking off."

"You'd better stick around. This might be a stiff one."

"Sorry, buddy."

"Okay, I'll see what I can do."

"Anything from the teams in the field?"

"Only that the last trace of Agrounsky was in the Myrtle Beach area."

"How about the Post Office Department?"

Charlie didn't answer for a moment, musing over the question. "You sure about that letter?"

"Check it yourself. Well?"

"They went through every General Delivery station in New York, Jersey and Connecticut and didn't turn up anything."

"So try Pennsylvania."

"I've already asked. They will tomorrow. Now what about Lavois?"

"Tonight I'll type out a report for your eyes only. Process as you think fit."

"Don't take too big a bite."

"It seems like I always do."

"Keep in touch."

I put the phone back, stepped out of the booth and carried my bag outside and walked two blocks before I picked up a cab and had him drop me a few blocks away from Fifty-sixth. When I was sure I didn't have a tail I cut east until I saw the sign that said *Shigley's,* found the doorbell and pushed it.

I had seen these strange people Martin Grady had in his employ before—funny little people who were well paid, asked for nothing, and did what they were told. I said, "Hallmark," and the little old man in the worn sweater barely gave me a second

glance over his glasses before taking a single key from his pocket
and pointing upstairs.

Grady took good care of his operatives. The three-room apartment had every convenience anybody could ask for, completely
antithetical to the outside of the house or the neighborhood. The
kitchen windows led to an exterior fire escape and a steel ladder
going to the roof had been recently installed outside the bathroom, not visible unless you looked up to spot it. Two escape
ways and a normal entrance. The back of the door was steel
plated and fitted with a massive slide bolt designed to give the
occupant time to clear out before it could be battered down.

I threw my bag down beside the bed, undressed, and got into
bed. For an hour I lay there thinking of the times Don Lavois
and I had had together since the first drop into occupied France
in '43 and all I could picture was him lying there on the floor with
a damn .22 bullet through his skull.

*Okay, buddy. The old ones are fading away, but we'll even the
sides up little by little. Virgil Adams didn't have to tell me what I
already knew . . . that Niger Hoppes was the man without a
face whose prints were on file, but of whom no photo existed. He
could come and go as he pleased and no one would recognize his
face. Except people on his own side.*

I met Dave Elroy at Newark Airport, told Mason Armstrong to
stand by and took Dave into the lounge where I briefed him on
events up to date. He was a tall, lean kind of guy, his face
weatherbeaten out of season, a little older looking than the thirty-
two years his staff card indicated. He wasn't the talkative type,
preferring to listen and to look, but every question was pointed
and direct.

He knew most of those involved in the international narcotics
cartel who lived out of reach of the law, but he enjoyed working
on a local level where his attitude and personality could make his
work profitable to the Grady organization. I didn't have to ask for
his record—he was fast with a gun and would go in anywhere
low and quick, able to make snap decisions and make them right.
In a way I envied him the plus ten years he had on me—he had

that much longer to go before something gave out that made you want a quiet life with a place in the country.

Dave wrote nothing down, committing it all to memory, then said, "That big a buy of H Salvi made would leave some taking behind it. No pusher handles that much stuff so it probably was made direct with the importers."

"Know who to contact?"

"For the kind of money I'm authorized to pay for information, I know a lot of them."

"Okay then, take it from there. We'll stay in touch through Newark Control. Adams will assign you quarters and you can handle it on your own."

"How're you going to play it?"

"From Hamilton's end. He's still the key." I gave him a copy of the Agrounsky photos and let him study them. "Show them around and see what you come up with. If Salvi was after him and Salvi was involved in a narcotics transaction there might be a three-way connection. We can't afford to pass up any possibilities. If you do get anything, contact me before moving in."

"Suppose there isn't time?"

"You know the answers then. Just make sure you leave a record behind in case you feel like keeping company with Don."

"Hell, you're a happy one," he said sourly, hiding a grin.

"It's happened before," I told him.

"All right, Tiger. Good to see you again. Sorry Don caught one, but we all know the risks involved. Nice to be working with you."

"Same here."

We shook hands briefly and split up at the cashier's counter. I started out to the cab stand, stopped just inside the door, then turned back to the telephone booths and called Charlie Corbinet. The police had already been notified about the body in my room, but I.A.T.S. had kept a lid on the news and Hal Randolph was raising hell about my involvement, threatening everything he could think of if I didn't show.

I said, "Relax, Charlie, I'll come in when I have something going for me. Look, I forgot to ask you something. . . . Doug Hamilton filed reports on everyone he investigated including the unsatisfactory ones. Washington has copies of his information. You know what bureau handles that sort of thing?"

"I can find out."

"Then get me the names of those not considered fit for jobs requiring security. I'd say hit the reports dated from the last two months. How long will it take?"

"If I call now and it's available it will be in the mail tomorrow and here the day after."

"Good. Suppose we meet at the Blue Ribbon for lunch then . . . twelve o'clock."

"In the open? I have a feeling Hal Randolph is going to be watching me a little closely now."

"So I'll give you something to ease the pain. You know the shot that killed Don?"

".22 Magnum. Nobody heard it so the gun probably had a silencer."

"Throw a net out for Niger Hoppes. That's his trademark and he's in this country now."

"Hoppes!"

"You remember him, don't you?"

"Certainly. He's been suspected of being the gun in quite a few high-level political kills in Europe."

"Check through ballistics. Interpol can get you a telephoto of the slugs they have there and if they match you know who to go after."

"Nobody's ever seen him."

"Don Lavois did," I said. "Somebody else will. I hope it's me."

"Okay, Tiger, if this matches out maybe some of the heat will come off you. Just do me one favor."

"What?"

"Pass on any information. Don't go into this alone."

"That's too big a favor to ask, Colonel. Don't forget, I have an official position now."

"And I outrank you."

"So I'll resign," I laughed and hung up.

It had started to rain again, a dreary, slow rain that seemed to ooze out of the cloud cover overhead. There was a chill in the air too, but I couldn't tell if it was the temperature or what—I was thinking.

And what was I thinking?

An annoying little faraway thought that was always there because I was playing in a dangerous game where the stakes were beyond comprehension and the rules limitless. If there were any rules at all.

By now the committee in Moscow would know how Vito Salvi died. They had their own ways of finding out things just as we did and the orders would be out. No matter where I went I would be a target whether on assignment or not. They wouldn't know just how I got involved . . . they wouldn't know what Vito Salvi had told me in a vain attempt to stay alive. They'd figure I was in at the beginning the same as they were and an obstacle to be eliminated in the search for Agrounsky.

Unlike Niger Hoppes, my photos were on file. I wasn't exactly unknown in the operational areas and until now could be reached without too much trouble. The only thing that slowed the process of elimination was that the Soviets had too much to lose by knocking me off as a direct project because they could expect the entire Martin Grady machine to grind into action and take their men out of play ten for one.

That was *before*. Now with the stakes what they were it would be worth the risk. Oh, they'd play their game well. It could be direct or insidious, but it would have a purpose. If they couldn't get me directly, they'd get *to* me somehow and that was the little faraway thought that was always there like a snake waiting to strike from the shadows.

I hopped in a cab and gave the cabbie Rondine's address and sat against the cushions while he threaded through the traffic to the Jersey Turnpike and in the Lincoln Tunnel. He cut right on Forty-second, turned north on Eighth Avenue, making the lights all the way, then eased across town and stopped outside her apartment.

The big doorman gave me a nod of recognition after I paid off the cab, his battered Irish face that had seen too many prelim fights in the Garden squinching up a little because he had lent a hand in a game before with me and knew the results. I asked, "Edith Caine at home?"

"Yes, sir," he nodded. "Came in about an hour ago."

"Alone?"

"Staff car from the U.N. brought her. Somebody was with her but didn't get out," he told me. "Everything all right?"

I knew what he was thinking. I said, "Anybody nosing around?"

He shrugged his heavy shoulders under his uniform, his mouth twisting into a thoughtful grimace. "Nothing I can say for sure."

"You don't have to be sure."

"So I know the regulars in the buildin', y'know?"

"So?"

"Like I know most of 'em who go up and down the street. People from the other apartments, tradesmen, the walkers from the other block . . . all that. Standin' out here all day for a few years you get to know them things. So today I get a cruiser in a cab, like a guy looking for a street number."

"What's so unusual about that?"

"Hell, man, the cabbies do the lookin' for you. They all know this number anyway. I see this guy just looking and the cabbie going straight ahead like he's been told to do or somethin' and it's outa place. Later he does it again. Sometimes they cruise for broads that way but not on this block. No hookers work this section. The next time it's the same face in a blue sedan."

"Think you could recognize him?"

"Hell no. It was just a face. It was what he was doing, I saw. He was lookin' only didn't want to be seen."

"When did he go by the last time?"

"Maybe a half hour ago."

I reached in my pocket and took out a ten-spot, folded it and handed it to him. "Keep your eyes open. I'll be upstairs if it happens again. Don't let anybody into the building you don't know and if one comes in supposedly asking for anybody else, call me right away. Watch the elevator pointer and tell me what floor it stops at."

"Sure enough." He put the bill in his pocket with a grin. "I could stop 'em here for you to look at if you want."

"Don't bother. Just make sure you'd be able to recognize them again."

"Expecting trouble?"

"All the time, friend."

"I'm on your side," he said. "If you need help I can always get Bert from across the street or Herman from next door. They was both heavies a few years back. They owe me some favors."

"I'll keep it in mind," I told him, then went inside and pushed the buzzer under *Caine* and waited impatiently for the series of clicks that would unlock the door.

When I reached her apartment I knocked on the panel, saw the light shoot through the thick glass of the peephole in the door, and heard her low, throaty chuckle behind it. She held it open, pleasure bathing her face, and reached out her arms for me. "Hello, my darling," she said and let her lips tickle against mine in a teasing gesture before I grabbed her with all the hunger I had built up inside me.

I kicked the door closed with my foot and held her off with a grin. "Ummm," I said.

"You Americans have barbarous reactions. Ummm indeed." She took my hand and tucked it under her arm, nestling it against the firm rise of her breast unconsciously. "I didn't expect you to-night."

"I didn't expect to be here, either."

"Then . . . ?"

"I don't like the idea of you being alone," I told her.

She turned and gave me a sober glance, the curious expression in her eyes telling me she had sensed the reason for my stopping by. "I see. This has to do with the Hamilton affair?"

"Make me a short drink, then sit down and I'll tell you about it."

"The usual?"

"Natch." Once again, out of sheer habit, I checked through the rooms while she mixed the two drinks, making sure we were alone and all points of entry were locked. Not that it meant too much . . . anybody who really wanted to could force an entrance anyplace but at least a lock breaking or a window snapping gave you a little advance warning.

When I got back to the living room she handed me the drink and sat beside me on the arm of the big chair beside the record console and ran her hand over my hair. "Do you think you should break security by telling me?"

I tasted the drink and leaned back into the chair looking up at her. "I'll pick my own security levels, Rondine. You've been trained in the British Intelligence Service and gone the route with me. Damn it, right now we need every experienced hand we can get."

"But that isn't the point you're trying to make, is it?"

"No."

"You rather think I might be a stumbling block to you, is that it?" she asked.

"In a way. I'd hate to have any heat put on me through you. Not now."

"Oh?"

"This is too big, kid. It's more than you or me. If someone got hold of you to force me into the open I might take up the challenge and land in their net. It's a chance I can't take."

Her fingers stroked my forehead easily, then slipped down the back of my neck and kneaded me there gently. "I don't think you would, Tiger. I really wouldn't expect you to."

The love was there in her eyes, bright and full, but knowledgeable love that realized the fullest extent of the job that had to be done. Before I could answer her she moved her hand and touched my mouth with her fingertips. "Don't argue against it. We have both adopted an ideal that can't be altered or destroyed no matter who has to fall. It's the chance we know we all have to take."

"You amaze me, doll." I squeezed her hand, then kissed it.

"If you want to tell me, I'll listen."

And I gave her the picture all the way. If she was going to be in it she had a right to know. An informed agent can make a lot more progress than one working in the dark. If you were alerted to an attack you could prepare for it and reach the enemy before he reached you and I didn't want her sticking her neck out any further than she had to. When I finished she took the empty glass from my hand, made another and curled up at my feet.

"What do you suggest I do then?" she finally asked me.

"Stay with me. If Hal Randolph puts a stakeout on you to reach me the operation can be slowed down if it works. If the Soviets corner you it puts a crimp in things because it diverts time and attention. I'd sooner have you within reach where nobody can screw things up."

"I have time coming to me," Rondine mused. "With this latest shakeup in the Kremlin our embassy will be holding fast awaiting developments before they set policy so there won't be anything critical for me to do." She leaned her head back against my legs and looked at me upside down. "So I await your command, master." She gave me an impish little grin and added, "Just don't yell at me again."

"Only if you need it, baby."

"Okay."

"So pack a bag, make your call to your boss and let's get out of here."

Rondine spiraled up from the floor with a single, smooth motion and held a glass out to me. "One for the road. You make them. I'll be ready in ten minutes. Do I leave a forwarding address?"

"No."

She gave me another one of those grins again. "Your country has a thing called the Mann Act, remember?"

"That's a different *Mann*, honey," I said. "If I take you across a state line it won't be for immoral purposes."

"You mean you might even marry me?"

"One can never tell."

She gave me a little laugh and said over her shoulder as she walked to the bedroom, "Either *Mann* sounds interesting. But I think I like your way better."

Inside, she went about the business of emptying drawers into a suitcase while I made a pair of soft highballs for both of us. My watch read a little past seven and outside the sun was fading into a hazy twilight that had the look of rain again. I walked over to the window fronting on the street and held the curtain aside, watching the traffic down below. The big doorman kept up a slow pace under the canopy, appearing on either side at regular intervals like a sentry on patrol, hands clasped behind his back while he watched each passing car. He wanted to really earn that ten bucks I gave him.

When I let the curtain fall back I crossed to the bedroom with the glasses and pushed the door open. And there are times when sudden movement just can't be accomplished . . . like being up-wind of a deer and watching him feed, unaware of your presence, or coming on a wild turkey, so normally given to flight they're never seen at all.

That was the way Rondine was, beautifully half naked, skin glistening in the light, her breasts arrogantly thrusting out and upwards from the athletic grace of her body, their ruby-hued tips like tiny warheads capable of destroying a man on contact unless they were disarmed first with a gentle touch.

She stood there, one foot up on a hassock, smoothing a stocking over her thigh, then clasping it in the hook of a garter belt to match the other. When she was satisfied she stepped into a half slip, adjusted it, then went to the full-length mirror on the opposite wall to be sure of the fit.

Then she saw me silently laughing at her, spun around grabbing for her blouse, then realizing how silly it was, gave me an impatient stamp of her foot and said, "How long have *you* been there!"

"Long enough."

"Well, it isn't polite. . . ."

"It isn't polite to undress a guy and put him to bed, either," I reminded her.

"That was different."

"I hope so," I said. I walked across the room and held out the drink. "You look better all the time, kid."

She took the drink, shook her head in feigned annoyance, and reached for her bra. "You keep it up and there won't be anything left for when we're married."

I gave her a long, long appreciative stare and grinned. "With you, honey," I told her, "there's always going to be plenty left over." Then before she could throw something at me I went back outside.

When she finished dressing I heard her call the embassy and arrange for a short leave of absence, then she came out carrying a leather suitcase and white trenchcoat slung over her arm. She let me take it from her, checked the windows and the lights and checked the door lock behind her when we went out. Downstairs she remembered another call she had forgotten to make, stopped at the wall booth while I waited near the door and dialed her number.

That was when the doorman came in. He started toward the desk, saw me and waved me over. "He went by again. Same car. I was just gonna call you."

"Get the number?"

"Damn right." He handed me a slip of paper with the license number scrawled across it. "Last year's Chevy, dark blue sedan and there's a dent in the left rear fender."

"Thanks, buddy. Can I use this phone?"

"Sure, go ahead."

I caught Charlie Corbinet at his apartment, read the number off and hung up while I waited for him to check it through. His contacts were damn thorough. In ten minutes he was back to me with the information that it was a rental car operating out of Surfleet Corporation on Fifty-first Street and a check there said it had been taken out two days ago by a John Clark identified by his driver's license. The same license had been reported stolen a month ago and reissued to John Clark with a Buffalo, New York, address.

Charlie let me note it all down, then said, "What's it mean, Tiger?"

"I may have to move faster. Anything from Interpol on the .22?"

"Uh-huh," he said. "You were right. Same gun used in those other kills. Hal Randolph is jumping all over the place. There isn't an agency left who hasn't been alerted. They're going all out now."

"And the by-pass control?"

"Nothing." He paused, then: "Tiger . . ."

"What?"

"We can't afford to miss."

"I know it, buddy."

"We can't afford to let this thing leak, either," he said. "One word and there will be a panic like we never saw before."

"Hell, the papers will cooperate. Washington is big enough to demand that if somebody tries to break the story."

"That isn't the angle I mean. Supposing the Soviets let the story out themselves. There are enough left-wing and liberal-type publications that drool the Moscow line to get it started. All it takes is one—one lousy do-gooder, one-worlder garbage-eater to get the nitheads screaming in the streets."

"Yeah, I know. All we have left is the element of time. If they're sure Agrounsky pulled the trick off with the by-pass control they might try it, but they have to be sure or it will backfire on them and at this stage of the game they can't afford adverse criticism."

"And how much time have we got?" Charlie asked softly.

"Hardly any," I said and hung up.

Rondine was watching me over the doorman's shoulder, keeping him out of earshot. I shoved the phone back, walked over and picked up her bag. "Where does that rear exit lead to?"

"Goes into the courtyard," the doorman said.

"There's a service alley that runs along the west side of the building behind this one?"

"You got to jump the fence." He thought about it a second and added, "The garbage cans are back there. You could stand on them. That fence is about eight feet high."

I took Rondine's arm. "Show me," I said.

With the doorman leading the way we turned left at the rear of the lobby, went through a fire door into a bare concrete corridor that had service rooms opening off it to the door at the back. At the far end was another metal plated fire door with a red exit bulb over it and a three foot horizonal latch handle stretched across its middle. Like all emergency doors, it opened out, but had an added safety lock of a length of two inch angle iron resting in arms attached to the door with the ends butted against the door jambs to keep it from being opened from the outside.

He pried out the bar easily, stood it on end, and pushed against the handle. The door swung out easily and he turned to me with a grin, half stepping outside to let us go past, and just as I reached for the bag the angle iron in his hand jerked back as if somebody had pulled a string and caught him flat across the forehead and he went down like a poleaxed steer, the door swinging shut until it hit his legs.

I gave Rondine a shove to one side, hit the floor and pulled the angle iron away from his face and checked the massive bruise that was beginning to show over one eye. His cap had saved him from cracking his skull on the floor but aside from the welt he was going to have when he woke up, he'd be all right.

Rondine stood there unmoving, then said softly, "What was it, Tiger?"

I pointed to the head high spot on the surface rust of the angle iron, a dimpled indentation the size of a nickel barely reflecting the dull gray color of freshly spattered lead. "We almost were suckered, kid. They pulled that cruising game out front to force us into a back exit. Somebody's been planted across the way waiting for us to show. They couldn't make a hit on the street without taking too many chances. We damn near fell for the bit."

"Are you . . . ?"

I shook my head. "Uh-uh, baby, I'm not going to do a thing. Whoever fired that shot expected to get me. He isn't the kind who misses, either. In this light all he saw was a body fall and the feet are still there to prove it. This guy and me are both about the same size and for now he'll think I was the one coming through the door. When our friend here comes around he'll go back on duty with a little larger hat to cover his bump and a pocket full of dough to salve his pain and we'll get out of here as nice as you please. If someone's spotted around to watch the action we'll make it nice and authentic for him."

She got the picture fast enough. A simple sketch was all she needed and she grinned from her position against the wall and said something soundlessly that would not have gone with the common concept of a cultured British broad and I grinned back because I knew what she said and that she meant it.

It was fifteen minutes before the doorman let out his first feeble groan and reached for his head and massaged it gently, his eyes flicking open a moment before he squeezed them shut again.

"Can you read me, buddy?"

"Yeah, but not too loud. What the hell happened?"

"Don't sweat it. I'll explain later. Stay right like you are and you'll get paid for the trouble."

"Somebody's gonna get his head in his hands for that one."

"That's not what you're getting paid for. You ready?"

"Okay, okay, just not too loud. Damn, who busted me?"

"Just figure yourself lucky. You could've been killed."

"So I'm lucky. Somebody else is going to be miserable. Wait."

"Concentrate on a grand in your pocket. You'll feel a lot better."

He opened his eyes all the way and peered at me in the near dark. "I feel better already. Tell me more."

"Later." I looked up at Rondine. "Can you handle it?"

"Go ahead," she said.

From the lobby phone I reached Wally Gibbons. He was still in his office at the paper and didn't bother going through the futility of asking questions. He arranged for the private ambulance to get to the address and forwarded my call to Charlie Corbinet so the timing would be right and the cover set through I.A.T.S. They weren't going to like it, but then, they didn't have to. All they could do was go along and let it ride like that.

There wasn't much time, but we worked it out. The ambulance got there first and before it was parked we had the doorman snaked out of his position. From outside all anybody could see was feet moving back through the door and that would have satisfied them. The doorman was back moving traffic along outside the apartment, keeping the curious away while they wheeled me out, face covered with a sheet on a stretcher, loaded me into the ambulance with a supposedly bereaved woman going along for the final ride at my side. We were making the turn at the corner when the first of the squad cars came screaming up the street and I sat up in the ambulance to look into the face of a completely cynical, white coated attendant who said, "What's the gag, friend?"

All I did was reach in my pocket, lay two big bills in his hand and answer, "What difference does it make?"

He took the cash, held out a clipboard with a printed form on it that I could sign, and when I did said, "None at all, friend. The bill is paid. What'll I do with the change?" he asked cautiously.

"Split it with the driver," I told him.

"Call on us any time. Here's our card. Now where to? We charge by the mile."

I gave him the corner two blocks away from my new quarters and he relayed the information through the window to the driver. The guy at the wheel said nothing. He turned off the overhead light, fired up a cigarette and relaxed back against the seat to enjoy the ride. I had thought the cabbies in New York were blasé, but they never came near these guys at all.

Rondine and I got out without attracting any attention at all, stopped at a deli to pick up some sandwiches long enough to make sure we weren't being tailed, then walked down to the sign that said *Shigley's* and went up to the apartment Martin Grady had so thoughtfully supplied.

In another couple of hours the evening papers would be carrying the story of the dead man shot in the classy residential district, identified by papers he carried as one T. Mann, an employee of the Martin Grady organization, the reason for his death unknown, but suspected of being caused by a prowler attempting to force an entrance into the building. I.A.T.S. had no choice but to go along, but the stuff was going to hit the fan when Hal Randolph and I got face to face.

The rain had started again. It slashed against the windows like fingers of an animal trying to get in, driving and clawing momentarily before taking a respite to make another attack, then under cover of the sudden glow of lightning and the rumbling of thunder from across the Hudson River it would charge in to beat and hammer in a furious onslaught of nature against man. There was a childish fury in the storm, an ineffectual pounding that was insistent and annoying, but lacking the cold skill of the adult beasts that were piling up in the Caribbean, massing themselves for a concerted attack in a month or so, disguised by innocuous female names they give to hurricanes in this age of suffrage.

A half hour ago the late news had mentioned the supposed killing at Rondine's address and somewhere out there in the city Niger Hoppes was sitting back smugly thinking his primary mission was accomplished and counting his reward when the report was in. Somewhere he was satisfied that he had won and the rest of the mission was a *fait accompli* because the biggest obstacle was already disposed of.

Somewhere out there was a guy who was going to get the biggest surprise of his life.

The phone rang, a jarring note in the stillness. I picked it up and waited, then heard Martin Grady code his identification. When I gave mine he said, "Newark Control just gave me the information, Tiger. Anything to add to it?"

"Not yet. Did any of our people cut it at Rondine's apartment?"

"We had two spotted there. Between the police and I.A.T.S., they did a good job, but some big explanations are going to be forthcoming. Your old Colonel put a tight squeeze on them. Incidentally, he passed on the information that the slug was a high-velocity .22, so the picture is coming together."

"But no sign of Niger Hoppes though?" I asked him.

"Not yet. We're trying some left-field tactics to get an ID on the guy. Somebody on his side will have to know him by sight and if we can run down just one we'll get a description. You'll get it the minute it comes through."

"Good enough. Any repercussions in Washington yet?"

Grady let out a chuckle. "Talk of reorganization in certain departments. That means they'll be promoting the eggheads up out of sight instead of dumping them. If the State Department would get on the ball they'd take an ax to some of their bunch.

When this is over we're going to concentrate on certain key personnel up there and get their activities out in the open."

"It's about time."

"Okay then, Tiger, stay in touch. Don't hesitate to ask for anything you need."

"Roger, Martin. As far as anybody's concerned, I'm dead, so get some light publicity in that department."

"Already done."

"Europe too?"

"The word was over there before it made the papers here. I don't doubt but that there is rejoicing in Red Square."

"Great," I said sourly. "Let's hope it gives us a little extra time."

I hung up and sat in the sofa, propping my feet on the window sill so I could look out at the rain. Someplace out there was the answer, the cause and the effect. Someplace out there Louis Agrounsky was still trying to make up his mind.

I felt Rondine sit beside me, her fingers slide up my shoulder and massage my neck. "Can it wait?" she asked.

"No."

Her lips brushed my cheek and she turned my head around gently. While I was watching the night she had changed into a cobwebby thing that was almost transparent. "But it'll have to," I said.

CHAPTER SIX

VIRGIL ADAMS AWOKE me at six A.M. with his call, a brief message
to make contact with Dave Elroy at a roominghouse so far downtown the river was in the back yard. He coded it urgent and
didn't give me any more details, so I knew Dave had buzzed him
from an open phone somewhere and didn't want to lay any explanations on the line at that point.

Rondine's eyes came open, still hazy with sleep, saw me
perched on the edge of the bed and smiled in that pleased way
women have after a perfect night and she squirmed under the
covers so that the sheet outlined the full sweep of her hips and
the lazy curve of her legs. "Who was it, darling?"

"Business, kid.

The hazy look faded and her eyes became bright with sudden
anxiety. "Something wrong?"

"I don't know." I climbed into my clothes as quickly as I could,
looked at myself in the mirror before deciding I could do without
a shave for a while, then dropped the .45 into the speed rig on my
belt and pulled on my coat.

"Will you be long?"

I bent over and kissed her lightly. Anything else and it would
be too hard to tear myself away from her. "I'll make it quickly as
I can. You just stay put, baby. Don't answer the door unless you

get a 'V' rap. If I call I'll let it ring once, hang up, then ring again. Anything else, ignore. Got it?"

She half sat up in the bed, the covers clutched at her throat. "Be careful, Tiger."

"You know me."

"That's what I mean."

Downstairs, the city was beginning to come back to life again. The early morning smells from the restaurants had seeped out into the canyons between the buildings to lure in the sidewalk marchers going to work. Two city trucks had already disgorged a dozen men near the corner where they were ready to finish a huge excavation in the street. New York, I thought, a self-perpetuating machine that never stopped. No matter where you looked, skeletal steel towered into the sky and gigantic troughs were gouged into the bedrock below. No place to build but up, and up they were going. I wondered what they'd do if they thought it could all come tumbling down in a single second.

Rather than take a cab, I let myself be fed into the maw of a subway entrance and boarded a downtown local. When I got off I spotted the house numbers, turned east and walked two blocks to the last remaining brownstones that had once lined the street and went up the steps to the vestibule and pushed the door open.

The greasy smell of cooking cut through the musty odor that was part of the building, coming from the apartment on the far end of the hall. Underfoot were a half dozen empty whiskey bottles, and the stairway to one side was packed with empty cartons and accumulated debris that would make a fire inspector turn green.

When my eyes were adjusted to the semi-gloom I snaked the gun out and went down the hall, staying close to the wall so the floorboards wouldn't creak under my weight. The signal I tapped on the door had been prearranged, but I still didn't take any chances. I stayed to one side ready to cut loose if anything was wrong at all.

Dave didn't forget his manners either. He tapped back the right answer to get me at ease, opened the door on a chain, made sure of the identification, then swung it open all the way.

"Greetings, Tiger."

"Yeah, sure."

"Come on in. We have a little party going."

I stepped in with the .45 still ready, cut to one side as I swept the room with my eyes, then stuck the rod back in my belt when I got the picture. There was only one other in the room aside from Dave, a scrawny little guy with a scared face who kept gulping rapidly even though he was dry as a bone.

"Couldn't you pick a better hotel?"

Dave grinned at me as he double locked the door. "His digs," he said. "Meet Earl Mossky. They call him The Creeper. That right, Earl?"

The guy's head bobbed and in a surprisingly deep voice he said, "Yeah, that's me."

Dave waved a thumb at me. "He's the one I told you about, Earl. Tiger Mann."

Earl Mossky's eyes narrowed and he gulped again. "I know about him."

"How?" I asked.

"Word gets around." He fidgeted in his chair and picked up the stump of a chewed cigar and lit it, never taking his eyes off me.

"What's the pitch, Dave?"

"Earl here is a pusher. Small time, but he's been at it a long time."

"Never picked up neither," the guy added.

"Deals strictly in H," Dave told me. "Poolroom trade, mostly, but it keeps him in bread and he doesn't have any big ideas about expanding."

"It ain't healthy," Earl muttered.

"So he's got a story to tell."

"Let's hear yours first," I said to Dave.

He pointed to a sway backed chair and pulled one up for himself. "I'll skip the details, but I picked up word of the buy Vito Salvi made. What Don Lavois found in the crapper in the guy's room wasn't the whole catch. That was only part of it. That right, Earl?"

"Hell, he went for a kilo. That's two-point-two pounds of junk and he got in at base rates. Paid five hundred an ounce off the ship."

I sat back and stared at the guy. "How do you know?"

The little guy puffed on the cigar, took it out of his mouth with distaste and stubbed it out under his foot. "You stick in this racket long enough and you get to know everything. Those guys transporting the stuff are like friends of mine, see? So they're footing the bill one night for a smash down at Pecky's Place and they let me in on this laugh how I should be on their side of the fence. They got two grand apiece for bringing the stuff in while I'm still hustling pennies."

Dave said, "Pure stuff. By the time they make the final cut a kilo of H is worth a few million."

"This guy who bought it," I said.

Earl shrugged. "I keep my nose long, buddy. I wanted a look at this character because he wasn't local. It was some kind of a special deal set up ahead of time. It was the same one this guy showed me the picture of."

"Salvi," Dave added.

"Go on."

"That's all. He took the can and bugged out. You think I'm gonna poke around?"

"How'd he pay for it?"

"Clean cash, buddy. Ninety G's and no arguing."

"Where did the split go?"

Earl Mossky shrugged again and squirmed in the chair. "I don't ask that either. The boys already left on another trip to the Persian Gulf and if you want you can find out from them. You won't get nothing though. The big ones don't leave no holes to look through. Someplace they just passed over the dough, got theirs and forgot about it."

"One more question, Earl," I said.

"Go ahead, you're giving the party."

"Where do you fit in?"

"I hear somebody's paying off big for some nice quiet talk, the kind that don't backfire. I want a trip to Miami for my health."

Dave said, "If you're satisfied, Grady's authorized a bundle for him."

"Let him have it then," I told him.

"Make any sense?"

I stood up and reached for my hat. "It will. There's a new dimension added now. I can think of only two reasons why they would want to make a buy as big as that and in so much of a hurry they'd have to take a chance and get it direct from an importer."

"Oh?" Dave was looking at me quizzically.

"You figure it out," I said. I started for the door.

Behind me Earl Mossky said, "What about my dough?"

Dave took a key out of his pocket and handed it to him. "In a locker at the bus terminal waiting for you. My advice to you is not to blow it around here or somebody else will be asking questions. Catch?"

"Buddy," he nodded, fingering the key with a hungry look, "I lived a long time and I figure to live a little while longer. I know the answers."

We waited until we got to the Times Square station before calling in our report to Newark Control. Virgil Adams was calling in another team to probe the area to see if any of the Salvi buy had been peddled off and putting through an overseas query to try and run down the reason for the direct contact. Dave Elroy was to stay on Don's original assignment of backtracking Salvi, and if possible, to pick up his source of financing. The Soviet network was tight enough to make it a tough job, but someplace there was always a hole you could sneak through if you found it.

At ten o'clock I angled over to Ernie Bentley's lab and went upstairs to where he was buried among his reports and poured myself a steaming mug of coffee. When I gave him the rundown he nodded as if I were reading off the ball scores and finished what he was doing before deciding to answer me.

"Got yourself a lot of pieces, haven't you?"

"Too damn many."

"Nothing leading to Louis Agrounsky?"

"No."

"Maybe I got something," he said. He walked to his desk, pawed through some mail and came up with a dye-smeared envelope and pulled out the letter inside. "One of the suppliers of sub-mini parts Agrounsky corresponded with. A few years ago he submitted several pieces for inspection and the manufacturer was pretty interested. Agrounsky came up with a few unheard of ideas that had a big potential. He wrote several times and got no answer until I contacted him. Right now he's pretty interested in re-establishing contact himself. In view of the new space developments Agrounsky's ideas can come in handy."

"No address?" I asked him.

"Just his Eau Gallie house."

"Damn!"

"But there's a lead. He apparently wrote his last letter on his friend's stationery. Guy named Vincent Small, address, 37 Meadow Lane, Eau Gallie, Florida."

"We're back to there again."

"It started down there, didn't it?" Ernie said simply.

"They've gone all over that route, Ernie. I.A.T.S., the other bureaus, our own teams. We have to pick it up closer than that."

"But *you* haven't, Tiger buddy," he reminded me.

I looked across the room at him, sipping at the coffee. "Okay," I finally said, "it might be worth a try. I'll clean up the loose ends here first and see what I can pick up in that section."

"Then keep the plane up here. If you need special equipment I'll send it down."

"Keep your toys to yourself," I said.

"They saved your tail a few times."

"I don't like the instability factors involved."

"So we all make mistakes. Besides, those details have been smoothed over. I have a new gadget here. . . ."

"Save it," I grinned at him. "I'll stick with the old fashioned way."

"You and that damn gun," he said.

At noon I met Charlie Corbinet at the Blue Ribbon, took a table upstairs and waited until our order was taken before I gave him the latest developments. Charlie let me finish and said, "I'll get with the Treasury Department on that heroin buy this afternoon."

"Lay off my sources."

"Don't sweat it. You know me better than that."

"What did you hear from Washington?"

Charlie reached down and laid a manila envelope on the table between us. "There's all the UR's from the security department. Doug Hamilton turned in thirty-four and half of them checked out with unsatisfactory reports from prior investigations. Several were known or suspected Commie agents and the rest we're working on."

"Any description fit Agrounsky?"

"None. But then, we haven't checked them all out yet. A batch are itinerant workers who showed up for simple laboring jobs, but their associations were listed as n.g., so they were disqualified. All this went through Belt-Aire Electronics before it was submitted to Washington anyway."

"That's what Camille Hunt told me."

Our waiter came along then, laid the lunch down with a flourish and went to get coffee. Charlie watched me across his plate, his eyes bright. "You two got along pretty well, didn't you?"

"Why not?"

"Hal Randolph dug into Belt-Aire pretty thoroughly."

"So?"

"You know they have top priority in the new space project?"

"Uh-huh."

"To what extent?"

"That's Martin Grady's business."

"Then let me fill you in. . . . What they're proposing can put the balance of power on our side. Mention Belt-Aire in Washington and you're in for a security check no matter who you are. They want nobody poking around. This is getting pretty damn touchy. Even we don't know the full extent of the operation. That's a highly sensitive area and if anything goes haywire there will be hell to pay."

"It can't be any worse than it is," I said.

"No, but now everybody is running scared. We haven't got much time to break something loose. I get the feeling the Reds are closer than we are and if they let the cat out of the bag this is going to be one shook up country."

"I don't need any reminding, Charlie. I was there at the beginning, remember?"

"Then keep your memory refreshed. What do you plan to do with this information?"

"Exactly the same as you—check it out step by step, only from a different direction. Can I have these names?"

"They're yours . . . all copies of the original."

I took the folder and put it beside me. "How does Hal Randolph like me being dead?"

"He'd like it better if it were true. My advice is to stay in touch, Tiger. Daily reports . . . the works. He's scared stiff you might do something that will trigger the works and I can't blame him. Right now we can't take any chances."

"The chance was taken when they hired Agrounsky," I said. "If he decides to use that by-pass control then we've had it."

"Hasn't everybody?" Charlie told me softly.

When we left I gave him a five minute start before I cleared out through the bar entrance. On Sixth Avenue I picked up a cab that was discharging a passenger on the corner, had the driver let me off a block away from my quarters, and walked the rest of the way.

I gave the bell the V signal, did the same thing with a tap on the door and let Rondine throw off the locks. Even then she was being careful, the little automatic in her hand being on full cock until she was certain it was me.

She shut the door, locked it securely and followed me inside. "I was beginning to get worried," she said.

I grinned and pushed a chair up for her at the table. "Don't waste time doing that," I told her. "It takes away from other things."

"There was an item in TV about the incident at my place again. The police are supposedly still investigating."

"Eyewash. They'll keep it up a couple of days and let it quiet down."

"Weren't you taking a chance going out in the daylight?"

I shook my head. "Not in this town, kid. People are like ants. You can't tell one from the other unless an army is searching for you. I played it cool."

"And your . . . meeting?"

Briefly, I gave her the details, then dumped the contents of the envelope out on the table. "I want you to do something for me. For a while you'll be free to move around and since you're not generally known it might work."

"Oh?"

I looked up at her, knowing my face had that tight expression again. "You've been well trained for this work, baby. You have the background and experience and I need your help."

She didn't hesitate. She knew the implications as well as I did and her own future was involved with everyone else's. "Just ask, Tiger."

"Here is a list of people I want you to run down. I.A.T.S. ran a check already with no results, but there's a lot of difference when they ask questions and a dame does. Even if these people aren't available, I want background material on them, their associations, and angle for any possible Commie affiliations. You have people attached to your British Embassy you can call in if you need help. . . . They'll know how to proceed . . . and I'll keep a constant contact with you here."

"And where will you be?"

"Eau Gallie, Florida. I'm picking it up from there." I wrote down two phone numbers, Ernie Bentley's and that of Newark Control with an identification name that meant she was clear to use our lines of communication and be given limited information. I let her study the numbers until she had them memorized, then burned the slip they were written on. "Dave Elroy will be available and if anything turns tough, you duck out and let him take over. Just make sure you don't stick your neck out. The ones we're bucking play for keeps and being a woman won't keep you alive. Understand?"

"I understand."

I slid a sheaf of bills across the table and said, "This will keep you going until I get back. If you have to pay off for any information, contact the Newark number and it will be arranged. And don't hesitate to buy what is up for sale. Money is the cheapest thing we have in our business."

"Tiger . . ."

"What?"

Something had changed in her face. There was a seriousness there I hadn't seen before and her eyes were those of others I had known before in bomb shelters, scanning the ceilings above them as though they could see through them to the hordes of death dealers flying high in the night above.

"Do you . . . really think you should have such a part in all this? Isn't it better left to those . . . equipped to handle a . . . a situation of this sort?"

My teeth were together so hard they almost cracked. "Like who, baby?"

"Our governments. They . . ."

"They're composed of great guys," I almost hissed, ". . . mainly. But in the ranks are too damn many selling us out through sheer stupidity . . . or cupidity . . . or avariciousness . . . or because they got caught with their pants down and face public exposure through blackmail. No, kitten, guys like me belong here. We've been here a long time and are going to stay. When one goes another takes his place, but somebody is always there to make up for the tacky ones who masquerade under cute government titles. They're not elected . . . the people can generally see through them if they try. But they're appointed or assigned to critical posts and suddenly we have a new pseudo-government functioning on collegiate political philosophy or the theoretics of some obscure but red-tainted brain hoping that someday he'll be holding the reins of a one world dictatorship.

You want me to mention names? Hell, I can give you fifty off-hand from your country and this one. I can make your hair curl with what I know and the public should know, but to protect themselves the biggies upstairs keep these babies under cover with a little pressure and promises here and there. So think it over. You've heard it all before from me. At least we're a damned talented bunch in a strange way, but we get things done nobody else can do and we're not hamstrung by niceties or afraid of losing our jobs . . . and we sure don't worry about what anybody else thinks about us, either."

Rondine absorbed it all, but the expression never left her face.

Age, *I thought*, she should have been there during the war. She was too young to know what it really meant, and unless you experienced the double dealing and the killing you could never really understand. You had to know the meaning of death and face it time after time before the calluses grew. You had to hold death in your hand and expose an enemy to it to stay alive yourself . . . then each time became easier and you became better at living and knowledgeable in the ways of this crazy world so that you became formidable as an opponent and could deal in extremes no matter the cost.

It was what I didn't say that made the impression. Her eyes seemed to bore inside me and search my mind for the hidden answers and what she saw satisfied her, and very slowly her face relaxed into that classic beauty so much her own. I felt that warm turmoil start in my stomach again.

"I'm sorry," she said simply.

"Forget it," I grinned. "It's a new game to you and I'm an old soldier."

Her teeth showed a flash of white in a terse smile. "*You're* forgetting, Tiger. In a way, I'm an old soldier too. Twice before . . . "

I could see the blinding sear of the explosion . . . remember the guns . . . picture her face . . . all when she was part of the deadly game the last time with me.

"Forget that too," I said.

"Should I?"

I studied her face, my eyes going narrow again. "No . . . maybe it's better you remember it after all. It might keep you on your toes."

Mason was at Newark Airport with the converted F-51 gassed and warmed up. While he filed his flight plan I stowed my suitcase in the wells that used to house the .50 calibre guns and climbed into the back seat. Ten minutes later we were airborne and headed south, climbing to eight thousand above the overcast that blanketed New Jersey below. When Mason leveled off he held the ship at maximum cruise, made a gas stop at Charleston, South Carolina and was back in the blue again in twenty minutes. An hour and ten minutes later we let down into the traffic pattern of the field a little south of Eau Gallie, landed and taxied up to the transient hangar.

The car I had arranged for earlier was waiting and I got in after telling Mason to be available at any time. He grinned, nodded, and headed off for a cold beer someplace. I didn't ask for directions to the motel I was quartered at until I reached town, then found the place not far from the beach and signed in under T. Marvin from New York City. Aside from Newark Control and Ernie Bentley, nobody knew where I was staying and until a break came, I wanted to keep as much of a cover as I could.

At eight fifteen I showered and dressed, grabbed a bite at the adjacent restaurant, got directions to Meadow Lane, and drove off in that direction. Number 37 was a red brick ranch-type house set back from the road, surrounded by a hodge-podge of foliage with huge red blooms that gave off a sickly sweet odor and seemed to attract a horde of pale blue butterflies. I turned in the driveway, parked behind a new Chevy convertible and killed the engine.

I didn't have to knock. The door opened as I went up the flagstone steps and a short, chunky guy with a big friendly smile grinned up at me and said, "Hello, hello. I'm Vincent Small. Something I can do for you?"

I shook hands with him, almost smothering his with my own. "My name's Mann, Mr. Small. I'm trying to locate a friend of mine and if I can bother you a few minutes, maybe you can help."

"Why sure . . . sure. Come on in. Always glad to help out." He ushered me in, closed the door and waved me into a spacious living room lined on two sides with fully packed bookshelves. "Make you a drink?"

"Fine. Whatever you're having."

"I'm for a beer."

"Good enough."

He popped open two cans, held one out to me and sat down in a wicker rocking chair opposite me. "Now," he said, "what's your problem?"

"You knew Louis Agrounsky, didn't you?"

"Lou? Why, certainly. Is he the one you're looking for?"

I took a pull of the beer and put the can on the floor beside me. "Uh-huh."

His grin took on a puzzled twist. "Now that's very funny."

"What is?"

"Poor Lou . . . having everybody looking for him and all the while he was right here he was a lonely guy who never knew a soul. Never saw anybody so much alone. Even after his accident when he couldn't work any more, nobody but Claude Boster or me ever saw him."

"He wasn't the type who made friends easily, Mr. Small. His work required so much secrecy the habit rubbed off on him."

Small nodded agreement, his mouth pursed in thought. "You're right there. Never could get him into conversation about his job. Never really tried," he added. "You understand that, of course. With Claude he always talked about his hobby—those miniature electronics he played with. Whenever we were together it was always philosophy."

"That your hobby?" I asked.

"Goodness no," he laughed. "That's my profession. Teach it over at Bromwell University. Lou and I both graduated from there. I was two years ahead of him, but we became good friends when we roomed in the same dorm. Lou never studied philosophy . . . majored in mathematics and all that, but after he had his breakdown he became interested in the subject and researched it as much as I did. It seemed to relieve him."

"I didn't think that breakdown was that serious," I said.

Small shrugged and sipped his drink. "It wasn't, really. Overwork, I think. Lou really crammed harder than most. He was capable of absorbing it all, but the late hours finally caught up with him. No sleep, hours of study, a part time job . . . that's a little too much for anybody."

"He really change after that?"

"He learned not to push too hard," Small told me. "He changed jobs and kept more reasonable hours." He frowned in thought a moment, then added, "He became more introspective, I'd say. Social behavior seemed to concern him . . . the state of the world . . . that sort of thing. We spent many an hour discussing it from a philosophical viewpoint."

"What was his?"

"Now that," Vincent Small said, "I was hoping you could tell me. Lou never did arrive at a conclusion. He would ponder the subject endlessly, but never found an answer."

"What philosopher ever did?"

He glanced at me, surprised at the tone of my voice. "Ah, Mr. Mann, I take it that you're a realist."

"All the way."

"And philosophy ; . . ?"

"Doesn't fit the facts," I answered him.

His eyes brightened with humor, sparkling at the possibility of argument, seeing me take a fall. "Offer an example."

"Where do you go when you die?" I said. Before he could answer I grinned and put in, "And prove it."

Then, like all the others who strive so hard to make the simple difficult, he threw it back to me again because he didn't know. "Maybe you'd like to offer your version."

"Sure," I said, and finished the beer. "Six feet down."

"Ah, Mr. Mann . . . that's so . . ."

"Practical?"

"But . . ."

"Ever go to a funeral?"

"Yes, but then . . ."

"And where did the body go?"

"Realists are impossible to talk to," he smiled.

"Ever kill a man, Small?"

"Of course not."

"Well, I have. Quite a few. That's fact, not philosophical nonsense. It's real and complete. It makes you think about more things than all the trivia Plato or Aristotle ever dealt out."

Small threw me a peculiar glance and put his empty can on the table beside him. "Mr. Mann . . . you're a strange sort of person for Lou to have known. May I ask how you came to meet him?"

"I haven't yet," I said. "I hope to before somebody else does, though."

"That sounds rather mysterious."

"It isn't. It's something that can't be explained because it involves his work, but it's damned serious and I want to find him."

"Yes." He nodded, suddenly concerned. "I can believe that."

"You mentioned other people interested in locating Louis Agrounsky. . . ."

"Several."

"They identify themselves as the police or a government agency?"

"It wasn't me they approached."

"Oh?"

"Claude Boster mentioned it. He was queried twice by persons saying they were Lou's friends and when he ran into one of Lou's former associates at the project, that one had been approached too. However, neither could supply any information. Lou seemed to have disappeared from the face of the earth."

"No communication at all?"

"None whatsoever. Now, may I ask you a question?"

"My pleasure."

"What is your interest in this?"

"Money, Mr. Small," I said. "My employer wants to purchase one of Agrounsky's inventions very badly, and if I can locate him before the competition, I'm in, so to speak."

"Then you're a . . . a . . ."

"Call it investigator."

"And you've killed people," he stated.

"Only when it was necessary."

"Do you think it will be necessary in this case?"

"There's a distinct possibility. We're at war, Mr. Small. Right now a cold war, but war nevertheless."

His nod was solemn. "I see. And the competition isn't the local commercial variety."

I didn't answer him. I didn't have to.

Finally he said, "Can you identify yourself, sir?"

"Curious?"

"All philosophers are."

"Then call the New York office of I.A.T.S. and ask for Charles Corbinet. He'll be glad to supply my ID."

"Perhaps I will," he told me. "You interest me strangely. This whole affair is very peculiar. It will make for some curious speculation."

"Don't philosophize on it, Small. If you can think of any place Agrounsky might be, keep it to yourself. I'll contact you off and on while I'm around. That is . . . if you don't mind."

"Not at all. Lou's disappearance disturbs me deeply. I'm quite concerned for him."

I got up, stuck my hat on and held out my hand to Vincent Small. "Thanks for the talk."

"No bother at all."

"Know where I might locate Claude Boster right now?"

"Without a doubt. He'll be in his shop behind his house, brains deep in hairlike wiring, circuits he's trying to reduce to pea size, and a headache as big as a house from squinting into microscopes."

And he was right. Twenty minutes after I left Vincent Small I was watching Claude Boster through the casement window of his small machine shop, back hunched over a small lathe he operated under an enlarging glass, stopping occasionally to rub his head over one ear and make a grimace of disgust.

When I knocked he shut off his power and shuffled to the door, opened it to peer out at me, and said, "Yes?"

"Claude Boster?"

He nodded. "That's right."

"Mann is my name. I just came from Vincent Small who suggested I see you about a matter."

Small's name wiped the puzzled frown from his face. "Oh. Yes, please come in."

I walked inside, took in the entire room with a sweep of my eyes, gauging the extent of his activities and cataloguing them in my mind. Although the layout was compact and gave no illusion of any size whatsoever, it was an extensive operation with equipment well into the five figure mark.

At one corner was a table with two metal chairs and Boster pulled one out, offered it to me and sat in the other one. "Now, Mr. Mann . . ."

"Louis Agrounsky. I'm looking for him."

A shadow seemed to pass over Boster's face and his eyes had a withdrawn look. "Yes, indeed," was all he said.

"I understand you've been approached before."

"That is correct. I also understand that Louis was engaged in project work that put him in a special category."

"There's no security involved now. There's a commercial aspect of one of his inventions I'm interested in. I'm authorized to locate him if possible."

"By whom, sir?"

Sometimes you have to go all the way and I did the same thing with him I did with Vincent Small. I told him to contact I.A.T.S. in New York and ask for Charlie Corbinet. He studied me a moment, then, without answering, pulled a phone out from under the desk, dialed the operator and gave her the information. The call went through in thirty seconds and Claude Boster had Charlie on the other end giving him my name, a description, then handed the phone to me. I talked for ten seconds more, enough so Charlie was certain it was me, then handed the phone back. What he said satisfied Boster and he hung up.

"Cloak-and-dagger business, eh?"

I shrugged, watching his face relax, and said, "Can we get to Agrounsky now?"

He opened his palms helplessly. "What can I say? Louis just disappeared."

"People like him don't *just* disappear."

"*He* did," Boster insisted.

"How well did you know him?"

"We were good friends, Mr. Mann. Closer, perhaps, from a technical viewpoint than a social one, but friends. I presume you know about his hobby."

"Slightly. You both seem to have the same one." I nodded toward the rest of the room.

"With me it isn't a hobby. It started that way, but it's serious work now. Miniaturization is a vital aspect of most engineering developments today and offers me a comfortable livelihood. I only wish Louis were with me now. I hate to admit it but he was well ahead of me in the major stages of mini-work."

"You familiar with the details?"

Boster shook his head. "Unfortunately, no, otherwise I would be tempted to duplicate his experiments. If his work is lost to the world, it's a great pity." He sighed and leaned back in the chair. "Louis was a genius," he said simply.

"How great?"

"Possibly one of the greatest. There was a power unit he developed that could be activated remotely, capable of lighting an entire house. The whole thing was small enough to hold in the hollow of your hand. His subminiature circuits, even at that time, were several times smaller than my most recent refinements, and I might say that I am foremost in this particular field at this moment. Yes, it was quite a pity." He looked up at me seriously and added, "Have you *any* idea where he might be?"

"No."

Claude Boster nodded again. "I believe you," he told me. He seemed to purse his lips in thought, then: "But it *is* strange. He was always so vitally interested in his work. You see . . . he too believed that subminiaturization was the answer to the complicated technical problems that beset space projects. He searched for the answers and found them. Then . . . it was all changed. It was that accident," he mused.

"The car wreck?"

"That's right," Boster agreed. "It seemed to be nothing at first. After he was released from the hospital everything seemed to be all right, then he started to change."

"How?"

Boster made an impatient gesture. "Oh, nothing definite. He . . . he seemed withdrawn, distant. We weren't as close any more. It was a surprise to me when he sold everything and left. I never heard a word from him."

"No complaints about the accident . . . no permanent injury?"

"He never mentioned anything and he seemed fit enough except for periods of extreme nervousness. At these times he'd leave for a few days and come back feeling better. I assumed he merely rested somewhere. We never discussed it." Boster paused, thought a moment, then went on. "Those periods became more frequent. Frankly, I couldn't understand it and since he was loath to talk about it, I never mentioned it. Such a pity."

"And he left no records?" I prompted.

Boster smiled wistfully. "None. I inquired personally. I searched what little effects he had here and found nothing. In fact . . . one day . . . it was one of those times when he was feeling very badly . . . he mentioned in passing that when he completed his special project he was going to destroy all written details of it. Frankly, I didn't think he would. It was much too unscientific a thing to do, so I passed it off to his condition. But . . . I guess he meant it, all right."

I took a cigarette from the pack, offered one to Boster, and lit them up. "He ever discuss politics with you?"

"Never. The subject didn't seem to interest him. Only his work was important."

I said, "He discussed philosophy with Vincent Small."

"That and politics are far different matters. Occasionally he would make statements that seemed to be connected with his work—whether or not the world should exist with such products in its hands . . . that sort of thing. A bit incoherent, I thought. The present world situation always distressed him, but doesn't it everyone?"

"Everyone with sense," I agreed.

"A few times he left and didn't return for three days."

"I see." I said absently.

"I wish I did, Mr. Mann."

"Well, thanks for the talk."

"Did I help?"

"Everybody helps somehow or other. I may call on you again. If anything occurs to you, keep it in mind."

"Gladly. I wish I could do more. He had few friends and I doubt if any of us could give a complete picture of him. However, you might consult the doctor who attended him after the accident. During that time he was fairly close to Louis. At least he saw him several times a day."

"Remember his name?"

"Carlson. Dr. George Carlson. He has his own clinic now one block from the shopping center."

I stood up and held out my hand. "I'll do that. And thanks. Hope I didn't put you out."

"Not at all."

Boster went to the door and opened it for me. I stuck my hat on and flipped my cigarette out into the night, watching it arc like a tiny flare . . . and that pinpoint of light saved my skin because it was cut off briefly by something that moved in front of it and I shoved Boster back with one hand and hit the floor even as two shots blasted above me and ricocheted around the room behind us.

There wasn't time to get the .45 out . . . barely enough to kick the door shut and yell, "The lights!"

Boster hit a switch by the door sill and the room went dark. I said, "Stay there," then yanked the door open, pulled the gun from the sling and cocked it, then went out into the night in a diving roll, hoping I wasn't going into a sucker trap.

I hit the bushes, waited, watched for movement against the lights in the background, but whoever it had been hadn't waited to see the results of his attempted kill. When I was sure the area was clear I went back inside, turned the lights back on and had Boster pull the blinds shut.

"Mr. Mann," he said, his breath caught in his throat. "What . . . was that for?"

"I don't know, friend," I said. "I'm just curious about one thing."

"What . . . is that?"

"Were they shooting at me . . . or you?"

CHAPTER SEVEN

THE POLICE BOUGHT an easy story. On three occasions in the past few months attempts had been made to burglarize Claude Boster's premises after a news story about his exploits had been published in a technical magazine. Now it was supposed that whoever was after his material was taking more drastic measures. The slugs they recovered were .38's and were to be sent to Washington for a ballistic check, and a uniformed police officer was assigned to cover Boster until they had the situation cleared up. I was simply a visiting friend caught in the middle and Boster went along with it, suddenly aware of the implications.

When they left I got back in the car, made no attempt to try anything fancy and deliberately left myself open for a tail. If those shots were meant for me the killer knew damn well he missed and would be making another try. I just wanted to make it easy for him.

Eau Gallie wasn't that big to hide in. But it wasn't that big to lay on a tail that couldn't be spotted, either. If those slugs were meant for Boster, nobody was interested in me. If they had my name on them, then the assassin was waiting for another time and another place.

I wanted to be sure, so I made my call to Newark Control from a well lit booth adjoining a service station. I parked the car to cover me from the dark area behind the building, so if anybody took me on it would have to be where I could see them and the .45 in my hand was ready to talk.

Virgil Adams taped our conversation completely, then told me he was sending Dave Elroy down by Martin Grady's orders to back me up. Dave was to register at an assigned motel and to stay on tap for any emergency.

"It isn't necessary," I told him. "I can handle it alone. Too many of our people around might cause trouble. Dave was on that narcotics bit in Hong Kong and the Soviets know him by sight."

"Just the same," Virgil said, "Grady wants you covered."

"So let him come then. Anything new on Niger Hoppes from London?"

"A curious bit of ID material, not that it will do much good. Johnson has been picking up bits and pieces about the guy and the latest is that he's a sniffer."

"A what?"

"Those nose inhalers to clear up the sinuses. Benzedrine compounds. Excitement clogs him up so he sniffs the stuff."

"Great, old buddy. So what do I do—check every drugstore and supermarket in the States to see who buys them? You know how many they sell every day?"

"I already checked," he laughed back. "About fifty thousand."

"Thanks," I said sarcastically.

"No trouble," he told me and hung up.

When I stepped outside I lit a cigarette, deliberately making a target of myself, but ready to move if anything showed. Aside from a few cars heading in either direction and two couples going by hand-in-hand the area was empty. The shift workers from Cape Kennedy had already made their swing and it wasn't the season for the biannual north-south flow of traffic. I took my time about getting in the car, then started up, cut out into the street and found an open diner where I grabbed a coffee while watching the windows, and when I was certain nobody was tailing me, I paid the bill and angled back to the motel.

I parked in front of the office, went in and hit the bell on the desk. The same man who had rented me my room said, "Yes, sir, what can I do for you?"

"I'd like a room, please."

"But . . ."

"No, I'll keep the other one. . . . I want a different one."

"Oh, I see . . . you're expecting company?"

"Not exactly. I may want to use it for a conference room later and I don't want one all cluttered up with my personal gear."

"Yes, yes, of course," he agreed quickly. "We don't usually get the salesmen trade here and I almost forgot their habits." He swung the card holder around to me. "Mind signing?"

I registered in the way I did before and paid for a day in advance. When I stuck the pen back I said, "Put any calls through to my own room, but if anybody asks where I'm staying, give them this number. I'll leave my car parked outside it, okay?"

"Certainly, sir. Glad to be of service."

"Fine. Good night."

"Good night, sir."

I put the car in the driveway beside the room, went in, kept the lights on about five minutes, cut them off, then eased back into the night and followed the shadows down to my original room, went in and undressed in the dark and lay back on the bed with the .45 beside my hand.

The shooters were everywhere and it was no coincidence. I went over every detail of leaving New York and convinced myself there had been no leak in security. No one but our own group had known of my leaving and no one but me knew where I was staying. Ergo . . . whoever shot into the door at Claude Boster's shop was hoping to get him. But why? What did he know? Or what did they think he knew? Could it have been a warning? I took a drag on the butt, then snubbed it out in the tray on the nightstand beside the bed.

In this case you had to go on suppositions. Louis Agrounsky's whereabouts weren't known to the Soviets . . . yet. They were processing it from all angles too. His incredible defection from principles had started right here and they, like us, were working it from both ends.

My eyes started to close and I was staring blankly at the darkened wall across the room through narrow slits. Then suddenly my eyes were wide open again and I said "Damn!" softly and shook my head at my own stupidity.

How would anyone know of Agrounsky's by-pass control?

Either he told them or they worked on it with him. Or . . . they could have suspected what he was up to and investigated his research enough to justify their suspicions. It was no secret that all our top priority projects were saturated with enemy agents skilled in the art of putting money to work. We used the device all the time ourselves. You could always find a price for almost anything. There was a probability that Boster or Vincent Small could unknowingly have leaked a little information on Agrounsky's activities to someone concerned who smelled the possibility and passed it on. Damn again!

I went to sleep trying to sort the mess out in my mind, but it was still a mess when I awoke at seven, showered, dressed and went back outside to check my other room.

Nothing had been touched. The strand of fine wire I had left in the door was still in position. I shrugged, figuring I went to a lot of trouble for nothing, then unlocked the car and got in.

It's all so automatic. You handle the everyday things until they become commonplace and you never give them a thought. You pick up a knife or fork with an unconscious gesture, flush a toilet without thinking beforehand . . . and those are the things they kill you with.

As I went to put the key in the ignition I remembered Caswell getting his in Trenton for not checking, and feeling a little foolish, got out and lifted the hood on the car. And I was lucky. I had gotten sloppy in my habits, but luck was there for one of the few times, nudging me with its tiny golden fingers, and made me look.

The package was a small one, but big enough to disintegrate the car and its occupants into a fine spray of metal and flesh the second the key was turned on, a taped grouping of six inch dynamite sticks artfully hidden under the transmission housing where a cursory inspection would miss them. But I saw the lead wires, followed them and cut the charge loose.

Cute, you bastards, you did a neat job. But why? Somebody was a lot more clever than I thought. Nobody tailed me so there had to be only one other way and it didn't take me longer than five minutes to find it. The tiny oscillator that could transmit a homing signal was fastened under the gas tank and whoever wanted me could take his time until I was where I was at, feeling perfectly safe, then move in and booby trap my car.

Now the next question. Was it a double precaution? If they wanted to knock off Boster they had to take a chance on a miss. But anyone interested in Boster, they'd be interested in too, and no matter who he was, they'd want him out of the way. So . . . who was the primary target?

I grinned a little, knowing that someplace an ear was glued to a receiver listening to the hum the oscillator was giving off, realizing that the second it stopped it meant the dynamite charge had done its work. I dropped the gimmick on the ground where it stayed activated, sending out its signal, and backed the car out of the drive, then turned and headed toward Dr. George Carlson's clinic a mile away.

The building was a one story affair, sprawled out like a T, of white brick with a red ceramic tile roof. The receptionist at the desk was a young girl with a tired smile who was just finishing stamping a pile of papers when I walked in.

"Yes?"

"Dr. Carlson, please."

"Are you a patient?"

"No, this is personal business. I'm not a salesman either."

"May I have your name?"

"Mann. I'm from New York. Am I interrupting anything?"

"No, I'm sure the doctor can see you." She smiled, dialed the phone and made a call that came over an intercom system from the closed doors behind her. There was a moment's conversation before she put the phone back and said, "Dr. Carlson will be right here."

"Thanks."

Dr. George Carlson was a tall, slim man in his early thirties, dressed in typical hospital garb, his eyes reflecting the things all doctors have seen and hope to achieve. He came through the doors, nodded to me and pointed to a door on my left marked *Private*.

Inside, he sat behind his desk and wiped his face with his hands in a tired gesture and said, "Long night. Two emergencies. Damn speeders." He looked up at me and leaned forward on his elbows, hands clasped together. "Now . . ."

"Doctor," I said, "I'm going to omit details unless you want them just to save time. I'm looking for Louis Agrounsky, who was formerly employed at the space project. . . ."

"I know him," he interrupted.

"He's disappeared. It's imperative that he be found."

Carlson made a wry face. "He was a patient of mine. That's all I can offer."

"Then let's put it this way. You can forget the doctor-patient relationship."

"No I can't, Mr. Mann."

"Then check on me." I gave him the same details I did Claude Boster and waited while he did the same thing and watched him while he hung up and nodded slowly.

"All right," he told me. "Shoot."

"First . . . his accident."

"Nothing serious . . . for most people, that is. The normal recovery period would have been much shorter, but with Agrounsky it was different."

"How?"

"Know what a pain level is?"

"Too well," I said.

"His was very low. This man could take any type of mental pressure . . . up to a point like any of us, but his physical pain tolerance was lower than most."

"Was he hurt?"

"Not too badly. You or I could have taken it and been ambulatory in a matter of days, but his acceptance of pain wasn't like ours."

"That's why he stayed here so long?"

"It wasn't the curing. It was the *un*-curing. His physical condition was fine, but in treating him we used morphine to ease the pain he undoubtedly felt and he turned out to be one of those rare specimens who become addicted almost immediately. Most of his stay here was devoted to taking him off the narcotic addiction."

I had it then. It was starting to fall into place.

"Did he ever talk to you?"

"Never about his work, if that's what you mean. He wouldn't speak about the space project at all."

"I didn't mean that."

Carlson waved his hands absently. "Oh, occasionally he'd go off into some vague ramblings. It wasn't the first I had heard. Look at how many scientists engaged in the original Manhattan Project suddenly became total humanitarians after they saw the damage inflicted at Nagasaki and Hiroshima. You can't engage in destructive enterprises without developing a guilt complex somewhere along the line."

"And what was his?"

"Worry about the world. He was afraid it would destroy itself and he was the one who gave it the means. Baloney. I tried to talk him out of it and I think I succeeded."

"You didn't," I told him.

His lips turned into a tight, thin line.

"Agrounsky's ready to do the job himself," I said.

For ten seconds he looked at me, then muttered, *"Son of a bitch!"*

"He was capable of it, you know."

Carlson nodded again. "Yes, I know. He was one of the great ones. What happened?"

"I don't know, but you might have a plausible lead. This addiction of his . . . how serious was it?"

"We caught it in time. It was all controlled and his treatment was the usual one prescribed in such cases."

"And when he left here . . . was he cured?"

Carlson licked his lips, chose his words and said, "I was sure of it."

"No recurrence?"

"There's always that possibility. It's like having an alcoholic teetotaler taste whiskey without realizing he's an incipient alcoholic. There's always that taste to remember. I never thought . . ."

"It isn't your fault."

"It is. I should have insisted on further checks."

"Look . . . you're a doctor . . . you know things and hear things. What's the situation on narcotic sales in this area?"

"Oh, hell, you have that disease in every damn city in the world."

"I'm talking about here."

"I've treated several," he said.

"Children . . . teen-agers?"

"No. Always adults. They came through the police courts."

"What's the source?"

Carlson made a negative gesture with his head.

"Guess."

"Imported," he said. "No reported incidents of break-ins that I know of. I've asked around several times and I've never heard of any. Listen . . . you get where money is big and you find vice. . . ."

"I know all that."

"And do you know that for some reason professional people seem attracted to addiction? They take a jolt now and then to keep going, to make up for the lack of sleep, the missed meals, the mental distress they undergo. Do you know. . . ?"

I said, "I know all that too." Then added, "You aren't one, are you?"

"No, I'm not."

"And what do you think Agrounsky's chances of remaining an addict are?"

"Too big," he told me. "If he stays away from the stuff he'll be all right, but if he found a taste for it he will wind up total. I gave him credit for having more sense than that."

"It's a disease, Doctor," I said sympathetically. "They haven't found a cure for the common cold yet, so don't blame yourself. It wasn't something you did. He had it in him all the time without knowing it."

"Nuts."

"I can give you some big names who are hooked right now if you'd like to hear them. It would surprise you."

"Don't bother."

"Thanks for the information," I said.

He didn't answer me.

The police had a report on the .38 used last night. Ballistics had come up negative and nothing useful had been found in the grounds outside the shop. It was supposed the gun had been a revolver since no ejected shells had been located, and it made a front page story for the local paper with the intimation that it was another robbery attempt, interrupted this time, by Boster and a friend appearing in the doorway and startling the heister. There were squibs in the Miami sheets and a brief recap on the TV news broadcast, but that was as far as it went.

I drove back to the motel and parked the car in its original slot, right over the oscillator, put the gimmick back in its place under the gas tank, hooked the charge up under the hood and went into the office.

The manager gave me a big smile, waiting.

"Any calls?"

"None, sir."

"Anyone looking for me?"

"No, sir, not a soul. Have a good day?"

"Profitable," I said.

"Care to keep the other room for tonight too?"

I threw a bill down on the counter top. "Yeah, I might as well."

He took the bill, stored it away and handed me my change and a receipt. "Just call me if you want anything."

"I'll do that."

I went back outside and stood in the fading light and looked over at the car. *They'd have to start wondering sometime,* I thought. *The bastards!* I grinned to myself, thinking through their minds. That oscillator had been put in place with masking tape and it could have fallen off. There was always the chance that a wired charge wasn't hooked up correctly too. I eased the oscilla-

tor down and let it lay in the sandy loam under the car, then re-
wired the charge myself from a different viewpoint. Up front, a
convertible drove in with a young couple in the front and *Just
Married* slogans chalked on the sides of their car. I checked the
room on the other side of the car, went back to the office and
registered that one in under my name too and paid for it. I was
getting to be the best customer the guy had. The newlyweds took
a room at the far end, giggling all the way, and the manager gave
me a knowing wink and a laugh as I went out.

Maybe they'd have a night to remember, I thought. At least
nobody could be in the area where they could get hurt. Only the
world was reserved for destruction.

The phone was ringing when I got in my room. I recognized
the voice but went through the coded check anyway and Dave
Elroy gave me the right answers. "Got in an hour ago, Tiger. I'm
at the Sea Cliff in room ten. Anything for me to do?"

"Yeah, probe this town and see if you can find any source of
narcotics. Look for H primarily and try to find out if Agrounsky
was a user."

"Any indications?"

"All of them," I told him. "Got hooked in a hospital, thought
cured, but was under a severe mental strain and might have re-
verted. He took off periodically and it might have been to see his
supplier. All I want to do is be sure. And see if he made any big
buys."

"Before he left?"

"Right. Try to date it."

"Okay, will do."

"You have an informant in this area?" I asked him.

"Not yet, but I know who can give me a lead. Tiger . . ."

"What?"

"Things are getting touchy. Hal Randolph is raising hell in
New York. They want you on the scene up there."

"Screw them."

"They have technicians breaking down all the circuitry of the
control system and they haven't come up with anything yet. Some

of the wheels are insisting that it couldn't have been done and are yammering to call off the search."

"The idiots."

"They won't do it, though," he said. "They can't take the chance."

"How about Niger Hoppes?"

"Not a thing. Grady has called in everybody and is pulling all the plugs. He's an unknown face. Johnson called from London again with another bit. . . . There's a possibility that he might have a slight limp now, but it wasn't confirmed. It could have been faked to throw off anybody looking for him in the future. You got the angle about him being a sniffer, didn't you?"

"Check."

"Then you got the latest. Johnson said he used the Bolatrine variety but that isn't sold in the U.S. at all. There are derivatives almost the same, so it wouldn't make any difference at all. I checked with Ernie Bentley and he told me all the inhalers conformed to the Pure Food and Drug Act . . . no bennies sold over the counters . . . but the only similarity was the containers. One firm makes them all in different shapes and sizes."

"Good enough. Call me back if you dig up anything."

"Roger. Off now. Behave."

I put the phone back and snapped on the television. I lay on the bed in the dark and watched the last segment of a western before the news came on, caught the news broadcast that mentioned that the sniper outside Claude Boster's shop hadn't been apprehended yet, then closed my eyes for a little while waiting for time to pass. Nobody was going to come near me until the night had quieted into that death-like quality that comes after a small town goes to sleep and the traffic has diminished to an occasional truck going up the highway.

But I was wrong.

Somebody had waited too long and couldn't understand why the expected hadn't happened. He didn't want to have to make excuses and be responsible for a bungled job and he checked to make sure. He must have found the oscillator and taped it back thinking it had fallen off from the heat and the vibration, then looked again to make sure the dynamite sticks were in place where they should be and when he wiggled the wires he had so carefully installed the night before they all seemed secure until the final wiggle touched off the cross wiring I had rigged and he blew up into a gory mess of parts and liquid slop and was plastered all over the remnants of the rooms I had rented on either side of the car.

The noise of the explosion was a terrible, flat, roaring sound that spread light and heat into the compound like the midday sun for one instant, then died away without leaving a trace of an echo. Only little noises came then—things falling back to earth . . . other things slowly giving way to fall from the impact of the blast. The silence was a stunned hush, then a woman's voice screamed incoherently, gaining in intensity until it was quieted from a lack of breath.

I was out of the door and on the scene before anyone else, standing there looking at the twisted wreckage when the manager came up, the expression on his face one of complete disbelief. "What . . . what happened?"

"Go call the cops. Shake it. Then come back and keep everybody away from here."

He gaped at me absently, swallowed hard and shuffled off, glancing back nervously over his shoulder. But somebody had beaten him to it. The wail of a siren tickled the air, coming from the east side of town, then another joined it from another direction. Already, the curious had started forward at a half-run, converging on the scene while the dust and fumes still hung overhead like a small cloud.

There was little left of the car at all and practically nothing of the buildings that had squeezed it in and softened the blast from tearing up the rest of the place. Blood-wet fragments of flesh glistened on metallic parts and larger pieces of the body were scattered in the rubble to the left.

One piece was intact . . . a hand. It lay there palm upward, expressing a peculiar bewilderment as if it still had life and could think and wonder. A section of plate glass lay on the ground and I picked it up, polished it with a handkerchief, pressed it against the fingertips, slipped it into my pocket. Then I flipped the hand as far as I could into the bushes.

The manager was still incoherent, still fumbling with the phone when I got in the office. He never even saw me poke around behind the desk until I found a heavy packet of fold-out cards that gave a picturesque view of the Cape Kennedy area, slip the glass into the middle where I held it in place with tape, then address it to Ernie Bentley and stamp it to go out in the morning airmail.

He'd know what it meant.

I only had a minute to do what I had to do, but it was enough time. I got back to my original room, stripped off the .45 and the speed rig, got the extra box of shells and the two clips out of my suitcase and stuck them behind the air-conditioner grill vent at the top of the room. No matter what happened, I didn't want anybody impounding my equipment for any reason.

Captain Hardecker got there in his own car, skidding into the drive ahead of the police cruiser and the two fire trucks that followed them. There weren't enough people around to give him trouble with crowd control and he cleared out all those who didn't belong in the motel area. The fire crew was quick and efficient, sizing up the situation immediately and checking for any unexploded dynamite sticks, standing by with the equipment to douse any flame that might occur. But like so many blasts of this intensity, combustible materials were disintegrated and the concussion blew out anything ignited before it could catch hold. Nevertheless, they dampened down the bedding remains and wooden splinters still showing, raking through the debris trying to separate the parts of the thing that had once been human.

We held the conference in the motel office, the manager out of it for the time being, trying to settle his nerves with a strong bourbon on the rocks. Hardecker sat back easily in a wicker rocker, scanning me through the blue smoke of a cigar while I told him I had rented both rooms and the car and couldn't explain why anybody would want to get rid of me.

When I finished he said, "Now that sounds like a reasonable story, all right, but between you and me, it doesn't make sense. You know what it sounds like from my direction?"

"Tell me."

"Like you deliberately parked that car there and took the rooms on both sides so nobody would get hurt if the car did get blown."

I agreed with a deliberate nod. "Except for one thing."

"Oh?" he said. "Now what could that be?"

"When somebody rigs a car to blow up they wire it so that they nail the occupant when he turns the key. I didn't turn the key, so either one of two things happened. The car was rigged and somebody tried to steal it or the guy rigging it blew himself up in the process."

"I can think of something else," Hardecker said.

This time I said, "Oh?"

"You rigged the car and waited for somebody to get in it."

"That wouldn't be very smart, would it? I'm still here."

"All these stunts aren't pulled by smart people. Nope, I don't like your story. Besides, there's something else."

"Now what?"

"You aren't scared enough, mister. You should be all shook and you're not even sweating. You act like it happens every day around you."

"I'm not the nervous type."

He grinned slowly, then looked up as the mailman came in, dropped a few letters on the desk and picked up what was in the receptacle. I watched my card folder go into his bag and felt better. "Fun this morning?" the mailman asked Hardecker without looking up from his work.

"Every day," the Captain told him. "If it isn't one thing it's another."

When he went out the uniformed cop outside the door spoke to one of the firemen holding a small basket in his hand, stuck his head inside and said, "Captain, they may have some identifiable parts here . . . a denture anyway. No clothes or labels yet."

Hardecker nodded solemnly and puffed on the cigar again.

"Get the teeth to the lab and process it. We'll find out who he was." He looked at me deliberately and tapped his cigar out and dropped the stub in his pocket. "And now for you. I think we'll print you up and find out all about you, mister. Mind?"

"Not at all."

"Unless you'd like to talk about it."

"I've said it all, Captain."

"Let's go then," he said and got up with a sigh to move to the door and wait on me.

It was the driver of the other squad car who recognized me. Before I could get in beside Hardecker, he came over and leaned on the window and tapped my shoulder. "You were with Mr. Boster when somebody shot at him, weren't you?"

There wasn't any sense denying it. "That's right."

"I think you got a live one, Captain."

Hardecker looked at me slowly, his mouth twisting into a small smile. "That true, mister?"

"I was there."

"Maybe we got plenty to talk about after all, wouldn't you say?"

"Not especially."

The Captain looked across me and said, "Follow us, Pete, then go pick up Boster. Maybe together they'll have something to say. You find anything in this guy's room?"

"Nope. Just clothes. He's clean."

Hardecker gave me another one of those funny smiles. "You don't happen to have a weapon on you, do you?"

"It's a hell of a time to ask, but I don't."

His voice rumbled in a deep chuckle. "Don't worry, I could have told if you had. I can smell 'em."

Just so he wouldn't feel too sure of himself I chuckled back and said, "I don't really need them."

"Uh-huh," he said, but he gave me a peculiar look as though he were seeing me for the first time and his smile faded completely away. He switched the key on, pulled the lever into gear and dug out into the street.

I let them put me through the entire procedure, mugging me

for their files, printing me, taking me into the office that served as an interrogation room, then being offered a chair and cigarettes across the table from Hardecker. The patrolman he had called Pete came in to report that Claude Boster was not at home, nor did he say where he was going. Hardecker told him to make periodic checks until he found him and get him down as soon as possible.

Only then did he sit back comfortably, his hands resting in his lap. After a minute of steady watching he said, "Now I know something is screwy here, Mr. er . . ."

"Mann is my right name." I grinned at him.

"By now," he told me, "most people would be screaming for a lawyer or wanting to make a phone call or yelling that we were violating their rights. That sort of thing, you know?"

"I know."

"Then why don't you?"

"What for?"

"You might have something to hide."

"Maybe I don't."

"It's more than that, isn't it?"

"Possibly."

"You know," he said, "you could have squawked and we never would've been able to print you." He leaned on his elbows and cupped his chin in his hands. "That isn't natural, is it?"

"I've been printed before."

"No doubt. So you're playing for time. I'd like to know why."

"It's easier this way than explaining," I said.

"Would it be easier if I locked you up until I found out what this was all about?"

"It wouldn't matter," I said easily. "Do what you like."

"Let's give it a try," he said.

The jail was clean and modern, the cell he gave me freshly scrubbed with a window facing the south that let in a fat rectangle of striped sunlight. "Any time you want to talk," Hardecker reminded me, "I'll be upstairs. I'm looking forward to some interesting conversation, Mr. Mann. The reporters are too.

There hasn't been this much excitement around here in a long time. All kinds of speculation going on."

"I'll let you know," I said and sat down on the cot and lit up a butt. The door clanged shut and they left.

I had to wait it out. It was all I could do. One thing going for me was that they couldn't locate Claude Boster. If he got picked up before I got to him and brought Louis Agrounsky's name into the deal, then everything could go to hell all at once. I looked at my watch. It was about two o'clock and I was hungry.

Maybe Agrounsky was hungry too. Not for food. For something more potent. For something he had to shoot into his veins to give him that thing he needed so badly. The pattern was beginning to make sense now. Dr. Carlson had nailed it down without knowing it, putting the lid on the kind of temperament Louis Agrounsky really had. Agrounsky was an addict. He couldn't stay away from the stuff, even after he was thought to be cured, and found himself a source of supply to take care of his needs.

That was as much as it took. Under the influence of the big H all his fears and frustrations came out of the shadows and he thought he was big enough to wipe them out by himself. But somewhere along the line he talked to somebody, or was recognized, and his addiction was stored away in the memory bank of a Soviet dossier until it was needed. To satisfy his need for the stuff he wiped himself out financially, selling everything, until he had nothing left to sell . . . except one thing.

And the Soviets had the payoff means. One kilo of H properly cut could serve an addict for a long, long time. It was a very tempting arrangement. Now the big question—was it planned or did it happen accidentally?

They brought the evening paper with my supper and I had a chance to see pictures of the devastation at the motel and my name in the papers as T. Marvin, the one I had registered with. I grinned at that, because whatever Hardecker thought, he was too wary to play with something that didn't smell right. There was always time later to correct a mistake like that . . . unless some reporter didn't take it at face value and checked the police blotter. The story was descriptive rather than informative and gave out few pertinent details. The identity of the dead man hadn't been established yet, nor his motive, and I was mentioned as simply being held for questioning.

At ten P.M. the guard came down the hall, turned the key in the lock and opened the door. "You got a visitor, Mann."

"Who?"

"Says he's a friend of yours. Dave Elroy."

"Sure." I got up and followed him down the corridor and up into the main building where I was waved into a room where Dave was sitting, a fat grin on his face. The guard left the door open and stood there unconcernedly, but taking it all in.

"Hi, Dave."

"Wait till the boys at the plant hear about this. How you doing?"

"Great. Nice suite facing the water." I looked around the room and spotted the two bugs without any trouble, letting my eyes deliberately point out the microphones. Dave nodded, having already seen them himself, and offered me a cigarette. I said, "What're you doing here?"

"What's a friend for? Want out?"

"Nope. I could have put up bail myself."

"Only you're the stubborn type. Who blew the car?"

"Beats me. Some nut."

"World's full of 'em. Anything you need?"

"Not a thing."

"No sense sticking around then."

"How you making out, Dave?" I asked casually.

"Fine. My old customers came through with some new contacts and it's paid off. This is virgin territory for a good salesman. Half the time you don't even have to sell . . . they look for you to buy from you. One guy was such a good customer he wiped out a stockpile in no time at all. Had to move on because he couldn't get goods any more. Business squeeze that was . . . one of the big companies put the pressure on the little guys so he was cut off and had to deal with them, only they cut their own throats because he skipped and got his material from someplace else. Business is rough, sometimes. Even with the anti-trust and monopoly laws they still pull that stuff."

I nodded. "Well, it doesn't pay to grow too big," I said.

Dave got up and stretched. "I'll stop around again if you need anything. Give me a call sometime. I'll speak to the Captain on the way out. He doesn't seem too unfriendly."

"Nice guy. Very patient."

"He can afford to be," Dave told me.

"So can I."

When Dave left, the guard took me back to the cell, locked me in and ten minutes later the lights went out automatically. An hour later a couple of boisterous drunks were brought in, locked up several cells down, and before dawn a pair of bearded teenagers staging some kind of a demonstration outside the project area were hustled in and tossed half crying into the can. What those guys needed was a tour of duty in some damn jungle.

Breakfast came at six and Hardecker at eight. He came down alone, opened the cell himself and nodded me out. I picked up my coat and hat, automatically went to the desk to collect my belongings that were held in a brown manila envelope and signed the receipt for them.

Hardecker let me put everything back in my pocket before saying, "Let's go into the office a minute."

"Sure."

He closed the door and sat down, his face tight and a wariness in his eyes. "You could have told me, Mann."

"Told you what?"

"Just who you were. I could have checked instead of sticking my neck into a goddamn noose."

"So?"

"There was a delay in getting a report back on your prints. Then the teletype started and I had to get on the phone to Washington. I had people crawling up my back wanting to know what the hell was going on and all I could give them was the details and that was enough. I got orders to lay off you and keep my big mouth shut and to play this your way no matter how you wanted it played." He paused and pursed his lips. "Who the hell are you, buddy?"

"Just a citizen, Captain."

"How big?"

"Big."

"Why?" he asked me seriously.

"If I told you you'd never believe it."

"And supposing I did?"

"Then you'd wish I had never told you so you could sleep at night without wondering when it was all going to end."

"What end?"

I looked at the sunshine coming in the window. "That," I said.

He waited a few seconds, tight lines drawing in around his eyes, before he said, *"Crazy!"* almost under his breath. "What do you want me to do?"

"Kill that story. As far as the press is concerned, the guy who pulled it was a mental case who had done the same thing before. He didn't need a motive . . . something like a firebug."

Hardecker looked down into his hands and nodded. "Okay, that's easy as long as a real ID doesn't show and the reporters don't get it if it does. Do you know who he was?"

"No."

"What else?"

"Forget Claude Boster. Don't tie us together. They were not related affairs."

"For my own information, were they?"

"I don't know. My guess is that they were but I'm not sure."

"Damn it," he said, "what kind of a lash-up is this anyway?"

"An international one, Captain. Nothing's being taken out of your hands. We're just requesting your help. That's why I preferred to spend the night in the cooler rather than spread the news around. Like I said, it's easier that way."

"Not on my nerves, Mann. Where will you be staying? . . . as long as you're here . . . and not that I expect you to be around long the way people are going after your skin."

"The same place," I told him. "It's as good as any now."

CHAPTER EIGHT

THE MANAGER AT THE MOTEL WOULDN'T have been a bit happy about seeing me if a TWX from Martin Grady hadn't arrived. It covered all his damages plus a substantial overpayment that could put a new wing on his establishment. Dave Elroy had been hard at it all night, smoothing things out even to the point of having another rental car waiting for me outside the office. It was from the same company who had supplied the first, so Grady had made his point with them too.

A work crew had already cleared away most of the rubble and I walked over and watched them a minute. I stared at them idly, then strolled past them to the clump of bushes thirty feet away where I had thrown the hand. It was still there, still grasping upwards stiffly at nothing. I wondered how many people it had killed before becoming a *thing* lying there in the grass, and I walked on down to my room.

The gun was still there, dusty now from the continuous stream of air blowing over it, so I pulled it down, disassembled the piece, cleaned it thoroughly, dropped it back together and put it on where it belonged. Then I lay back on the bed and picked up the phone.

Claude Boster still hadn't returned, though he had called his housekeeper and told her he would probably be back in the evening. Vincent Small's phone went unanswered completely, so I quit trying and stayed there, waiting. An hour later Dave Elroy rang, told me to meet him at the Rose Bar in fifteen minutes, and hung up.

It was a small unit built to accommodate the construction crews working at the space project, a combination bar and restaurant that had been added on to several times, primitive enough to keep down the overhead, but stocking enough liquor to account for heavy payroll tastes.

Dave was at a table in the back where he could see everything going on, next to a window so he could watch outside too. I walked up, ordered another beer, and slid in opposite him.

"Hello, jailbird," he said.

"Drop dead."

He grinned at me and sipped his beer. "Tell me something, Tiger, why didn't you nail that guy who tried to disintegrate you beforehand?"

"Because he might have been too damn smart to get caught. Once away he would have stayed away and somebody else would have been brought in. At least this way we scratched one assassin and got an ID besides."

Dave's eyebrows went up questioningly.

I said, "I found the hand and got prints from it. Nobody else got anything. I should be getting a report from Ernie sometime today."

"Clever, Tiger, clever. Excuse me for asking."

"What about you? I got the double-talk, all right, but how about the details?"

Dave finished his beer and signaled for another. "There was some H flowing in here, all right. Not much, but enough to supply a couple dozen users. One guy handled it all from a jobber in Miami. Then he turned his trade over to somebody else . . . a guy they called Fish. No other name. Just Fish. He laid it on heavier than his predecessor, so he either located some new customers or built up the old ones.

"Now, here's the part you're waiting for. When the squeeze went on, Fish was supplying an addict that was identified as

Louis Agrounsky. A couple of other users recognized his picture. They had seen him make the contact and one came through with the bit that he even sold some to him when he was told there was none available. My guess is that Agrounsky was deliberately cultivated by Fish. The stuff he was selling Agrounsky wasn't the usual cut . . . it was a hell of a lot hotter. Agrounsky was shooting with damn near pure stuff and with short cuts he couldn't make the grade. He was hooked all the way on big loads and had to have the best he could get. Then, all of a sudden, Fish dropped out of sight and Agrounsky was stuck. He had gone through his bundle, his source was dried up, now he had to make do with whatever he could get, and he couldn't get it around here."

I raised my beer and tasted it. There was something sickly sweet about it until I saw the lipstick on the rim and told the waiter to take the damn thing back and get me a new one in a clean glass. "They missed their timing," I said.

"What?"

"Agrounsky couldn't wait. He needed it worse than they thought he did . . . or else he let somebody else have enough of his stuff to diminish his own supply so that he went short before they figured it."

"So that's it," Dave mused. "That's why the kilo was picked up in New York. They thought he was heading for there. They were going to make it available for him."

"He wouldn't have had any trouble getting it in the city," I said.

"No, not with the right contacts . . . and those guys can always find them. But what would he use for money? That early cut stuff costs pretty big."

"That's what I'm wondering. . . . You know anything about the Myrtle Beach area?"

Dave took a pad out, flipped over a couple of pages, and looked up at me. "A dead spot. Nothing there at all. If he sold his car there it was to get transportation somewhere else. There's no known narcotics traffic in that section at all. If he worked according to form he had enough H on him to keep him running on the edge. That car of his could have been giving him trouble and he didn't want to take the chance of a breakdown that could cost him money."

"Could be."

"So where do I go from here?"

"Look for Fish," I told him. "He's right in the middle, so start the word going."

"Hell, he's been off the scene pretty long."

"Then put him back on again."

"Okay, you're the boss."

"I'm going to register at the Sand Dunes Motel. It might start to get hot and I'll need an alternate contact point. The name will be Gerrity, T. Gerrity out of Miami."

"Got it."

"If I'm not there leave word where you can be reached. Scramble the number the usual way."

"Expecting trouble?"

"Plenty."

I got up, laid a buck on the table for the drinks, nodded to Dave and left. If Fish were still around he'd have him spotted before long, but it was still a good bet that Fish had pulled out.

At the door I looked up at the sky. One of those freak Florida storms was moving in and the clouds were a blue gray, rolling along ahead of a stiff breeze and the smell of rain was in the air.

Just like always, I thought, a kill smell—getting ready to wash away the blood before it had been spilled. I walked across to my car, pulled out of the drive and headed toward Claude Boster's house. A police car was there, the driver talking to a uniformed patrolman who had been assigned to watch the place, and the garage door was open showing both spaces empty inside.

I didn't stop. I went up the road, turned north, then angled over to Vincent Small's. Nobody was there either, so I cut back to the motel as the rain started and got into my room just before it turned into an oblique, slashing downpour.

The phone was ringing as I turned the knob and when I picked it up Ernie Bentley identified himself and said, "Are we clear?"

"Go ahead, Ernie."

"I got the prints from that glass. Your person is one Henri

Frank, age fifty-two, naturalized Austrian subject, five foot, eleven inches, brown hair, chest tattoo that . . ."

"Any photos?" I interrupted.

"The usual ones taken when he was naturalized."

"Get them on the teleprinter to the local police office right away. Put it through as a missing persons report."

Ernie chuckled and said, "Boy, you're getting official. Ready to wear a badge?"

I ignored his sarcasm. "What else?"

"Suspected Commie affiliations. This came from our own files. You want the entire sheet on this?"

"No." I was looking at myself in the mirror above the dresser. The name of Henri Frank had rung a bell someplace and I was trying hard to locate the source. I said, "Who did the footwork?"

"Checking out the prints? No trouble . . . Charlie Corbinet put it through. What kind of hell are you raising down there?"

"I wish I knew." I paused, looked at myself again and said, "Special detail, Ernie. How many manufacturers of true sub-mini components are there?"

"Five. All reputable."

"Would they be interested in Agrounsky's work?"

"Damn right."

"Contact them right away. See if he made a sale of anything to any of them. They might not want to talk about it if there are patent complications, but put any kind of heat on you can, assure them they'll stay clean, but find out."

"Will do, Tiger. They're easy to speak to."

"If necessary, let Martin Grady do the talking. He's got the power to push it through if he has to."

"I think I can reach them," he told me. "By the way, we had a signal from London ten minutes ago on Niger Hoppes. He goes for one brand of inhaler called Bezex. It's made in West Germany and imported here. Sells for one ninety-eight and isn't an item generally stocked. One national drug chain handles it in limited quantities, but the main sale is to independent stores in areas where sinus trouble is prevalent. Martin staked out people wherever he could to watch sales, working from the manufacturer's sales guide he got, but you're not on the chart. The nearest place to you that handles Bezex is Miami. I've sent you a carton of twelve to plant somewhere if you want to try to lay a trap for your boy. I would have sent the other twelve, but I needed two containers to work out a gimmick."

"Ernie, look . . ."

"You'll get two in a separate box," he told me. "Don't try using them. They look alike and they're packaged alike, but unscrew the cap and sniff once and all you'll get is a nose full of cyanide gas. Life expectancy after that is about two seconds. Beware the innocent bystander. I'll get that photo off right now."

"Hurry it up."

"Right. Watch yourself."

I hung the phone up, frowning. *Henri Frank.* It *was* a name I had seen before. I ran it through my mind several times before I placed it. Henri Frank had been one of those listed in the Unsatisfactory Reports Doug Hamilton had submitted to Washington. At some time he had applied for a job at Belt-Aire Electronics and Hamilton's check had found him to be a security risk.

I grabbed the phone, dialed the apartment in New York over Shigley's to try to reach Rondine, listened to it ring a dozen times before I hung up, got a new connection and called Newark Control.

Virgil took my identification and said, "Clear, Tiger."

"Try to make contact with Rondine at the apartment. Tell her to forget the others and concentrate on Henri Frank. She has Hamilton's UR's and will know what to do. If she comes up with anything, have her contact me at this number. If she can't reach me, tell her to stay put at the apartment until I get a call through."

"Got it."

"Ernie's got photos of Frank he's sending down. Have him make copies and spread them around the city. He was pushing narcotics down here, but that was an assignment, not a trade. Check him out with those who might tie him into a Commie setup."

"What do we do with him?"

"Nothing. He's dead. I want to know his associates. He's part of the machine working against us, but so far he's the only one who can give us a direct contact if we can locate it. His prints were on file in Washington, only not through a police record, so there's no angle there or Ernie would have notified me. This guy's managed to stay clean in that department."

"Okay, Tiger, check back tomorrow. Time enough?"

"No. I'm going to try a couple other ways too."

"Keep us informed."

"Roger."

I held the phone down to break the connection, lifted it and gave the operator the number of Belt-Aire Electronics. The girl at the switchboard answered, took my name and put me through to Camille Hunt's secretary, and after a few seconds Camille said, "Well, hello, fly."

"Hi, kid."

"You've kept me waiting."

"Not you, baby. You don't wait for anybody."

Her laugh was a low, pleasant thing. "For some unaccountable reason I've been waiting for *you*. It's an admission I don't like to make."

"Flies make a lousy meal," I said.

"Ah, but you said you were the mud dauber type. They're tastier."

"Oh, shut up."

She laughed again. "Now . . . are we on business or pleasure?"

"Business."

"Damn."

I grinned at her through the phone. "Favor, honey. Take a quick check through your records and see what you have on Henri Frank. He made an application there and Hamilton's check rejected him."

"Frank, Frank," she mused. "Wait a second. I don't think I have to." I heard a drawer open and shut, pages being ruffled, then she said, "Remember I told you I took notes on certain people?"

"Uh-huh."

"Well, he was one. I have it here . . . wait a second." She paused and I could hear her whispering to herself, trying to decipher what she had written. Then: "Strange little man. My impression was negative. He applied for common labor and gave half a dozen former places he had worked in the Florida area."

"What are they?"

"I . . . don't know offhand. I seem to remember something he said . . . oh, damn . . . I didn't write it down. These were personality notes. Lack of sincerity, hesitancy in offering information, no apparent ambition."

"How about the files?"

"If he were a UR only Washington would have them."

"Then think about what he told you."

"Tiger . . . that was some time ago. Perhaps I can recall, but . . ."

"All right, do this then . . . hop a plane down here. I'm at Eau Gallie, Florida, right next to the Cape Kennedy project. I'll check the schedules myself and meet the flight you'll be on. Don't bother packing . . . just get on the first one out. Think about it on the way down and we'll pick it up when you get here. And forget the job . . . this is a Martin Grady authorization." I laughed and added, "Besides, you can use a vacation."

"Sure, without clothes?"

"What better kind?" I said.

"I didn't mean it like that," she told me, a lilt in her voice, "but you're making it sound awfully interesting. I'll see you shortly, mud dauber."

Captain Hardecker was rolled back in his desk chair when I opened the door. His feet were propped on the window sill, the stub of a cigar clamped in his teeth while he looked at the tele-photo in his hands. The look he gave me was hard, but not too unfriendly. "I've been expecting you," he said.

"Henri Frank?"

"A missing person. Do I get an explanation?"

I took the picture he held out to me, a front and profile view of a guy who would always be missing. "You got it," I said. "He's disappeared."

"Can I make a guess?"

"Go ahead."

"Like blown to bits?"

I shrugged. "It's a possibility."

"How distinct?"

"Very "

"I'm glad you admitted it."

"Why?"

"Because some kid at the motel found a gun that had been blown fifty yards away and his old man turned it in to us. We checked the ballistics and the slugs matched those used out at Boster's place."

"It figures," I said.

"Then why the picture?" he asked.

"To find out what's known about him. I want some b.g. on the guy."

"Nobody here knew him."

"I didn't think they would."

"Since it came in on the printer as an m.p. I took the liberty of running off a few copies. Two of my men are asking around. Know where they might hit pay dirt?"

"Not the faintest."

"And if we hit it anyway . . . ?"

"Any cooperation would be appreciated."

"You scare me," he said bluntly. "You and that goddamn attitude, that look in your eyes. It's not like I haven't seen it before. I've been in this business a long time and I can classify types automatically. Like in the movies, there are good guys and bad guys and if I had to put you anywhere it would be the bad guy department, only bad guys don't have your connections and that's what scares me. This whole damn situation is unreal, and that's what makes it too real for me. This town is a hotspot to start with and someplace the Soviets have an ICBM lined up to pop right down our throats like they have all their other primary targets. I don't enjoy sitting on my thumbs having nothing to do while something is ready to claw me up." He pulled the cigar out of his mouth and tossed it into the metal wastebasket where it hit with a wet *plop*. "How bad is it?"

"Bad," I said simply.

"Then why are you alone on this?"

"I'm not. You just haven't seen the others."

"Publicity could blow something then?"

"All the way."

"Okay, I'll go along. I'll be damned if I don't dig something up on this guy." He caught the look on my face and said, "Don't worry. We know how to ask questions too. We have our own ways and our own people. I'll give you a call if something turns up."

"Thanks." I flicked my finger against Henri Frank's picture. "Mind if I keep this?"

"It's yours." I looked at it again, saw the face of the one who wasn't any more, a partially bald-headed guy with a sallow face and eyes too close together. He had a mouth like he had just tasted something sour and the expression of those who had nothing but dislike for the rest of the world. Perhaps before he would have seemed ordinary, another guy out of step with himself, fighting everything because he was inadequate for survival unless he was handed it on a platter, but now, knowing what he was really like inside, the picture fitted him perfectly. I stuck it in my pocket, nodded to Hardecker and left.

Outside the rain had lost its original fury, settling into a monotonous drumbeat that raised the salt out of the sand and laid the smell of the sea on the air. The quiet of a small town at rest was almost a strange noise in itself. Like someone waiting, I thought. It was sitting there marking time, knowing something was going to happen and almost anxious to be an unseen spectator.

I jumped in the car, made a U turn and picked my way back toward Vincent Small's house. The time-drag was beginning to get me. Impatience made me run through the pack of cigarettes and rip the top off a fresh deck, swearing softly at the inconvenience. The whole situation was like a huge bowl of Jell-o that was liquid-hot and you had to stand by until it set before it could be handled properly. And you knew there wouldn't be that much time allotted you.

It needed a catalyst. It needed an agent to cool it suddenly and shorten the time period. Somewhere in the night hundreds of personnel were on the hunt. A thousand technicians were running down the circuits of Agrounsky's electronic installation looking for the bug. The night was crawling with faceless men, looking for one lone man who seemed to have removed himself from the world . . . and in their midst was another loner, another faceless one who might be steps ahead in the game, getting closer all the time to Agrounsky who was holding the world in his hands, trying to decide just what to do with it.

There was a light on in Vincent Small's house, his car back in the garage. I nosed up the driveway, cut the engine and hopped out. Before I rang the bell I glanced in the window beside the door and saw him pacing the floor, talking heatedly to someone in a chair with his back to me. The figure shifted slightly and I saw the side of Claude Boster's face, his mouth drawn tight with some fierce emotion.

Vincent Small opened the door, nodded as though he were expecting me and stepped aside to let me in. "Ah, Mr. Mann. Please join us." A worried expression creased his forehead and he couldn't seem to keep his hands still.

"I've been trying to reach you," I said.

"Yes, indeed. I have been . . . out." He waved with one hand. "This way, please."

Claude Boster made a noncommittal gesture with his head when I walked in, looking at me with that strange stare professionals have for someone not in their field, and picked up his drink. He fidgeted nervously, squirming in his chair, sipping at his drink every few seconds.

Small said, "Can I get you anything?"

"No thanks."

"May I ask a question then?"

"Go ahead."

"That bombing affair at the motel . . . did it have anything to do with—" he glanced around and added with a helpless note—"us?"

"It was meant to take me out of the action," I told him, "the same way those shots were supposed to remove Boster or me the other night. So, friend, it has a lot to do with you. The key factor is Louis Agrounsky and unless we turn him up soon you'd better get used to the sight of dead bodies."

"Mr. Mann . . . please."

Vincent Small gave me a glance of pathetic hopelessness and sat down on the edge of a chair, staring at his hands in his lap. "We . . . we've talked about it." He looked up at Claude Boster who tried to shrink back into the overstuffed cushions. "It . . . well, begins to make sense."

"How?"

"Louis . . . the way he acted. Something was wrong."

"Did you know he was a narcotics addict?"

Once again there was that quick exchange of glances, the slight hesitation and the feeling of nervous tension in the air. This time Claude Boster wet his lips and said, "We . . . thought it was something like that. Vince and I . . . talked about it."

"Recently?"

"No . . . earlier, before Louis disappeared. He was developing some peculiar traits . . . and we both noticed how quickly he could recover from a tense period by a trip to the bathroom. There were . . . other things, too."

"For instance?" I asked them.

Small said, "I laid his jacket on the bed one time and a packet fell out. There were . . . well, he had a syringe and several capsules in there. At the time I assumed it was all prescribed by a physician following his accident and had no reason to believe otherwise until . . . well, as Claude mentioned . . . he began to act rather strange at times."

"I'll tell you how strange he was," I said. "This man has an unusual susceptibility to narcotics. He became an addict accidentally but immediately, and it's distorted his entire personality."

Vincent Small's face paled and his lips were held together tightly. "To . . . what extent, Mr. Mann?"

"Let me shock you . . . but first let me remind you that if this goes any further you'll both find yourselves in the cooler so fast your eyes'll cross . . . and you'll be lucky because otherwise you might be dead." I let it sink in a moment before saying, "Agrounsky holds something that can tumble this whole world. He gimmicked our ICBM system with a by-pass control that gives him the ability to activate or deactivate it. If we don't get him before he makes his decision we've lost it, buddies. Either way we can all go down the drain."

Vincent Small swallowed hard, fumbling for words. Boster just sat there staring at his hands. Slowly Small raised his eyes to mine. "Louis used to talk . . . about a place he had. He was very . . . secretive about it."

And there it was. Close. I could feel my hands tighten and the muscles bunch up in my neck.

"Where?"

Vincent Small made a tiny negative with his head. He looked across at Boster, shoulders bent in a slump of defeat. "We . . . talked about it. He mentioned a few things . . . a fish store run by a man named Wax . . . Louis liked fish. He said it was perfect for what he needed . . . a place to think or to work out what he called . . . his problems."

"And you found it?"

"No. We asked the realtors in town and saw people Louis knew but they couldn't tell us anything. We even tried locating the fish store and the man he called Wax, but that wasn't any good either."

I could see everything going up in smoke. Here it was in my hands, right on top of me, yet a million miles away. But if Agrounsky had said one thing he might have said another they didn't recall yet.

"How often did he speak about this place?"

Claude Boster said, "Just twice to me. Both times was when he was . . . feeling sick."

K

"Like he needed a boost," I suggested.

"Yes."

I looked at Small. "And you?"

"Several times. Casual remarks, but strange for him."

"Why?"

"Because he was used to big laboratories and the finest equipment. In his work he needed other technicians to perform minor time consuming tasks and it wasn't like him to seek solitude."

"He was a loner, wasn't he?"

"Quite so, but only in regard to his personal association with people. Other people were a necessity in his profession."

"And you can't think of anything else he might have said or done that could locate this place of his?"

In a soft tone Boster said, "It wouldn't have been up north."

"Why not?"

"Louis had a touch of rheumatism. He couldn't stand cold weather."

"So that narrows it down to half a continent," I mused. "Nuts."

"We tried, Mr. Mann," Small said apologetically.

"The next time don't try it alone. I'll get some people on this and see what we can run down. My advice to you both is to stick close to your homes and stay locked in. There are others who know of your connection with Agrounsky and if they think you have anything that might locate him you'll be a target. You've already seen an example of what they'll do so don't play it down."

"But . . ."

"I'll arrange for police protection. You're public property for a while and you'll need it. What I want is for you to think. Go over every damn detail of your talks with Agrounsky and see what you come up with. If there is anything at all . . . any little thing, you call me." I wrote down the Sand Dunes number on separate slips of paper and handed it to them. "If I'm not there, contact the I.A.T.S. offices in New York or the local F.B.I. and they'll have an agent here in a matter of minutes."

Both of them nodded silently.

"You realize how critical this is?"

They nodded again.

"One of you might be holding the key to saving your own hides. You haven't got much time. Maybe none at all."

I.A.T.S. was in emergency session when my call got through. Charlie Corbinet took the message and put Hal Randolph on the line. The edge was off the usual gruff tone and he sounded tired, and all he could say was, "Yeah, Randolph here."

"Tiger Mann. I have something." I gave him the details of Agrounsky's narcotic condition and the possibility of his having a hideout somewhere near a fish place run by a guy named Wax. "You'll need a damn big team to run it down," I said. "It could be a store near a river or a lake as well as the oceanside. That gives you a lot of country to cover, but it's the only lead I have."

"Okay, Tiger. You sure that's all?"

"Push it from the narcotics end and you might get something."

"Don't worry, we will." He paused, then added, "You get off it now."

"Like hell I will."

"Orders, Mann."

"Shove 'em. I'm closer than you are and I'm staying on it."

"You were told you'd risk a court-martial," he warned me.

"You scare me, big daddy. You need every person you can get."

"Except you," he said. "This is a matter of national concern. There can be no instability factor. . . ."

I hung up on him and grinned to myself. Hell, they weren't worried about me. They didn't want to risk putting the Martin Grady organization in a position of power if we broke through. They still wanted us destroyed and if they could keep us from gaining strength the odds were still going for them.

My watch read ten after nine. Another hour and the men Hal Randolph would have assigned would be flooding the area, some with orders to hold me. Well, they'd have a time of it if they tried squeezing me out.

. I got back to my motel, paid two days in advance, took a few necessities out of my suitcase and drove over to the Sand Dunes Motel and registered in under T. Gerrity, getting a corner room on the northeast end of the building.

When I finished putting my gear away I called Dave's motel, left word for him to meet me outside the police station in twenty minutes, then ducked back through the rain and took the highway down to the precinct station and asked for Hardecker.

The Captain opened the door himself, looked me over as if I were a bug of some kind and waved me in. "You're a pain in the butt, Mann."

"So I've been told before."

"What's it this time?"

"A constant stakeout on Boster's and Vincent Small's places."

"Why?"

"You could have a repetition of the other night. Cover all doors and keep a car ready to roll."

"Just like that, huh?"

"Just like that."

The faintest grin showed around his mouth. "I don't know why I like you," he said. "You scare me, but you make life kind of exciting. Okay, I'll get somebody there. I don't suppose you can explain."

"That's right."

"And nobody's to know about it, right?"

I nodded.

"Son-of-a-gun," he almost whispered. "I get the feeling I'm being made a sucker."

"You're not."

"I know that too, but I can't help the feeling." He slid into his chair and rocked it back, picking up two report sheets from his desk in the same motion. "We're not so stupid around here, Mr. Mann. I have a little news for you."

"Oh?"

His fingers flicked the sheets. "Something on Agrounsky. We work pretty closely with personnel on the space project . . . continuous surveillance on certain people engaged in classified work . . . for their own protection as well as security reasons."

When I didn't say anything he looked down at the sheets again. "This is confidential. Duplicates of these reports were never submitted to any agency because we checked every detail out thoroughly."

"Go ahead."

"Louis Agrounsky was a bachelor with pretty sedate habits. He didn't drink and he didn't consort with women. That is . . . not often. When he did it was with two professionals on six different occasions over a period of thirteen months. Now we don't condone or protect prostitution, but we face the facts and know it exists. These two women were informers for us and notified us of the contact and we bugged the rooms to make sure Agrounsky didn't talk out of turn and become a security risk."

"Did he?"

"Nope. It was all very physical and very professional. And understandable," he added. "He satisfied a need and left. In case you're wondering, this situation has arisen before and . . ."

"I get the picture," I interrupted. "It's nothing new."

"Naturally, we kept a check going and on several occasions had the report that Agrounsky was seen with a woman. No identification. They met for supper twice and went to the picture show once. No further contact."

"No attempt was made to establish identification?"

"There was no necessity for it. He was allowed to lead his own life. She wasn't a known person and the association was casual. It wasn't an overnight affair and the police officer seated nearby said the conversation was inconsequential."

"Description?"

Hardecker shrugged. "Female, early thirties, well built but on the plain side. Their relationship seemed friendly. Nothing more."

"It doesn't sound like him."

"Friend, if a man is a male, sooner or later he's going to get that yen for a broad. In Agrounsky's case it was on rare occasions, but enough to satisfy him even if it was only a matter of getting into a conversation."

"How far did you go in checking her out?"

"She was registered at the Sinbad as Helen Lewis, giving an address in Sarasota. A call there verified it. The manager said she had lived in an apartment there the past two years."

I held out my hand and he dropped the reports in it. I scanned them quickly, picked up the address and phone numbers listed there and handed them back. "Could be okay," I said.

"We're still asking questions. If there was anything irregular, we'll dig it out."

"Mind if I drop back?"

"With your connections I don't mind at all."

"They may go sour," I told him.

"I run my own department," Hardecker said.

I looked around for Dave and didn't see him outside anywhere. The rain had put a glaze over the street lights and hammered at my face as I walked into it toward my car. When I reached it I pulled the door open and slid into the seat.

Behind me Dave said, "You're getting careless, chum."

I grinned at his reflection in the mirror. "Not really. You ought to try squatting in the middle. All your weight was on the one side."

"Forget it." He clambered over the seat and got beside me. "Anything new?"

"Nothing in your department."

"Well, I have something. I had to use a little heat to get it and it cost Grady two grand, but a fairly big buy was made from a peddler in Savannah who palmed off a lot of low-grade stuff to a sucker for a bundle. The contact was a guy named Sonny Kipton who had a reputation for this sort of thing. The same sucker called back here to a friend to make the original connection for another contact and was steered to a man in Charleston."

"We're working our way north into the Myrtle Beach area."

"Check, buddy. Remember me telling you about the guy Agrounsky took off the hook by selling him some of his supply?"

"Yeah."

"So he talked some more. He used to be located up there and put Agrounsky on both of them."

"He made his deal?"

"Yeah, and got the same old switcheroo. The guy's contacts were lousy. The Kipton punk tried it a week later and got knocked off for his trouble by a hophead who's being held for it. The other one can't be located. They don't stay put very long. Want me to scratch him up?"

"No. I want Fish."

Dave shook his head. "Not a sign, and brother, I looked."

"Keep looking," I said. I reached in my pocket and brought out the photo of Henri Frank, stared at it a moment, and held it out for Dave to see. "Here's another one we're after. This one's dead, but he ties in someplace."

Dave took the picture from my hand, glanced at it, then frowned at me. "Hell, Tiger," he said, "this is Fish. The description matches every damn detail."

CHAPTER NINE

THE STREET THAT ENDED at the beach was deserted, flanked by two empty summer cottages with shuttered windows that accentuated the eerie feeling of desertion. Wind had blown the sand up into a soft roll at the edge of the concrete, partially covering the walks on either side. I cut the engine and sat there staring out into the rain toward the blackness of the ocean, occasionally taking a drag on the cigarette.

Dave said, "Spell it out, Tiger."

"They had this going a long time, buddy. It was no sudden thing. The Soviets keep their people around all our hot spots looking for a weak link and somebody spotted it in Agrounsky."

"When he went back on the needle?"

I nodded. "They ran their own supplier in and got him hooked but good, then cut his source off to put the squeeze on him. When an addict is cooking he'll talk, rationally or not, and someplace he let the cat out of the bag about the by-pass control. That put the finger on him. Once he was on H strong enough they could control his supply and make him come across. They just didn't figure on him doing a disappearing act, that's all. He was important enough to call in their best man to run him down, so Vito Salvi got the job."

"Salvi was working in New York," he reminded me.

"Hell, they knew where he was heading. They were lined up

waiting for him. Agrounsky was out of cash and the biggest source of the stuff was the city. And don't bet his moves weren't prearranged. That little guy he did the favor for by sharing his junk was probably part of the setup. He put Agrounsky in touch with the other peddlers who slipped him out cut loads and reported back to Fish where Agrounsky was."

"I can check it out fast enough."

"Then do it."

"Where did they slip up?"

"I'll know for sure when I contact Ernie Bentley." I turned the key in the lock and started the engine. Dave had left his car back in the middle of town and we drove over to it. When he got out I said, "Locate your contact and call me at the Sand Dunes." I looked at my watch. "I should be back in an hour."

"He may not be available that fast."

"I'll wait. If he's in on it he might steer us to somebody else."

"Okay, Tiger. See you later."

Flight 804 was taxiing up to the ramp as I parked the car. Four men came down the anus-like stairs in the rear of the plane before I saw Camille Hunt. She had her suitcoat over her shoulders, leaning against the downpour with her head ducked into it. I ran over, took the briefcase from her hand and said, "Hi, spider."

"You would drag me out into this."

I grinned at her. "You don't know how easy you have it. The car's over here."

She got in, shook the rain from her shoulders, and tossed the silly hat she had on in the back seat. "My goodness, Tiger, is this really necessary?"

"It was."

She gave me an exasperated glance. "*Was?* You mean I made the trip for nothing?"

"*I'm* here."

"That's a consolation."

"I'll try my best."

Camille nudged me with an elbow, her face still shining wetly from the rain. "Seriously, what is this all about?"

As I threaded my way out to the road I said, "I wanted you to make an identification. It isn't important any more. Henri Frank is dead."

"Dead? But . . . how?"

"He blew himself to bits trying to knock me off. It was a case of a guy who couldn't understand his own failure and tried to check on it. I was there before him."

"Tiger . . . this whole thing . . ."

I let it hang there. "Don't worry about it. I'll get you back to Belt-Aire in the morning."

She gave me a long, steady stare. "You just haven't read the weather reports. My flight was the last one in. They expect everything to be grounded tomorrow. If it weren't for some slight mechanical trouble we would have gone on into Miami."

"So you got an unexpected vacation."

"My foot," Camille exploded. "With all the work piling up I can't afford it. Do you know orders came in from Martin Grady himself this morning to arrange for an expansion program? The Belt-Aire project has been approved and goes into full production at once. I shouldn't be here now."

"Well, I'll try to make your stay enjoyable."

"Swell," she said with a hint of sarcasm. "Where will we go?"

"First, to a whorehouse."

She turned her head to see if I were joking or not, then decided I was serious and frowned with annoyance. "I don't understand you."

"That's good. We'll never have any trouble then."

Louis Agrounsky had frequented a place that had all the earmarks of respectability if you didn't know what it was. The house was a two story affair barely different from its neighbors; better kept, if anything. The lawn and hedgerow were trimmed, the siding freshly painted, and the two cars in the double garage were both late model Fords inconspicuous anywhere.

The woman who answered the bell was the full-blown type, tall and pleasant, with a ready smile under vivacious blue eyes and a pert tilt to her pretty blonde head. She started to say something, then saw Camille and divided her glance between us, as though we had come to the wrong house.

"Yes?"

"Lisa McCall."

Her eyebrows went up questioningly. "Yes, I'm Miss McCall."

"I'd like to speak to you about a friend of mine. Can we come in?"

The blonde nodded and opened the door wider, the smile curious now. She could smell the trouble, but rather than be frightened she was curious because of it. When she shut the door behind us she walked ahead and ushered us into a well appointed living room dominated by a masculine bar that was out of place among the obviously feminine decorations.

Out of routine, she went behind the bar, waited until I said I'd have a rye and ginger with Camille nodding for the same, then mixed the drinks and placed them in front of us.

"I know you," she said quietly.

"Do you?"

"La Plata Bar in Rio. Four years ago. There was an attempted revolution and you killed two men who tried to take the one you were with. He was a General named Ortega Diaz."

"You get around, kid." Beside me I could feel Camille tense suddenly, then relax. In the mirror behind the bar I could see her eyes watching me as if I were something in a zoo.

"I don't know your name."

"Tiger Mann."

"Yes. I have heard it mentioned. There were a lot of stories about you in Rio."

"They were troubled times. But I don't remember you and I don't like that. I don't generally forget faces."

The girl made a sad motion with her hands, but smiled and said, "I was younger then, and pretty. Time and this business does things to one. I was twenty pounds lighter and my hair was black. A nose job to correct what a drunken seaman did to me makes a big difference." She stopped smiling then and looked at me seriously. "But you came to see about a friend."

"Louis Agrounsky. Hardecker gave me the tip and told me about bugging the room for information. Now I want your version."

Her expression was bland a moment, then a furrow appeared between her eyes. "But what is there to tell?"

"Your reaction. I'm more interested in your opinion of the association. You've been with enough men to read through them."

Lisa McCall dropped her head a moment, then peered up at me. "It probably was as professional as it can get." She looked over at Camille and the corner of her mouth twisted in a funny smile. "Am I embarrassing you?"

"No . . . not at all." I caught the implication in her tone of voice. Camille was quietly objective, observing every facet of a type she had never come into contact with before.

Lisa said, "There was little conversation. Mr. Agrounsky wasn't given to talk and it was obvious that he was inexperienced with women. He called here and I immediately called Captain Hardecker who installed the tape recorder in the room. When he arrived he simply paid his . . . fee, then we left for the bedroom. He demanded nothing out of the ordinary, was quite incompetent sexually from lack of experience, thanked me when it was over and seemed a little bit shaken for having resorted to such an extreme."

"He was here on six different occasions."

"That's right," Lisa agreed readily. "Twice when I wasn't here Marge attended to him. Each time Captain Hardecker was notified. There never was any change in his routine. If anything, it was very formal. I know why Captain Hardecker was interested . . . it wasn't the first time this happened nor the last. Several times this . . . establishment has been useful to him."

"So I understand. I'm not complaining. But I still want your opinion."

"Of . . . the arrangement?" she asked me.

"No . . . just Agrounsky."

Lisa let her eyes wander to the wall, then came back to me with a knowing expression. "For what it's worth, I'd say we were substitutes."

"For what?"

"Your friend wasn't a forward type at all. Under all that reserve he still had masculine drives but didn't know how to compensate for them. My guess is that he visited here after he had had some previous contact with a woman. She probably aroused him somewhat, but he was unable to approach her and came here as a last resort for . . . physical release."

"Did he ever mention this?"

"No, but it was a very familiar attitude. It isn't at all unusual." She stopped a moment, touched her lips with her tongue and said, "I didn't mention it to Captain Hardecker because it slipped my mind, but once after he left another . . . client saw him go and made a remark about it when he was with me. Something about Mr. Agrounsky being so aloof at the project when all the time he had the hots over some young technician in his laboratory. He used to blush whenever he saw her legs but never bothered looking away, either. It was sort of a joke with the men, I think."

"This client . . ."

"No use, Mr. Mann. I told you what you asked me."

"The girl?"

"Never mentioned her name. You can probably ask around."

"I'll do that. Thanks for your trouble."

"My pleasure, Mr. Mann. I've been around enough to realize the possibilities in this sort of thing. I hope everything comes out all right."

"So do I," I told her. "If you think of anything else, I'm at the Sand Dunes Motel. Or you can call Hardecker."

Lisa went ahead of us and opened the door, smiling politely at us both. As I went out she said, "Hurry back," but before I could answer Camille gave me another short jab in the ribs and grimaced as the rain sliced into her face. She wanted to say something, but a sneeze stopped her short.

"Damn," she told me as she climbed into the car, "if I get a cold out of this you're a dead fly."

"Mud dauber, remember?"

"All I remember is that I came down here without a thing to

wear and I'm soaking wet. What are you going to do with me?"

"Get you in a motel and dry you out."

"That's the first exciting thing you've said to me today," she chuckled.

The little old lady at the desk of the Sand Dunes gave me a knowing nod when I checked Camille in and asked if I wanted an adjoining room for her. Rather than shake her faith in her supposed powers of observation I tossed a bill down and said, "Why sure. I'm too old to be chasing around in the rain."

Her mouth pursed with indignation and she didn't know whether to believe me or not, so she just handed over the key, a late paper and asked if I wanted ice water in the room. I told her no and drove on down to the end of the row.

"Man and wife?" Camille asked with a small leer.

"That takes all the fun out of it," I told her. "It's better to have to kick your door down."

"You would too, wouldn't you?"

I shook my head. "I'm too handy at picking a lock."

"Well, never mind either. I'll leave the door open. I have my own way of handling you virile types." She stifled another sneeze, shook her head with annoyance and got out of the car in front of her room.

It didn't take her long to get in the shower. I heard the water run at full blast and a short yell as she found it too hot and settled it down to an even temperature.

I picked up the phone and called Ernie Bentley. I gave him the coded ID and said, "Tiger. Did you follow up my request?"

"Got it right here. Hit it with the second call and no protest. Louis Agrounsky sold two patented devices to D.L.W. Enterprises for a thousand dollars apiece. The deal was made by phone, confirmed and paid for by telegram sent and received out of Wilmington, North Carolina, with a following letter from the same city signed by Agrounsky assigning them all rights and residuals. The patents comprised mini components for TV transmitting cameras and were worth a hundred times that but all he wanted was immediate cash and a deal that could be made without going through lengthy legal maneuverings. D.L.W. was happy to go through with it and even took the chance on it being a phoney to wrap it up."

"The telegraph office demand identification?"

"They did . . . and he presented it. The check was cashed at the receiving office in small bills. The clerk remembered him well enough to describe him and there's no doubt about it being Agrounsky. I passed the information on to Newark Control and they tried to pick it up without any luck. He never checked in at any of the local hotels or motels and the clerk didn't remember him having a car."

"He could travel a long way on two grand."

"Or he could stick around and spend it," Ernie said.

"That's what I'm thinking too."

It was making better sense now. Wilmington was a seaport and a possible drop for narcotics that flowed into the country. If Agrounsky drew a blank in the Myrtle Beach area after he sold his car he could have headed north by bus looking for another supplier and Wilmington was the next logical spot on the route to New York. If a source had been prearranged for him he'd know where to go, but he wouldn't be taking any chances on being caught short again. Even though he was still an amateur in the business, a hophead could be crafty. He had to learn fast to stay on his kick and keep the monkey off his back. That was where the Soviets went wrong. They weren't dealing with a rational person at all. Agrounsky the scientist they could deal with. Agrounsky the addict was unpredictable. He wasn't taking any chances getting screwed with a cut deal any more. He had picked up his own bundle and was getting the H his own way now.

Ernie cut off my thought with, "Your package will be at the post office in General Delivery tomorrow morning. There's still a check on all Bezex sales and one was reported at the Atlanta air terminal yesterday. If Hoppes is on his way down it's along the route. Other sales were scattered. Miami reported several, but the salespeople knew the buyers."

"What's the life of the container?" I asked him.

"About two days of constant use. Built-in obsolescence, European style. Potent, but of short duration. A real sales gimmick. Scatter the batch down there and watch for a reaction."

"Will do, Ernie." I paused, thought a moment and said, "Has Rondine made contact yet?"

"No. Your message will go through when she calls. Virgil Adams said she and her friend Talbot went to Washington but haven't been located yet. They may still be there or on the way back."

"Right."

"Now here's one direct from H.Q. Grady wants action fast. You're not getting through often enough and he's hot. Word has leaked out of some of the ICBM installations that something big's going on and the newspapers are yelling for official statements on what's happening. A smart assed reporter dug out a history on Vito Salvi and wanted to release it but I.A.T.S. reached him in time and he's been in protective custody since this morning. It's gotten as far as overseas and there's a storm brewing, Tiger. Nobody is going to be able to sit on this much longer."

"But nothing's been located?"

"Not as far as we know. They completely cut off the installation at the March Station and are rebuilding the system. Unless the bypass is found they'll eventually do it all over, but that will take a year anyway and will leave us in the cold. Technical crews went into the Nordic and Vesper Stations in California, but that's only a drop in the bucket. All it takes is one and Agrounsky was involved in nine of the projects. Damn, this thing even has me shaking."

"It should."

Ernie's voice changed then and he said almost quietly, "How does it look, Tiger?"

"Lousy," I told him and put the phone back.

Next door the water was still running hard and I heard Camille's voice half muted in some song. I lifted the phone again and gave the operator the number of Helen Lewis' apartment in Sarasota I had picked up from Hardecker's report sheet.

After a two minute wait I got the superintendent of the building who came on with a high flutey voice and told me who he was. I said, "Can you reach Helen Lewis for me?"

"Miss Lewis? Why, I don't believe she has a phone."

"Can you get her to this one?"

He giggled, then said, "I'm afraid not. Miss Lewis has been on vacation and isn't expected back for some time. Can I take a message?"

"Do you know where I can reach her?"

"You might try Rome," he giggled again. "That's where she said she was going. She travels a lot, you know. In fact, if she weren't paid up for a year in advance I'd be tempted to rent her apartment out."

"Don't do that," I told him.

"No, of course not. I was only joking. Sorry I can't be of help."

"Tell me one thing . . . is her apartment furnished?"

"Naturally, all of our apartments are. Why, may I ask?"

"No reason. Thanks anyway."

"Certainly," he said, and broke the connection with another giggle.

And there it ended again. A short road with nothing around the bend. Everything petered out into a puff of dust. The whole world was sitting on the thin edge of destruction, never knowing how close to the edge it was, and every thread to the man upon whose whim annihilation or life depended was broken off short.

The trouble was that it wasn't a planned arrangement. It was something totally accidental that was stumbled upon, and before an arrangement could be properly set up, circumstances became accidental again. Agrounsky's condition was seized upon quickly enough. The importance of his defection from logical principles was recognized, but he couldn't be handled in an ordinary manner, his susceptibility to narcotics was minimized, and he got out of the circle because of his immediate need for the big jolt.

He was fair game now, but above all, he was his own biggest target.

Next door the water stopped and I heard the shower doors

L

open and shut as Camille Hunt stepped out to dry herself. I opened the bureau drawer, took out a blue oxford shirt and unfolded it, then stepped outside and knocked on her door.

When she called to come in I pushed the door open. She hadn't bothered to lock it. The electric wall heater was going full blast with a chair drawn up in front of it, her clothes draped over the back to dry off. Tendrils of steam still came from the partially opened bathroom door and I walked over and stuck my hand in with the shirt in it.

"This is all I could find," I said.

"Gee, thanks."

"It ought to be long enough to cover up the goodies. Tie the tails between your legs and be glad I'm so thoughtful."

She snatched it from me with a laugh and slammed the door shut just as I got my hand out of the way. A minute later it opened again and she came out. Camille hadn't tied the tails like I told her, but it was long enough. She stood there smiling at me and said, "Damn you. It's indecent."

"I saw your picture in the office, remember?"

"That's not the same," she told me.

And she was right. Her body was still damp from the shower and the fabric clung to her skin, her breasts full and high, centered with emotional punctuation marks she couldn't hide, rising pertly with each nervous breath she took.

The taper of the shirt was too big, blousy at the waist, but swelled out over hips that filled it and draped down across a flat stomach that arched outward gently from her navel before outlining the female beauty that lay beneath. The shirt ended at the middle of her thighs and somehow she seemed more naked than if she had been wearing nothing at all, and with the light from the bathroom behind her, filtering through the cloth, all the essence of the woman in the picture was magnified in front of me.

"This is all I could find," I said.

"Yes, I know. With an oiled feather."

"I'll go dig up a chicken."

"Don't bother. Just help me get my clothes dry."

The black half-slip, bra and bikini pants hung across the slats of the ladderback chair were barely damp, but the wool skirt and suitcoat were heavy with moisture, dripping on the floor while tufts of steam rose lazily upward. The room was beginning to have the feel of a Turkish bath.

"Those things'll shrink," I told her.

"And I'll charge it all off to Martin Grady. Tomorrow, a new suit and you can pay for it."

She had been smoothing the skirt out on the seat of the chair and stood up suddenly, turning around with a smile, close . . . too close, and my hands went around her waist. There was a startling warmth to her and under my fingers I felt her body tighten, tiny muscles responding to the unexpected touch. Her smile dissolved into a half-helpless look and the rich, ripe mouth that was about to say something parted wetly and her breath was like a stifled sob.

Camille Hunt had spent too many years being objective. She had been the watcher, not the doer—her reflexes were geared to the other person's reactions and someplace she had forgotten about her own. She came to me with an instinctive gesture that had been inborn in women thousands of generations ago, yet conscious of the bewildering fact that she was capable of it and moved to its demands with a volition she couldn't and didn't want to control. Her eyes were sleepy things, knowing, yet pleading for it to happen quickly before the trained consciousness could reject the animal impulse that was activating her.

Her body began to press against me in a rolling motion, coming to me in a slow arc, her thighs touching first, then her belly in a timorous touch that changed to a powerful thrust as she ran her hands up my back and pulled me against her breasts that had stiffened into hard probing mounds of pure desire and when our mouths met it was with a fierce, driving contact like being sucked into a hungry vortex of violent passion. Her lips and tongue were lively things that worked to drain away the last reserve and with a mewing little cry her fingers tore open the shirt so that the buttons fell to the floor like raindrops and she crumpled slowly, pulling me down on top of her.

The reflected warmth of the heater was lost in the glow we

created ourselves. Her hands were wild things working at me to
expose flesh to flesh, her desire for satisfaction beyond belief, her
imagination transcending that of any woman I had known before.
Time after time we fulfilled ourselves until sheer physical limitations put an end to it and we lay there amidst scattered clothes in
the exhaustion only pleasure can bring.

We would have stayed like that if I didn't hear the muffled call
of a phone from my room next door. I snaked myself loose from
her arms, hearing a small, disappointed protest, and picked up
the receiver from beside her bed and told the switchboard in the
office to transfer the call there.

Dave Elroy caught the change in circuits and coded himself
properly, then waited for my own proper ID before he said,
"Tiger . . . what the hell's going on? Trouble?"

"Everything's fine," I told him and he knew by my choice of
simple words we were clear to speak. "What's up?"

"This town's crawling with Federal men. C.I.A., F.B.I. and
I.A.T.S. are stationed all over the place. I spotted those who
would know me and stayed out of sight. Charlie Corbinet's in
with them and they've shaken your other hotel room down, so
they want you."

"Where's Corbinet at?"

"He checked into your old digs and is waiting around. As far as
I can tell he's the only one there."

"Good. I'll make the contact then."

"Let it wait. I need you, old boy."

"Why?"

"I found the guy you wanted found. Get over here now . . .
and I mean *now*. I'm at 124 Pino Lane . . . and expedite." That
was all he said. He hung up on me.

"You have to leave?" Camille was looking at me through eyes
half closed in sleep. Stretched out there naked with the reddish
heat from the wall unit lighting her body, she looked like a big,
lovely doll, languid in repose, the tiny smile showing the pleasant satisfaction of a woman who had enjoyed the completeness of
her womanhood.

"I have to."

"Don't leave me here, Tiger."

"Business, kid."

"I don't care. I just want to be with you for a little while longer."

"Okay, get `dressed," I said, then finished buttoning my shirt. Camille wrinkled her nose at me, rolled into a ball for a second, then pushed onto her knees and stretched, holding a statuesque pose for a moment before getting to her feet.

"Turn around," she told me.

"Now you get modest," I said, laughing at her. "Great." I checked the clip in the .45, jacked one in the chamber, put the hammer on half cock and slid it in the holster. By the time I had finished knotting my tie and getting into my coat she was almost finished. I looked at her, wondering why it was some women could come out of a rainstorm and a flurry of passion in a matter of minutes with nothing more than that look in their eyes and others couldn't be budged for hours.

Evidently she knew what I was thinking because she smiled with those sleepy eyes and said, "Treat it like enthusiastic applause, my Tiger. The desire of a woman who has found her desire and wants to keep it as long as possible." Her hands made a pass at her skirt and blouse for those small adjustments that build clothes onto a woman. "Neat but not gaudy. Can you stand me a little bit wrinkled?"

"As long as it isn't deception."

"Oh?" She glanced at me, eyebrows raised.

I said, "Isn't it at this point the spider takes her victim? The male performs, the male satisfies, the male dies from a lethal bite."

"Ah, but that's only between spiders. You're the wasp, the mud dauber. There seems to be something indecent about the relationship and we'll probably breed a hybrid. However, this is one spider who knows when she's well off despite the basic biological premises. I like you."

"You're weaving a web again."

She laughed at me, a low, throaty chuckle, and said, "Well, let me try, anyway."

The storm had taken on a new tone. Thunder rolled out over the ocean, lightning flashes illuminating the terrain briefly with a startlingly white brilliance. Rain drifted in front of the wind, angling sharply as the gusts increased momentarily, then came straight down to flatten out the ripples that disturbed the great puddles that ran from curb to curb.

Pino Lane was a dead-end street in a section that had started as a new development, then was discarded when progress stretched the city in another direction. Number 124 was the last house in the row, a small boxlike affair, never completed. Paint had weathered the siding and the path to the door was a line of two-by-eights laid from the curb to the house through the mud and weeds once intended for a lawn.

No lights were on behind the windows, but Dave's car was parked fifty feet away in a turning area, nosed back for a quick move if he had to get away fast. I drove by slowly, looking for any sign of movement or fresh tracks laid in the muck, and seeing none, turned beside Dave's car and drove back to the front of the house.

I didn't like it at all. There were too many places for a quick gun to be crouched in the shadows, waiting. The thunder could cover the sound of a shot and a getaway would be an easy thing through the brush to a car parked on the next street. I sat there with the .45 in my hand and let the lightning brighten the area twice, scanning the spaces between the houses during the momentary daylight.

Nothing moved.

No dark blotches indicated a possible assassin.

I touched Camille's arm and said, "I'm going in first. When I reach the door and wave you run for it."

She nodded curtly, her tongue a nervous little thing that wet her lips. She was scared now, her voice stuck in her throat, but I knew she'd do as she was told so I opened the door, slid out and ran up the planking to the house, ready to dive into the mud if anything at all showed. I reached the two unfinished steps, flattened against the wall, turned and waved to her. She came out of the car running, hobbled by her heels and tight skirt, head down against the rain, but didn't stop until she got to me. I grabbed her arm, pulled her behind me and waited.

Still nothing.

Then the door opened and I had Dave lined up on the end of the .45 when he said, "I was covering you all the way, Tiger. Come on in. No lights."

I pushed Camille in first, closed the door and stood there listening.

"We're clear, Tiger," Dave said quietly. He flipped on the narrow beam of a pencil flash and pointed it across the room. "How about this?"

The shaft of light hit a worn mohair armchair in the corner of the room, then ran down until it traced the outline of a shapeless bundle sprawled on the floor. Nobody had to be told he was dead. There's something special about the human body that has stopped functioning. There is a release from all tension, an attitude of terrible finality in the way it can sag and drape itself in total relaxation as it kisses off the world and goes about the business of death. Even the terror and pain of dying disappear and it's a thing in clothes that never fit over an incongruous posture impossible to attain in life.

"Beezo McCauley," Dave said. "Puncture scars up both arms and legs. He was holding four caps of H and a new kit with two syringes in his pocket. The house has been leased to him three years; he's got receipts showing a total disability pension from the Army, deposits in a checking account to match with occasional one-thousand-dollar discrepancies here and there, and the stubs show withdrawals that could mean a big blast off every so often."

"What's the rest?"

"I went through a few leads, got one that located him and came right here. Nobody answered the door so I came in a window. He had been dead about a half hour by then."

"How?"

"Small calibre high-velocity steel slug through the heart. Damn good shot and close. The bullet penetrated his chest with a minimum exit hole, went through the chair and is still in the wall. My guess is a Magnum."

"Niger Hoppes."

"He's caught up with you."

"Not yet," I said. "He's just here."

Behind me Camille let out a strangled gasp and turned her head, covering her mouth with one hand. "It's . . . terrible."

Dave lowered the flash to hit the floor at our feet. "I shook the place down as well as I could but there was nothing here. The door was unlocked and one light on by the chair that I switched off. It looks like the killer simply came up, opened the door and shot McCauley while he was sitting in the chair. No wet tracks on the inside . . . nothing. The rain would have obliterated all footprints outside anyway. Beezo has a fresh hole in his leg and one of the needles was still wet from being washed. Evidently he had mainlined one and was sitting back to enjoy the effects when he got hit. A nice clean wipe out."

"Where are his papers?"

Dave reached in his pocket and took out a half-empty checkbook, a pack of receipts wrapped with a rubber band, a few folded papers and handed them to me. I didn't bother looking at them then. Time for that later.

"You calling this one in or letting it stay this way?" Dave asked me.

"Nobody can help him now. Let's leave him sit. If we stir things up now we'll be doing too much explaining. If Hoppes is in the area it means he's here to eliminate us or else he has a line on Agrounsky."

"Hell, Tiger, with all the Feds around they ought to be able to run down a new face in the town. It isn't that big. Hoppes has to hole up someplace."

"He's a pro, Dave," I reminded him. "He won't take a room where he has to register or be cooped up in a dead end. Either he's moving around or he has himself a spot where he can stay buried until he wants to come out."

"Still, it might be worth a try."

"Let's not scare him in deeper. If we curtail his activities he'll be all the more careful. I'd rather give him latitude to pull something in."

"Somebody else can die too."

"Like the man said, you all got to go sometime. The picture's bigger than just that."

"Those thousand-dollar deposits . . . ," Dave started.

"McCauley's payoff for his part in steering Agrounsky to the contacts up north. We'll check out the dates and they'll match. The nut never figures the final payoff would be bigger than he bargained for. The Soviets aren't going to leave anybody alive who can mess up their play."

"Then they wouldn't run Hoppes in alone."

"He won't be alone. They're screening every move down here. You can damn well bet the C.I.A. and I.A.T.S. have specialists on this operation that can identify all known Soviet operatives, so they'll have people in they've been holding for an emergency. No . . . the faces will be new, all right."

"That leaves us holding the bag."

"Like hell it does," I said.

In the semi-darkness of the room, lit by occasional strikes of white lightning from the outside, Dave watched my face and grinned. "What have you got going for you, boy?"

"Some thinking people whose memories need jolting," I said. "I'll wait."

"Won't we all?"

Camille's fingers plucked at my sleeve. "Tiger . . . can we go? I . . . feel sick."

"Sure, kid." I tapped Dave with my thumb. "Cover us going out. I doubt if anybody's around, but no sense taking chances. We'll run right after the next flash. You get to the motel and stay there until you hear from me. I'll make all the contacts. Call Newark Control and give them a full report. Tell Virgil not to assign anybody else down here, but keep a team on tap if they're needed."

"Roger."

I led Camille up to the door, waited until there was another sudden stroke of white from the rolling clouds overhead, then

opened it and ran down the plank walk to the car and held the
door open for her. Dave would make his own way out after making sure no prints or tracks were left to identify us. Camille
slumped in the seat, her body heaving with an occasional convul-
sion of nausea, hands covering her face. I started the car, drove
down to the intersection, then turned north up a road flooded
from side to side.

Overhead, the world seemed to crash down in an exhibition of
its own fury.

I left her at the motel still shaking, but better than she had
been. She was wet from the rain again and her voice had gone
hoarse, and although she grinned at me between a sneeze, I knew
she was calming down after going through the experience of
seeing violent death for the first time. She didn't want me to
leave, but knew better than to ask me to stay.

Her hand fell over mine and squeezed. "Will you be long?"

"No."

"Tonight . . . you'll stay with me?"

"Tonight," I said.

"I'll weave another web. You broke the first one."

I kissed her lightly, then pushed her from the car. When she was
inside I turned around in the gravel drive and cut back across the
highway.

Vincent Small came to the door, saw me and opened it without
a word. When I stepped inside I had a chance to look at a face
that had become haggard with worry and the drink in his hand
was potent enough so that I could smell the liquor through the
mixer and the ice. His eyes had a hazy look, requiring seconds to
focus, and his expression was drawn. Somehow he seemed ten
years older, a philosopher drowned in his own subject matter. He
finally frowned, peering at me and said, "The police . . . "

"Sitting in a car out front. I parked around the corner and came
through the back."

"What . . . has happened?" The ice clinked in the glass as his
hand shook.

"We found a guy who had contact with Agrounsky. He was part of the pattern. Maybe you'd like to see him."

"No . . . no, it doesn't matter." He swallowed hard and waited for me to speak.

I said, "The contact was minimal but important. Like yours. He's dead. I thought you might like to know because you might be next in line."

Small backed away, staggered to a chair, and sat down heavily, the drink forgotten in his hand. "But why . . . why me?"

"Louis Agrounsky talked just enough. They all do when they're riding the *horse*. If he told you and Claude about his little hideaway he could have told somebody else about that too. Narcotics addicts don't keep secrets very well, especially when they're hurting for the junk."

"Mr. Mann . . ."

I stopped him short. "You call Boster and tell him what I told you. Then sit and think. You go over every word he ever said and chew it good. Between you and your friend, you're holding this explosion in the palm of your hand, and buddy, if you think your own neck isn't on the line, you're wrong. If you doubt it, a short ride across town will prove it to you. A dead man is pretty convincing evidence."

"I never thought . . ."

"That's the trouble with everybody . . . they never think," I said.

CHAPTER TEN

When I tapped on the door of the room Charlie Corbinet said, "Come in, Tiger." He was sitting there in the light of the TV watching an old movie, his coat off and his sleeves rolled up. "You took long enough. I don't like to wait. You ought to remember that."

"Those were the old days, Colonel. Now you wait if you have to."

"Quit getting raunchy," he said testily. "You're the one on the hook now."

"Nuts."

His smile took the sternness from his face a second. "I wish I could have trained more respect into you."

"What's the pitch?"

"Hal Randolph wants you out. The other agencies are squeezing."

"Let them squeeze. They haven't got anything to yelp about."

"They're dismantling the installations."

"I know. It won't do them any good."

"They know it, but they have to try something."

"Sure, and leave us hanging on the ropes again."

"Have you got a better answer?" he asked. "We're waiting for one."

"Soon."

"Not quick enough."

"Then add something to the picture."

Charlie Corbinet sat back in his chair, crossed his arms with that old familiar gesture and looked at me across the shadows. "Randolph kept the pressure on Doug Hamilton's secretary. She began remembering things. Some fast footwork dug out a few facts that may or may not have a bearing on the case."

"Like what?"

"Like he was efficient but not clean all the way. It looks like he had a sideline of blackmail going for him. Not too big, but not too little either. In checking out the backgrounds of potential employees he ran into some odd arrangements involving people in the upper brackets who scorned our capitalistic system and took up with ultra-liberal types for lack of something better to do. He put it to his own use. Most of them were the student types with sneakers and beards who should have known better, but you know this younger generation. Anything for a kick, anything to show their own self-importance and to break loose in an orgy of self-indulgence."

"Little bastards. They need a hitch in the Army and some time laying face down in the mud while the ones they admire try to take their hides off. All the guts they've got is to wave placards and wear hair like the girls. Their grandfathers fought Indians and built this country out of the bare dirt and the only kind they ever see is under their fingernails."

"So be it."

"They don't inherit over *my* dead body, Charlie."

"Nor mine. Like you said, there are still some of us left. Doug made money out of it."

"But how does it stand here?"

"I don't know. It may not mean a thing."

"Maybe it does."

"Then figure it out." His eyes came to meet mine, half closed in an attitude of study. He was trying to read me again and annoyed with himself because he couldn't do it. Lightning swept through the night again, a bright swelling light with a strange tremor to it, lasting a few seconds before fading out. We both waited until the thunder came on, slowly at first, then with a dramatic crash of sound that burst directly overhead.

"I'll be waiting," he told me at last.

"You'll know when," I said. He nodded and turned back to the TV set deliberately ignoring me the way he used to do when he was finished explaining. I opened the door, backed out after checking around me and walked to the car. The rain laughed and rumbled deep in its throat, slackening long enough for me to get in before clawing at the windows again.

When I reached the highway there was a casual roadblock at the intersection, four patrolmen inspecting licenses of passing vehicles and going through the backs of trucks. I saw it in time, swerved into an empty driveway, waited a while, then backed up and took a route that led me around them. At a diner a mile north I had coffee and a sandwich beside a pair of truckers who bitched about being stopped and having to shift cargo in the middle of the night and rain for no apparent reason at all. When I finished I picked up my change, told the counterman good night and left.

But you could feel the *thing* in the air. Impending action. Coffeyville waiting for the Dalton gang to pull the raid. Too many cars cruising. Too many people where there shouldn't have been any. Too many cars parked where the sweep of headlights could pick up the outlines of men sitting waiting for a call. The sky was cooperating and a dead man on the floor a short drive away said it all.

The *thing* was there.

It was coming.

Or was it here already?

A family of tourists was disgorging itself from an overloaded station wagon at the motel when I got there, two small children squalling in protest at being disturbed, two others dragging themselves behind their father who had driven too far and wasn't in a mood for arguing. A woman stood at the door of the wagon, holding it open until a white poodle jumped out, cringing at the rain before making a dash for the shelter of the roof of the building. Down further a white Jaguar and a pickup truck were nestled in their ports, lights on in the rooms.

I switched the lights off and drove to my own complex and cut the engine. Behind the drawn curtains of Camille's room a pale yellow line of light showed through the break in the drapes. I tried the door and it swung open easily.

Camille was lying in bed, the night light on beside her, the covers rising and falling with her breathing. I watched her a minute until she coughed in her sleep, turned on the pillow and rubbed at her nose with the back of her hand. She sneezed once, almost awakened, then squirmed back to her original position and relaxed. I adjusted the catch on the knob and pulled the door shut, then went next door to my own room.

Automatically, I felt for the thread I had left caught in the door. Nothing was there. I had the .45 in my hand without realizing it, knowing it was too late to back off without alerting the one who was waiting inside. Two windows led off the room, one to the back, the other to the side, and if I didn't make an entrance he could be gone if he had planned it right.

I put the key in the lock, turned it and shoved the door open as I stepped aside waiting for the muzzle blast that would locate my target.

Captain Hardecker laughed in the darkness and said, "Don't be touchy, Mr. Mann. It's only me."

"Show a light."

A lamp clicked and illuminated the room with an unreal reddish cast. Hardecker was propped up in a wooden chair tilted back against the wall, his feet on the side of the bed.

"That's a good way to get yourself killed," I said.

"We all take chances in this business."

"How did you locate me?"

"No sweat. I'm local, remember. A few diligent calls, a few out of my jurisdiction like here, and we got complete cooperation. I further instructed my friend at the desk not to inform anyone else of your whereabouts."

"Why?"

"I told you. I like you. You scare me. I want to know what's happening in my own back yard. The city is full of Feds and I'm out in the cold. Nobody seems to want our services and I'm getting curiouser by the minute."

"About what?"

"Let's say a guy shot with a .22 Magnum nobody bothered to report."

"Somebody did apparently."

"A good citizen thought something funny was going on in a darkened house when three people came out, got in their automobiles, and drove away. A phone call brought a prowl car, then me. The dead man was a narcotics addict. There were no prints on the door knobs, walls, light switches and any other normal places. Tracks on the floor had been wiped clean."

"Who made the call?"

"Unidentified male who didn't want to get involved. Most calls are like that when they mean anything."

"Nice. Now what?"

"You're not thinking fast, Mr. Mann. I said I was out of my jurisdiction. I'm just curious."

"I didn't see any cars outside."

"My driver dropped me off. He'll stop by later to pick me up. I don't want to interfere with your program."

"You're bugging me, Captain."

"I had hoped to."

"So tell me the real reason for the visit."

His smile was a hard thing that started at the corner of his mouth and gradually drifted across his face. "I checked on you," he said. "The report was extremely interesting. The available information on you was pretty livid. I'm surprised you're still alive and operating out in the open."

"Maybe I don't give a damn any more."

"It isn't that," Hardecker said. "It's the necessity, isn't it?"

"Perhaps."

"It excited me. I don't usually get excited."

"Never pays."

Hardecker paused, looked at me, and let the smile stretch

wider. It was damn near impossible to tell what he was thinking. "One of my men came up with something," he said.

I waited.

"He has a photographic memory."

"Good for him," I said.

There was a dark depth behind his eyes watching for my reaction. "He remembered Helen Lewis. He had seen her twice with our piecemeal man named Henri Frank. Later he saw her with Louis Agrounsky. I thought you may find a connection."

"I have."

"So?"

"She's a Soviet agent who rented a place in Sarasota and never used it except as a temporary address in case of a check."

Hardecker let his smile drift away gradually. "They have a fine network, haven't they?"

I didn't say anything. He had put some of the pieces together himself and knew what he was talking about. He said, "You won't find the Lewis woman. She's one of the unidentifiables. Ordinary, medium, no outstanding characteristics, no record we know about. One in the crowd, the way they pick them. They can appear and disappear and nobody knows the difference. Just a person."

"She'll show," I said. "They all do, eventually."

"They're smart."

"Wrong, buddy. If they were, they wouldn't be on that side."

He rubbed his hands along his legs and stretched, the deep yawn filling his chest to barrel size. "But if they have the edge somehow it will be worth it to them, won't it?"

I shook my head. "Never."

Captain Hardecker got up as if he were tired, but it was only a pose that could trap you if you weren't careful. He hitched the gun up at his belt and looked at his watch. "Maybe for . . . let's say a day . . . we'll keep the killing of Beezo McCauley a local affair. After that, well . . . we'll see."

He walked to the door and stood there beside me a few seconds. I said, "Why, Captain?"

"There are still some of us left," he told me.

The words were very familiar.

I closed the door after him, switched out the light and watched him walk across the gravel to the street and stand there ignoring the rain until a car drove up, made a U turn on the road and stopped to let him get in. When the red of the taillights had disappeared in the distance I let the curtain fall back in place and went to the dresser.

Captain Hardecker hadn't been that curious. Nothing there was out of place and I had left everything arranged to be able to discern any sign of a search. Hardecker had been playing it square. The only thing that bothered me was the quick way he ran me down. He was in the position to do it, but so was anybody else if they figured out the angles. Nobody is really hard to find if you wanted them badly enough and they were available.

I was available.

And Niger Hoppes was looking.

The faceless one was out there in the night with a .22 Magnum that had proved its point all over the world and now it was ready to do it again.

Thunder came in a slow drone that sounded tired and the lightning lost that quality of wild intensity it had had an hour ago. Even the rain seemed to have settled back into a period of waiting, knowing that what it came to see would be seen.

All it had to do was wait.

When you've been exposed enough you begin to sense things. Proximity with death makes you familiar with his aptitudes. Some conditions expedite his activities, like a spring thaw bringing out the snakes. It's too early, but they respond to the stimuli of nature and poke a cautious head out of their lair, winter vicious, angry at the disturbance and ready to strike even if the time isn't *the* time.

I could sense it. He was out there somewhere. It wouldn't have been too hard at all. In the bad light at McCauley's place he wouldn't have chanced a long range shot, not with two of us there and the prize at stake. But he could have laid a tail on me with a set of cars operating by radio. I hadn't been careless. The thought had always been there. I was a thorn that had to be plucked out, the one who wasn't stymied by rules and regulations and could operate on a level with them, backed by an organization as coldly efficient and as deadly as any they ever possessed. I was letting myself stand in their sights and asking for it, hoping to get in just one return shot. Take out a key person and the structure would sway long enough to topple it from another direction.

I knew I was laughing without making any sound at all, enjoying the moment to the fullest, tasting the sense of that other one who was out there waiting, watching, planning how to eliminate me. I took the safety off the .45 and thumbed the hammer back, feeling the live weight of the piece in my hand. It was old and familiar, worn smooth by much handling, as much a part of me as my thumb and forefinger, a metallic monster that could say yes or no to life or death.

I went to the windows, parted the blinds enough to study the terrain outside and see what spot I would pick for an ambush if it were me out there. The area in front of the crescent shaped line of double rooms was too well lit with nothing to afford concealment, while the brush cover on the other side of the end room I occupied didn't give a view of the front door. That left just one spot, a clump of palms diagonally off the corner where a killer could cover all exits of my room.

And damn it, I could feel him there. He was outside!

Now I had to make him show himself. I went to the bathroom, turned on the light and closed the door so none of it would seep in toward me, but out there he would know I was up, that I wouldn't sleep because time couldn't be lost to that factor. If they had kept a check on me they'd know I had spent time with Camille and might go back. They'd have seen Hardecker come and go, but not knowing what was said, would wait for my reaction to whatever had passed between us. Once I stepped out that door I'd have had it. They had to kill me alone and on their own terms so there wouldn't be any sudden repercussions, giving them back the time advantage. Even hours counted.

But I had to go out that door.

If I didn't they would come in and if there were more than one they could clean the job up even at the risk of losing some of their own. But one man could handle it. I'd done it myself. One gas bomb or a grenade could ax me fine.

The night laughed at me with a staccato drum roll of thunder and threw the rain at the windows like hands full of pebbles.

It didn't take long to fold the bedding inside my other clothes and drape the almost-human figure on the lamp. I forced the window open an inch, just enough to admit the snout of the .45. Then I unlocked the door, swung it open and pushed the dummy into the darkened aperture and waited for the next flash of lightning that would reveal it.

Perverse nature wanted to savor the moment. It sat there and enjoyed the tension, tasting the nervous excitement of the approaching climax like a lover bringing a virginal partner to slow and complete sexual fulfillment that would erupt in a searing highlight of ecstasy for them both. It nursed the breasts of the scene, stroked its belly and kindled an agonizing flame of desire in its loins, stimulating passion by its very reluctance to light the stage until the orgasm of violence could no longer be contained.

And then nature gasped, succumbed to its own uncontrollable release and split the sky with a blinding forked tongue that kissed the earth in an orgy of pleasure that gave an aurora of midday to the landscape and in the middle of it I saw the shaft of flame come from the group of palms and the thing I had built slammed backwards into the room while wood splintered and brick crumbled behind it.

I fired seven rounds into the trees as fast as I could pull the trigger and was out the door slapping a fresh clip in the rod before I knew I had been suckered. The shot that had come through the door had come from a rifle, not a .22, and I was alone in the middle of the arena if nature laughed again.

She did. She clapped her hands for an encore like a single neon tube and I was in the gravel and rolling when the second shot came. But this time it wasn't from the palm grove. It tore through the collar of my coat, splattering fragments of stone in my face that stung as they gouged into the skin and ricocheted off in front of me. In the brief light still left, I turned, saw him on the roof of the middle building and snapped a booming shot off that threw up pieces of tile at his feet even as he was aiming across one arm for another burst. He didn't wait for it. He spun and clambered over the ridgepole as the sky roared its thunderous applause and doused its lights.

Some late tourist still fighting the weather gave me my life back. His headlamps made a yellow background that outlined the single massive figure plunging out of the trees still clutching a rifle, running erratically, trying to pick me out against the rain-dimmed floods of the courtyard beyond. He was on me before I could get turned, his yell one of startled satisfaction, the rifle barrel swinging toward my head. I ducked under it, lunged into his legs, and took him down on top of me.

He liked it that way. His laugh was raw as he groped for my neck, one balled fist smashing into my ribs. One huge paw wrapped around my hand holding the .45, forced it back until the gun dropped from it, then his knee ripped upward aiming for my groin, and when he missed, started rolling over on top of me, utilizing every ounce of power in his great body. He laughed again, enjoying what he was doing. He liked it.

He forgot one thing.

I liked it that way too.

I let him get right in position before I did what I had to do. I broke his voicebox with one stab of my fingers and while he groped at his throat with surprised urgency, screaming in absolute silence, my fingers wrapped over his and broke every one of the bones from the palm to the tip. My knee didn't miss. It rammed the socket between his thighs, turning his whole belly into a mass of terrifying pain that bulged his eyes out into great white orbs. He had been too used to winning. He had been too confident that he was the best. He had been too used to watching the terror in others, and now it was on him. It wasn't a little thing now. There would be no stopping point and he knew it. He started to shake his head, unable to speak at all, consumed by physical agony he had never known before, yet even then, given any release, he would have done anything to avenge the terrible thing done to him.

Before he could I reached up, had his head wrapped in my arm and with one furious twist I broke his neck and threw him off me like a lump of dirt.

There was another one in the palms. He was a little guy with a birthmark on the side of his face and a hole in his chest from one of the shots I threw at them. A loaded but unfired .303 rifle lay under him and a .38 snubnosed revolver was in his belt.

I dragged the remains of the big guy back and piled him on top of the other one, then threw the rifle down on the wet earth. Nature appreciated the gesture, let me see the tableau in her fiery brilliance a few seconds, gave another booming sound of gratefulness for the entertainment and watched me walk away.

Nobody was watching. The noise and fury of the storm had covered it all.

I found the ladder that had put Niger Hoppes on the roof and went up it, reached the slippery wet tiles, and made my way to the other side where he had stood, the place marked by the chunk my .45 had taken out of the ceramic. Clever. He had played it cleverly, covering me from front and rear, thinking ahead the way I would have myself. He would have a feeling for these things too, knowing the possibilities, realizing others could be sensitive to an unseen presence and prepare for an eventuality.

How long had he stood there waiting for the right moment? And was it really Niger Hoppes who had chosen to accomplish the mission? He answered it for me himself. It was lying there in the rain gutter caught in the overlap of the tile, a slender white tube, finger-long, stamped with the name BEZEX.

I tossed it back, satisfied, then climbed down and found his tracks faintly etched in the wet soil, leading to a path and angled out toward the road. I didn't bother following them. He had had the time and the facilities to make his escape. Now he'd have to choose another time and another place.

Niger Hoppes wasn't around any longer. I could feel it. The *thing* was gone.

With very little work from a standard pick I got Camille's door open. She hadn't changed positions at all. Her breathing was heavy, forced through accumulation of mucus in her throat. She sniffled once and coughed as I closed the door.

Dave Elroy picked up the package Ernie Bentley had sent me through General Delivery and dropped it off a little after eight. The cloud cover still obscured the sky, the rain falling monotonously, and even at that hour there was a dawnlike quality to the day. He handed me a container of coffee he had brought along, then sat down and listened to what I had to tell him about the night before.

When I finished he whistled through his teeth, grimacing. "You can't leave those bodies out there."

"I'm not going to get tied down making big explanations yet. That's all we need to blow the act."

"Okay, it's your baby. Check their ID?"

"Nothing there. The usual assortment of junk that would have been faked. When the police get to them they'll check out the specifics. At the moment they can't help one way or another."

"So who's on the hook?"

I grinned at him slowly. "That's where my 'official' status gives me a degree of immunity, buddy. Self defense in the line of duty. I'm not worrying about the future. You call in to Newark and let them sweat it out."

"You sure like to take chances, kiddo," Dave said.

"What's it like in town?"

"Crowded," he told me. "More are coming in all the time. They're not the tourist types. It's worse than Los Alamos when the Manhattan Project was in full swing. I hear a dozen people have been rounded up on general charges and are being held incommunicado in a government depot until the air clears. The hustlers saw them coming and cleared out overnight. You can't even find a bookie in town."

"It doesn't matter."

"What's with the package?" Dave asked.

I opened the wrapping and took the top off the box inside. A pair of finger-length inhalers made of white plastic bearing the

Bezex label were nestled inside with Ernie's note on top of them.
I looked at the addresses he delivered the real things to, then
went over his explanation of how he had cut their effectiveness in
half. If anybody used them they'd be needing another in a hurry.
I peeled off the cellophane wrapper from one of the deadly little
containers, remembering the way Ernie used to look when he
read one of the reports, thinking *we* were the hard cases. Hell, he
was in a class by himself. He invented death and we just pushed
the buttons. What he didn't invent was the way I could pull the
switch on Niger Hoppes, hoping it was Hoppes who got the
cyanide capsule and not some poor slob who didn't deserve a
killer's death. The best idea he offered was spotting the samples
around. I dropped the capsule in my coat pocket and put the
other one in my shaving kit, then handed Dave the list of stores
that would have the Bezex.

I said, "Check with the owners of these places and get a description of anyone who buys the things. As far as they're concerned, you're a follow-up representative for the company and
make it look good."

"And if there's a contact?"

"Cover it. Stay with him out of sight and get to me through
Charlie Corbinet. I won't check in around here at all. It's better if
I keep moving. Just don't close in on the guy unless you have
help."

"Hell, Tiger, I've handled them before."

"This is a top gun, buddy. Your action has been investigative
more than trigger jobs. If you get that close and you're sure of
your man, don't take a chance. Kill him."

"No talk?"

"No talk," I repeated. "There isn't time for it. We want Agrounsky, not Niger Hoppes. He's only an obstacle."

Dave lit a smoke and smiled at me across the room. "You guys
are like fighter pilots during the war. One of you has to be eliminated so the bombers can either get through or be shot down."

"So let's keep the odds on our side," I said. "What are you
packing?"

"A .38 and a shiv on my leg."

"Remember your training."

"How could I ever forget it?" He laughed. "Take care, Tiger. You're the real target." He went out, shutting the door quietly, and I heard his car start up and drive off. I piled all my loose clothes into a laundry bag, threw them in the back seat of my own car and hung a Do Not Disturb sign on the door of my room. I didn't want any cleaning woman coming in and finding that hole in the closet and the chipped brick from the wall just yet. There was time enough for that when somebody stumbled over the bodies in the palm grove.

I rapped on Camille's door three times before I heard her stir. She came awake slowly, got out of bed and walked across to open the door and peer at me through the opening. I got a sleepy smile and stepped inside. She had my shirt on, clutching it shut at the middle.

"You left me," she accused.

"The way you were sleeping I didn't want to bother you."

She tucked her head against my shoulder a moment, then looked up at me. "It's my fault, really," she said. "After seeing . . . that man, well, I took a couple of sleeping pills and on top of the excitement I sort of faded out." Her nose crinkled and she stifled a sneeze. Her eyes had a watery glaze and I could hear a wheezing as she talked.

"Forget it. You needed it."

"Has . . . anything happened?"

"Plenty. You slept through it all."

"Can you . . . ?"

I knew what she was going to say and shook my head. "Get dressed. We're moving out."

Without another word she nodded and turned back to take her clothes off the hangers in the closet. Outside, the rain hammered down and from afar off there was a majestic rumble of thunder as the storm paraded by over the state.

Camille went into the bathroom to dress and I sat on the edge of the bed waiting for her to finish. Beside her handbag on the night table was a packet with the top torn off, a prescription issued to her from a New York pharmacy with the instructions to take one or two capsules before bedtime. Idly, I flicked the ten remaining from the original dozen back in the envelope and stuck it in her bag.

And outside the world churned in utter anxiety, stirred by contemptuous nature who laughed gleefully at the pitiful efforts being made to emulate her strength and fury.

Outside was a killer and a team behind him checking and double checking, following every lead, hard on each trail that would take them to the ultimate survival factor.

Someplace out there Agrounsky was still sitting, coming to his decision, and sooner or later something or some*one* was going to make it for him. With all the deviousness of a warped mind, he had chosen his place well. He had left no track, no trace. The hungry animal of embittered philosophy had commandeered a genius' mind and guided it to where it could do the most damage. Now it just sat and ate away at the vital parts until it was self-consumed by its own destructiveness.

I picked up the phone and dialed Vincent Small's number. It rang a half dozen times before a querulous voice said, "Hello?"

"Small?"

"Yes, this is he."

"Mann, Vincent. You alone?"

"Quite. There are . . . policemen outside."

"Everything all right?"

There was a hesitation before he said, "Yes. I'm all right."

My voice felt tight and edgy. "Talk to me, friend."

"There's nothing really. It's just that . . ."

"Well?"

He sounded tired, all the jubilance he'd had when we first met gone from him now. "I . . . you remember how we asked the realtors about Louis possibly buying a place somewhere?"

"Yeah. What about it?"

"I don't know. One of them called last night. He said there was another man asking the same thing."

"Local?"

"No . . . a stranger. He only called because he wanted to locate Louis if he was interested in property. He had a few sites available."

"Any description?"

"Very vague, that's all. The man had on dark glasses and, well . . . it was raining out and he had on a slicker with a hat pulled down low so he really didn't get a good look at him."

"Then why are you scared?" I asked deliberately.

Vincent Small didn't answer at first. He took a long time before he said, "I called some of the other real estate people. He was there too."

"You're not saying it all, Vince."

I heard his swallow audibly, then he blurted out, "The first one told him we had been asking the same thing too. He didn't mean anything. He just said it and . . ."

"Did you call Boster?"

"Yes." His voice turned tinny as he said, "He . . . didn't answer. It may not mean anything. . . ."

As quietly as I could, trying not to scare him, I said, "You call in those cops and have them sit there beside you. Don't you let anyone else in unless you know they're from the police. *You sit tight, understand?*"

"Yes, I understand."

He was still talking when I held the button down long enough to break the connection, then dialed Claude Boster's home.

Nobody answered the ring.

She came out as I put the phone back, saw my face and said, "What is it, Tiger?"

"It's breaking." I looked at her, debated the advisability of leaving her alone, realizing she could be used as a lever against me if it became necessary, then said, "Let's go, kid. You stay with me."

She didn't argue and didn't ask questions. She went out and got in the car, her eyes following me all the way as I went around and got in under the wheel.

I looked up at the sky and somehow I could feel the *thing* again. It was out there waiting. I cut by the spot where two men were still sprawled in the brush with sightless eyes open to the rain, bodies stiff in the penalty of death, waiting to be found and remembered, then angled up the drive and took the highway back to town.

The gas gauge was almost on empty, so I stopped at the nearest service station and told the attendant to fill up the tank. While he did I went inside to the pay phone and dropped a dime in the slot, then dialed Captain Hardecker's number.

When the desk sergeant put me through I said, "Mann, Captain. I need a favor."

"Naturally." There was something funny about the way he said it.

"Okay, do I ask or not?"

"You're sharp, Tiger." I heard a pencil rap against the phone and he added, "They've removed your cooperation factor."

"Nice of them."

"My information on you gets wilder all the time. Nobody tells me anything except about you."

"I'm available."

"To me, but not to them. They'd like very much to have you out of the picture."

"Sure, I know."

"And what's the favor?"

"Do I get it?"

"Why not? I have the feeling that if you're forced to you could trade goodies with me."

"If I have to," I said.

"So ask."

"Call your men outside of Claude Boster's place. I want to see him."

"Consider it done. You're on the hot sheet and they've been given some pertinent instructions over my authority to nail you, old feller, but in this district I still pull a little weight. I may need some excuse to explain the move if the roof comes in though."

"You have it then. Will you hold it?"

"Shoot."

"Two dead men in the palms beside my hotel. I killed them

both. The bullet hole in the room will fit the picture so use it as a diversion. I'll give you the details later."

It stopped him a second, then he told me, "That comes under county business."

"The sheriff will be glad to have your help, Captain. Inform the boys pushing you of what happened and you'll see some jumping after they identify the characters. It'll make you look good." I glanced at my watch. "Give me an hour first."

"No more. If I had any sense I'd play this by the book and roll all over you."

"There's no job security in being dead," I told him and put the receiver back.

The attendant had filled the tank, checked the oil and took the bill from my hand. He gave me back the change wishing I had never stopped there in the first place because he was soaking wet and tired of bothering with outsiders who didn't know enough to stay out of the rain.

I got in the car and turned the key.

Camille laid her hand on top of mine. "Tiger?" she said tentatively.

"I'm scared, kid," I told her.

CHAPTER ELEVEN

THE TWO COPS IN the prowl car had discreetly pulled up fifty feet away from Claude Boster's drive to avoid seeing me in case they had to answer questions later, but both of them made a careful check through the rear window and satisfied it was me, went back to their conversation. Footprints in the wet lawn made a continuous path around the house, evidence of constant patrolling, an occasional rain drenched butt flipped here and there.

I rang the bell, waited, looked back at Camille who was peering through the dripping windshield anxiously, then rang again. When nobody answered I told her to wait, then went around and tried the back door. That brought no response either.

The only other place he could be was in the workshop and if he had the phone cut off it would explain his silence.

My feet slipping on the wet grass, I cut diagonally across to the gravel path, reached the door, and hammered on it. I called to him, the heavy air muting my voice. I kicked at the bottom of it, then put my ear against its solid bulk and listened.

Inside there was the faintest tinkling sound, that of glass breaking against concrete. I said, "Damn it!" softly. I tried the knob of the door again, but knew it would be no use. Even the .45 couldn't tear those locks loose in time. I hugged the side of the building, edged around the side under one of the windows, hoisted myself up enough to see part of the unlit gray interior of the building, then figured the odds and swore again.

Someone cornered there could take me apart with no trouble at all. A shot fired from the inside wouldn't be heard at all, an escape would be quick and easy with the cops pulled off their beat. He could even have watched the entire action, realizing why it had happened, and could have waited for me knowing it would be worth while.

But I couldn't take the chance.

I swung the nose of the .45 against the window, smashed it, broke out the jagged shards left in the frame, then tore the metal blinds out and threw them down behind me. It wasn't time to think or consider the consequences. It had to be done *now*.

My hands grabbed the sill, I lunged in and over with one motion and fell hands out to the top of a bench, the gun almost going out of my fingers. I didn't stop . . . I kept on rolling, got to my hands and knees and skittered beneath a bench to a packing crate and crouched behind it.

For five seconds I had been exposed. An expert marksman would have had the time.

I crawled out, stood up, and saw the glint of light from a broken flask on the floor. Next to the pieces legs lay sprawled limply, half hidden by the top of a metal lathe bench. I found the light switch, flicked it on and twisted the gooseneck down to one side.

Claude Boster lay there almost unrecognizable, his face bloodied and swollen beyond belief, fingers disjointed and broken back, jutting out at odd angles. A wide piece of surgical tape still hung from one cheek where it had been used to muffle him while the job was done.

But he was still alive. There was a flutter to his eyelids and somehow he had managed to knock over that flask when he heard me at the door.

I said, "Claude?"

His mouth moved and blood spilled over his lips. I saw his apron front then, torn and powder-burned directly over the heart. Gently, I felt the area, probed the heavy canvas and picked out the flattened lead slug that had smashed into him from a .22 Magnum.

Someday Claude Boster would realize how lucky he had been. In the top pocket of the apron he had dropped three small steel crescent wrenches that had absorbed the murderous impact that would otherwise have torn his chest inside out. They lay in my hand, bent and split, but lifesaving armor against a shot fired to silence him permanently.

"Can you hear me?"

A small nod indicated that he could.

"I know you're hurting, but you'll be all right. Now even no matter what it takes, don't pass out. I have to talk to you."

Boster nodded again and said weakly, "Yes . . . but . . . hurry. I can't . . . stand it."

"What happened?"

For a second he closed his eyes and I thought he had drifted off, then he opened them and looked at me, pain showing through the slits. "There . . . was a knock . . . on the door. I thought it . . . was a policeman. He . . . came in . . . hit me."

"Who, Boster?"

"Thin. He was . . . tall. Face was . . ."

"What? Come on, snap out of it!"

Boster spat out blood from his crushed mouth, eyes pleading with me to stop, but I couldn't. He said, "Right side . . . scarred. Glass eye. He had a . . . funny gun."

"What was he after?"

The pain receded then, horror taking its place as he remembered. His jaw came open, trembled, and he moaned and tried to turn his head.

"*What was it, Boster!*"

He rolled his head back slowly. "I . . . told him," he said, his voice accusing nobody but himself. I waited, knowing there would be more. Finally he moved his mouth again. "I had remembered . . . a place Louis . . . mentioned. Leesville. He beat me . . . did things to me . . . and I told him." His eyes squinted shut and a tremor went through his body. One hand twitched with the terrible agony in it. "I . . . couldn't help myself."

I tried to keep my voice quiet. "When, Boster? How long ago?"

"Right . . . after daylight."

That gave Niger Hoppes a few hours' start!

"Leesville . . . where is it?"

He tried to talk but wasn't going to make it. One hand reached out feebly as if it were pointing. A glassy stare was coming into his eyes again. He made one final attempt and got out, "Map . . . pinhole," then relapsed into total unconsciousness.

Like that the pain was gone into the darkness the body reserves for such moments and there was nothing I could do for him that couldn't wait. I straightened up, shoved the gun back and scoured the room for a map. I tore the place apart, throwing drawers on the floor, slamming papers and blueprints from the shelves, looking for the thing and finding nothing. Boster had tried to point, but where?

I went back to the inert form wanting to yell at him, make him tell me, then I saw the bulge in the lower pocket of his bench apron. It was just a standard East Coast roadmap issued by a big gasoline company, but it covered the area from Florida to Maine, and in the southlands there could be hundreds of Leesvilles that were no more than intersections of county roads. I spread the map out, checked the important cities listed in the corner without finding any reference to a Leesville.

But Claude had said a pinhole.

I stretched the map face down on a bench and ran my hand over the surface, feeling for any raised edge from a perforation. When my fingers came away empty I held it up to the light, let my eyes roam over the area inch by inch, concentrating in the lower quarter.

It took five minutes, but I found it, buried in the crease of a fold, just the tiniest pinprick as if someone had looked at the map once and absently touched the spot with a pin. That's what Louis Agrounsky had done, and Boster had seen him do it.

Alongside the minute hole in fine blue letters identifying a blue dot near the coastline was the legend, *Leesville*.

I shoved the map in my pocket and picked up the phone, waiting impatiently for Charlie Corbinet to answer. I heard the phone connection open and the hum of voices in the background before he said, "Yes?"

"Tiger, Charlie. Can I talk?"

He recognized the urgency in my voice and kept his friendly and disarming in case anyone else was listening. "Certainly," he said cheerfully.

"I have the spot located."

Then his tone was forced and his breathing was hard. "Yes, yes, go on. I'll be glad to help."

"No thanks. We haven't got time. I don't want anybody moving in or we'll scare our boy off. You get the information firsthand the way I did. Niger Hoppes reached Claude Boster somehow. It wouldn't have been much trouble to do . . . the grounds were patrolled and he came when the cop was on the other side of the building. Boster needs help and fast."

"Fine . . . I understand." He knew it was useless to argue at that point and didn't try. But he could try a different approach just to keep me there and said, "Your . . . friend has been trying to call you."

"Dave?"

"That's the one. You're to call your . . . fiancée. Apparently it's important."

"You trying to keep me here, buddy?"

"It's for your own good," he said, but he didn't mean it at all. They wanted me out of the way.

I grinned at the phone mirthlessly and said, "I'll leave the name of the place on the workbench. Let's see you find it ahead of me. You'll have the same chance as Hoppes, only he's got a bigger start."

I hung up, scribbled *Leesville* on the desk pad for him to find and went over to the door. The chain hung there, but the other two automatic locks were still in place, pulled shut from the outside. Niger Hoppes had had it too damn easy.

Not now though. Right then he was activating every source at his command to locate the possible sites of Leesville along the route Louis Agrounsky took and the faceless underground was going to find it for him.

I ran to the car, got in, and backed out of the drive. By the time I reached the corner, went down a block and reversed my path I heard the moaning wail of the police car's siren in front of Boster's house as they got the call to intercept me.

There wasn't time for explanations. Camille could see it on my face and stared straight ahead. I took the back roads, picking my direction carefully, heading continuously toward the airport on the other side of town. They'd be out in full force now, knowing I knew the actual location of the place, ready to tear it from me any way they could. I couldn't blame them. Their concern was as great as my own, but I had been there at the beginning and I was going to be there at the end. I was closer than they were and at this point better prepared.

Beside me Camille sneezed into her handkerchief, sniffling hard as she fought the cold the rain drenched her with. Her eyes were watery when she looked at me through a forced smile and said, "Can I help somehow?"

"Keep watching those side roads. I can't see too well."

"Where are we going?"

"The airport."

She spotted an intersection and cleared me with a nod. "You found . . . your friend?"

"Yeah, I found him. He was supposed to be dead." I described the scene briefly to her and her shoulders shook with some inward revulsion. "I'm . . . sorry. I'm not very . . . good about these things."

"Forget it. We're almost on target."

She took the handkerchief away from her mouth and wiped at her eyes. "Tiger . . . I'm frightened."

"Don't be."

"I can't help it. Maybe it's silly . . . but I haven't . . . before I haven't been part of anything. . . ."

"You did fine, kid."

"I wasn't any help. . . . You'll leave me here?" she asked.

"I have to."

"But . . . "

"Nobody'll bother you. The action's left this place. It'll be in Leesville now."

"Where?"

"A spot on the map in North Carolina near the ocean. The killer I want has a few hours' start, but it won't do any good."

"Hours?"

"I have an F-51 waiting, honey. It can bore right through this weather ahead of any transportation he can pick up. Even if it only took him an hour to locate the right Leesville I can beat him in. The benefits of the Martin Grady organization."

The wind shifted, bringing the crosshatch patterns of the sirens coming from my left as cars toured the main roads in their futile searching. Twice, I had to follow a sandy side road too close to the highway, but each time another strip heading south showed up and I took it, plowing past rough holes and shoulders that fell off into drainage ditches. All I had was a rough idea of my position, but it was enough. A white arrow nailed to a tree read AIR-PORT, and I cut sharply, took the branch road and stayed on it, until I reached the fringe of the field, then turned into the first opening, picked up a runway and laid on the gas as I tore down the paved surface to the hangar area.

Mason Armstrong was inside with a steaming cup of coffee, idly reading the NOTAMS posted on the wall when I walked in. He put the cup down and said, "Going somewhere?"

"What's the weather?"

"N.G. They're holding everything down. All commercial flights are canceled."

"Can we move?"

Mason shrugged and grinned. "Not unless you want trouble."

"A little more won't matter," I told him.

"A Piper Comanche took off a while ago. They raised hell in the office, but the pilot had a happy look like whatever he was paid was worth losing a license for."

That cold, bleak feeling traveled up my back again. "You see who rode with him?"

"Just from the back. Tall skinny guy, but I didn't see his face."

I pulled the map from my pocket and opened it. "Check your sectionals. See if you can get down someplace close to here." I pointed out the dot that was Leesville. Mason gave me a strange look, shrugged again and went over to his mapcase.

Down on the far end of the wall was a public phone. I dropped in a dime, gave the operator two numbers Rondine could be reached at and waited while she tried to connect me. Neither one answered. I gave her Ernie Bentley's and waited again, knowing that if a call to Newark Control had gone in from Rondine it would reach him too.

Ernie was there, his voice choppy. I identified myself and said, "Rondine call?"

"Damn right, but she wouldn't talk to Newark. Virgil contacted me but I couldn't put him on you when I didn't know where you were."

"No message at all?"

"Nothing. She was pretty well shook up about something . . . said it was absolutely imperative that you reach her, but she wouldn't talk. All I gathered was that she found something. She said she'd be at the place you told her to stay at three this afternoon."

"I just called there."

"It isn't three yet."

"Okay, I'll make the call. That's the roominghouse you quartered me at. Get some of our people over there and have them stay put with her until I call in. But in any event, get her to talk, damn it. Hell broke loose down here. . . . I have the spot Agrounsky's holed up in but Hoppes is ahead of me. Anything that can rush things, do."

"Get him with the Bezex?"

"Sorry, buddy. This time your gimmick was no good."

I hung up and turned back to the counter Mason had his maps spread out on. "What's there?"

"Nothing but farmland. The nearest strip is ten miles away and all dirt. This weather would have turned it into a mudhole. Nothing's getting in there."

I pushed his maps toward him. "*We* are," I said.

"You're nuts, Tiger."

"So I've been told. But we have no other choice. That Comanche was heading for there too."

"He's light enough to make it in the strip with that but we can't."

"Ever come in with your wheels up?"

"Not when I didn't have to, friend. I hope you're not thinking what I think you are."

"You'll be right if you do."

"Look . . . ," he started.

I cut him short. "There won't be a world worth flying in if we don't."

He took two seconds, no more. He had been around with us before. He saw my eyes and the set of my face and said, "What are we waiting for?"

I pulled out the keys to the car and went over to where Camille was sitting quietly, coughing into her handkerchief, and handed them to her. "Stay here an hour, honey, then check into a motel until it clears. There ought to be flights leaving in the morning to New York and you be on board. I'll see you there."

She turned her eyes up to me, a sad, tired expression emanating from their beautiful depths. "Will you really?" she asked with no inflection in her voice at all.

I reached out my hand. She took it and stood up facing me, her hands touching my waist with a gentle pressure. "Maybe," I said.

Her smile had a little-girl quality. "No . . . it's over. My web . . . wasn't strong enough." She let her smile brighten a little. "But I tried, you know."

"I know."

"And it was worth it. I only regret one thing."

"What?"

"You didn't get to paint me with the oiled feather."

My mouth touched the wet spots on her cheeks and brushed away the dampness that clung to her eyelashes. Under my hands she began to tremble again and her lids half closed as she choked out a tiny sob I stifled with my lips, fanning the fire in her to immediate and violent life. Her mouth was a wild thing, sucking hungrily, tasting quickly to absorb the present and the future in the few seconds left to us, then I pushed her away when I didn't want her to go at all.

"Be careful, Tiger."

I nodded.

"Will you see me . . . sometime, perhaps?"

"Sometime. It has to happen again."

"Then I'll weave a new web," she smiled. "Be careful, darling."

Behind me Mason said, "Ready, buddy?"

"Coming," I told him.

The Mustang was chocked and tied on the ramp area at the end of a short line of private planes, its WWII fighter silhouette towering over the other craft, the menacing nose pointing skyward as if sniffing out an enemy hidden there.

Mason had pre-flighted the plane earlier, part of his normal routine, so we were ready for immediate take off barring any interference. The rain solved that problem nicely. The field was officially closed and anyone present was behind closed doors sipping coffee near electric heaters that took the bite out of the air.

I climbed in, strapped on the shoulder harness and seat belt while Mason pulled the chocks, then put on the headset and plugged it in while he was getting set. With the canopy closed and the rain obscuring us, no eyes caught the preparations until Mason flipped the starter switch and the four great paddle blades whipped into life.

No other sound in the world is like it. The twelve massive cylinders of the Merlin coughed once, then roared alive with a snarl of gratitude for being awakened, and as the radio suddenly took on life with the startled voice of the tower operator questioning us, Mason pulled out to the taxi strip, went downwind to the runway where he checked the mags, then kicked the tail around and gave the Mustang full take off power into the wind. He went on instruments fifty feet off the ground, broke out of traffic and started to climb, saying the things softly to himself all pilots say when they're hoping there are no other chunks of metal in the sky ahead.

At thirty-five hundred feet we broke out into a bright, beautiful day that was like turning on a switch. Beneath us the rolling clouds that had been dangerously black from the inside took on the soft mounds and valleys of hilly country under a fresh snowfall. The shadow of the plane was encircled by a tight spectrum, a rainbow in full, that rode the crests and dipped into the recesses of the whiteness that capped the hell going on below.

Mason had estimated the time en route at an hour, forty minutes, carefully ignoring the fact of what we might find when he tried to let down. Those things he could think about when he got there. One bridge at a time. Somewhere up ahead another plane and other people were facing the same situation. Mason's calculated voice told me the answers he had worked out on his computer. The Comanche's start was a good one. There was a probability he could find a hole in the overcast and make the field. Maybe not. Leesville would have to be selected by dead reckoning and both planes would face the same difficulties. The best he could say was that it looked like a tie. We could overcome the time lag, but getting on the ground was going to be the big problem.

Time, always that time element, always pulling it up to the last impossible second. I closed my eyes and sat back, letting Mason do the worrying until the time came, and thought about Rondine.

What would she tell me she wouldn't reveal to the others? What was so important? Her assignment was simple and could have given me a lead if the right answer hadn't broken under my nose. She couldn't have made contact with anyone out of the ordinary, but there was always that outside chance that it happened. The Soviets weren't playing this one on a solo basis. Their teams were in there the way our own were, every man alerted, every possible phase of action being explored regardless of how remote it seemed. They had their own experts, their own killers ready to move when necessity demanded it and were forced to do what they had to do to win this crazy game.

Their philosophy for winning was better, too. It was the combat philosophy that the end justified the means and no matter how softly they talked or broadly they smiled in those conclaves at the U.N. they treated the play as war and geared their moves to fit it.

And now they found themselves right on the goal line because we had fumbled the ball through the fault of a player, and they were going to take every advantage of their position and try for the touchdown strategy even if they had to sacrifice their players to do it.

I was the safety man.

Great.

The wind was at their back and the dirt was in our eyes. We couldn't afford to lose, but neither could they. In one sense, we could lose by winning, so if the laws of luck and circumstance turned back to us again it would all be a game played in front of a blindfolded audience. They'd only know the score if *they* won.

Twice, Mason let down through the overcast, feeling his way on the instruments. The second time he waved and pointed toward the ground and I saw the bleak rain-drenched expanse of a field, but there were no identifiable landmarks.

He switched to intercom and said, "The crosswind was stronger than I thought. We're too far west."

"What now?"

"We'll turn east, pick up the ocean and beat up the coast until we locate ourselves. Ceiling here is too low to mess around in. Hundred feet tops and goes right down to the ground in places."

"Let's go then."

It took another fifty minutes before he found a small summer resort nestled in the sand dunes and circled it, then, satisfied, picked a southwest heading and hugged the treetops at minimum altitude, tensed for anything that might jut up out of nowhere. Once he hurtled a power line, then followed it to a road, banked ten degrees away from it until he reached another highway and stayed with the dull white concrete ribbon several minutes before starting a slow turn to the left.

I looked down, following his glance. Directly below us was the outline of an airstrip, the tracks of three wheels gouged into it before slithering off to one side where the Comanche sat mired in the mud.

There was something else, too.

Face down beside it, half covered by a pool of water, was the body of a man.

Mason said, "They beat us, Tiger. That pilot knew the area too well."

"Can you get in?"

"No chance in that slop. We'd do better grinding in on a paved road."

"Any around?"

Mason shook his head. "None on the map. All dirt roads between here and Leesville."

"Then let's get as close as we can. Our boy would have gotten transportation one way or another. It's ten miles between here and Leesville and he's had the time to do it in. We haven't."

"Ever tried this before?" Mason asked me flatly.

"There's always a first time for everything."

"Sometimes it's the last. It's a good thing I'm a company man," he said. "Damn."

Leesville was only a cluster of stores, a gas station and a few houses at a crossroads. We went over it, flaps down at traffic pattern speed, looking for any cleared area that gave a reasonable chance of a landing, both of us trying to fight the restricted visibility that was turning the whole thing into a joke.

I saw Mason nod and his eyes met briefly with mine in the mirror. "Button up."

I yanked the harness as tight as I could, set myself as he picked his spot, dumped full flaps and came in nose high over a grassy pasture that had taken on the appearance of a lake.

He made a beautiful job of it, the tail dragging first, then the fuselage pancaking down with a heavy thud as a crazy scream came from the engine as the prop bit into the earth and the blades bent back in despair. The roar of the Merlin was wiped out almost instantaneously, replaced by water and mud tearing at the metal, biting out pieces and spewing them back into our faces. The seemingly interminable slide came to an end at the rise of a drainage ditch embankment and both of us were out of the cockpit in a second, running for cover in case something blew.

We stopped fifty yards away and Mason looked back ruefully. "What a hell of a thing to do to a lovely airplane."

"Grady'll buy another," I said.

Overhead the sky chuckled with a faint roll of thunder. Mason pointed the direction out and we started walking toward Leesville a half mile away.

The old guy in the jeans and flannel shirt at the gas station took the twenty dollar bill from my fingers, looking at it suspiciously a moment before tucking it in his pocket. He had a languorous drawl that couldn't be pushed and an attitude that any strangers walking in the rain were open to question before they got any answers. I simplified it by saying we were stuck down the road and he agreed with that, though what we were doing there at all puzzled him.

"Come to think of it now," he said, "a car did go by some time ago. Old pickup truck. Used to belong to Henny Jordan. Sold it last year though. New feller on the Dexter Road bought it."

"Near the airfield?"

The man made a surprised grimace and nodded. "That's the one. The crop dusters use his place sometimes. Not much business so he runs a farm on the side."

"He ever come over here?"

"Never see him outside his own place. He deals at the Dexter stores."

I looked at Mason and saw by his face that he knew what had happened too. I took out a cigarette, lit it and said, "There's supposed to be a fish house around here. . . ."

The old man cut me off with a wave of his hand. "Only open in the summer. Guy who runs it has a shack in the woods right back of it. You know him?"

"No, but I'd like to talk to him."

"Well now, you might just do that. He's there, all right. Stocks up for the whole year with groceries and magazines right after Labor Day and just sits it out nice and cozy."

I reached in my pocket and took out the photo of Louis Agrounsky. "Ever see this man before?"

His eyes got cagey and he barely glanced at the photo until I dropped another twenty in his palm, then he studied it carefully. "Lot of tourists come to fish here in the summer. Surfcasters."

"How about this one?"

He held the picture closer to his face. "Could be. Yep, could be he was around. Not that many I shouldn't remember, but I saw this one, all right."

It was coming now.

"Does he own a place around here?"

He handed the picture back with a friendly smile. "Now that, mister," he told me, "I can say no to. Been living here thirty years and there ain't a dirt farmer or registered voter I don't know about."

"Any property change hands?"

He shrugged, spreading his hands. "Does that lots. Good years a man lays in more land, maybe even builds a new house or adds a few rooms. If you mean has your friend in the picture moved in, then it's nope. Three tourists got beach shacks they bought 'bout five years ago . . . come down summers and fish. Nice people. Never see 'em 'cept when they spend money."

I stuck the photo back in my pocket. "Where's this fish house?"

"Mile and a half down the road. Not far from the beach. You figuring on walking?"

"No. I'm figuring you have a car to rent for a price. How does fifty suit you?"

"Suits me fine," he said. "She's sitting outside, that black Ford." He took the bills from my hand and fondled them a moment and as we left he grinned and said, "Hurry back."

The fish house, with the sign that read *Wax's Fish* made nearly illegible by wind-driven sand, was buried behind scrub pines, shutters propped across the windows and a plank holding the door shut. No paint had ever touched the bare wood, and except for the smell that was part of it, the place was perfectly camouflaged. But anybody who could survive a year with two months' work had to do a good business—the pile of clam and oyster shells, almost covered with pine needles at one side, were mute evidence of it.

The shack was behind it, similar in appearance except for the tendril of smoke that came from the brick chimney and the faint glow of light from one window. I knocked on the door, waited, then pushed it in impatiently. Over at the far end, stretched out on a cot and reeking of whiskey, was a bearded old fat guy in dirty long underwear, his breath wheezing from his mouth in drunken monotones while a calico cat perched on the wrinkled newspaper he had draped over his mountain of a stomach. A pair of empty bottles lay on the floor beside him, the remains of a sandwich being attacked by a mottled kitten who looked up at us and growled at the intrusion.

We reached him together, tried to shake him awake, then doused him with a glass of water from the hand pump beside the sink. Mason said, "Hell, he's out."

The guy stirred a moment, grunted something unintelligible, and tried to roll over. I got my hand behind his neck and jerked him upright. "Wax! You hear me?"

"Get him on the floor on his stomach and I'll make him toss his cookies."

"Hell, we haven't got time to fool with him, Mason."

"Let me try anyway."

Both of us pried him off the cot, rolled him on some papers, and Mason went to work with his fingers. In a second Wax was gagging and coughing, trying to push himself up, bleary eyes searching for his tormentors. I turned on a gas jet, put a pan of water over the flame and found instant coffee that I loaded into a chipped cup, and when it was hot enough, forced it down Wax's throat.

It was thirty minutes before he was alive enough to say, "What . . . the dickens you think . . . who you people?"

Money makes the loudest sound in the world. I let him see a fifty dollar bill in front of his eyes, feel it, then look up through a dreamy haze and nod. "I need information. You up to talking?"

Mason handed him another cup of steaming coffee and he drank half of it greedily, then made a face and looked around for a bottle. "Maybe . . . if I had a drink . . ."

"Talk first." I held Agrounsky's photo out in front of him. "Ever see this man?"

He leaned forward, glanced at it once, and nodded again. "Buys fish from me."

"Where does he live?"

His mouth gave a negative twist. "On the beach someplace . . . I guess. Never said. Hardly comes down. Saw him 'bout three, four times. Sick man."

"Do better than that, Wax. Where on the beach?"

This time he shook his head decisively. "Dunno. Maybe he camps like some do. Couple shacks there, few houses."

"But he's from the beach . . . you're sure?"

"Uh-huh."

"Why?"

Wax gave me a silly grin like I should know better and said, "Come in with sand spurs on his pants like the rest. No sand spurs this far in. Always droppin' the damn things where I step on 'em. He's from the beach. But not now. Nobody there now."

I didn't wait to argue. I nodded to Mason and we got back to the car and headed toward the ocean. Sometime in the last half hour the rain had let up and holes were showing in the clouds, big patches of incongruous blue against the dirty gray. The sandy road had drained quickly, the coquina base firm under the wheels. Barely visible were tracks partially filled with water, but the car that made them, having taken the center of the road, could have been going in either direction.

Somewhere above the cloud layer a flight of jets screamed by, cut out to sea, then circled back, challenging the thunder of the broken storm front.

The road began to bear to the left, then angled sharply and intersected a rutted strip that paralleled the beach. Once past it we would lose the cover of the tree line, so I braked, backed into an opening in the pine grove, and cut the engine. South of us we could see the boxlike shape of the beach houses perched on the dunes, abandoned now for the season.

Mason said, "How do you figure it?"

"Agrounsky could have bought one of those places from a summer resident. The transaction wouldn't have gotten any attention if he didn't use it often. My guess is he stocked it with groceries and equipment he needed and let it sit until he was ready to use it."

"Which one?"

"That we find out the hard way." We reached the end of the road and I looked at the line of poles running in both directions. "They're all power serviced. Any not being used will be shut off at the meters, so we'll see who's using juice. Don't you stick your neck out."

"Now you tell me."

The jets roared by again and somewhere the deep growl of thunder talked back to them. The hole in the sky overhead closed in menacingly and the soft blanket of rain moved in from the ocean like a heavy fog, cutting off sight of all but the first beach cottage.

Aside from the dunes there was little natural cover and we made use of every hillock and the weaving fronds of sea oats that crested them. The rain was a veil of protection, but an enemy in itself because it could work to shield another as well as us.

We reached the first house, checked it thoroughly, and satisfied it was unoccupied, started for the next one a hundred yards away. We stayed split up, separate targets if shot at, ready to build an effective crossfire if anybody showed.

It was Mason who spotted it first, a beat-up old pickup mired in the sand off the road where it had been forced after hitting a pothole, leaning into the trees and brush, obscured from any angle until you were right on it.

"He's here," Mason said.

I nodded. "Go see if any tracks lead from it. I'll hit the next house and keep going until there's a contact. If you spot anything, cut back to me and we'll take him together."

"Hell, Tiger . . ."

"Look, buddy, this is a pro. He's a killer, you're a flier. He's ready for anything and knows we're behind him. This is one guy you won't slip up on from a blind spot. He hasn't got any."

"So you're going in and . . ."

"I don't have any either. Now move on out."

He threw me a mock salute and grinned, then drifted off into the rain toward the car while I went back to the dunes. Two minutes later we had lost each other in the haze of rain, but up ahead in fuzzy outline was the squat shape of another weatherbeaten house that leaned a little to one side as if it were tired of it all.

I got to it, flattened against the side, and hugged my way around it looking for any indication of its having someone inside. The electric meter was silent and still, covered with fine sand, both doors partially ramped by drifts. Nobody had used the place for months.

For five minutes I scanned the area, trying to locate the thing that was wrong. Neither at the first place nor this had there been any tracks. For some reason Niger Hoppes had a definite direction in mind. Why? He had no more information than I had.

Then I saw it and cursed myself for being stupid. The poles bringing in the electric power had another service wire below them, one that hadn't cut off to the other house yet, a phone line. Louis Agrounsky wasn't there on a vacation. He was there for a reason and had provided for it. He was a man used to the immediate conveniences and would have installed a communication system without thinking twice about it.

I couldn't wait for Mason to show. I lowered my head against the rain, holding the .45 in my fist, the hammer back and my finger nestled against the trigger, running in ankle-keep sand as hard as I could, picking my way through the valleys in the dunes while I watched the faint threads between the poles that marked the power lines.

A full minute before I reached the last weary looking building that sat there on spindly pile legs I heard the crack of a shot that hung heavy and muffled on the air for a full second before losing itself in the rain. I tried to place its position, but it was impossible and there was no time to waste in locating it.

Around the house the sand dunes crept in away from the sea and I crawled face down behind their cover. I went as far as I could without exposing myself to direct fire from the house, ready to pull the trigger if there was any movement at all.

That was when I saw Mason. He was belly down in the sand, head twisted to one side, blood streaming from one side of his head. Somehow in falling he had rolled into a gully the wind had etched out behind a mound of clam shells and one hand moved feebly in an unconscious gesture.

But I couldn't go for him. Hoppes would be waiting for that. I'd be out in the open and he'd never miss. Not killing Mason was a deliberate act, designed to bring anyone else into view who might have been with him. He could afford to wait, not too long, but enough to make sure he could do what he came to do.

Niger Hoppes was thinking wrong. Sometimes you had to sacrifice somebody when the necessity was great enough. Mason was down where he wouldn't be hit again unless you stood almost over him from the front and he'd have to stay right there until I could get to him later.

If I could.

I inched backward into the vee of the dunes. Hoppes would have picked his position carefully, commanding the area that led to the house. I could see across the four-foot-high emptiness that was between the sand and the floor of the house and no dark splotches of a hidden figure behind the pilings were visible. The couple of steps that led off the front porch facing the ocean seemed unlikely because anyone there would have had a blind side.

He had to be in the dunes.

There was little necessity for being quiet, the sand giving off no telltale sounds, the rain and the dull roar of the surf not far off obscuring any small noises completely.

How many times had he done this? How many times had I?

Somewhere there was always a crossroad where you eventually met and only one would take the path leading away. No matter how good you were, there was always someone better. Both of us had beaten the leading contenders and now it was a playoff game to pick up the big prize. No factor would be left out of the winning potential.

I nearly hit the thread before seeing it and grinned at the trap. It wouldn't lead to him. It would trigger the movement of one of the sea oats in the sand and he'd know I'd be closing in and would be ready. Without touching it, I rolled over the fine strand, crawling toward the water. It wasn't the logical move. An approach through the dunes would have afforded greater protection, but it could put me there too fast. A man moving couldn't get ready as fast as one entrenched watching the approaches.

I came out of the dunes to the flats that angled into the breakers, then inched along the sharply rising slopes toward the house. A dozen timid sandpipers watched me curiously, never breaking their endless run and peck as they followed the surge of the breakers that tongued at the beach.

The house was close now, looming there, a silent witness of the ominous present, glass eyes gaping at the scene expressionlessly. I stopped long enough to study the topography, trying to choose the exact spot he would have picked for the ambush.

There was only one, a peculiarly shaped dune that seemed to have a dish-shaped back that covered all fields of fire and could hide a man completely from anyone making an assault. I could feel the rain against my teeth, wetting my lips with a malicious kiss of death, wishing me luck.

I started up the incline.

Above me the low flying gull wheeled suddenly and made a startled ninety degree turn toward the water, flapping in to land beside the sandpipers.

It was enough. The gull had seen him first.

That dune was a clever trap too. It was the spot I'd look for. There was only one other left.

The waiting was over. I ran.

He was half buried in a hollow he had dug for himself, secure in the knowledge that he controlled the action. He lay there balled up, the long nose of the pistol aimed to his right and the grin gave his face the appearance of a skull. *One hand held a Bezex inhaler screwed into a nostril.* At any other time he could have passed for any face in any crowd, but with the kill look of pleasure tightening every muscle in his body he was like all the others I had seen before, typed down to the hard glint in his narrow eyes, the thin, bloodless mouth stretched tight in anticipation, and that strange tensed relaxation of a pure killer, highlighted by the facial scar.

He had it too, that feeling for the *thing.* He knew I was there when I came over the rise, and even in the fraction of time that I had to study him he had done the same and I knew he saw the same expression on my face that he wore on his own. His twisting motion was like that of a cat, swinging the gun and firing as he rolled toward the cover of a dune.

There seemed to be no separation of the two blasts. Both merged into one gigantic slam that split the air with their combined fury and I felt a tug at my side just below the rib cage, a hot dart that went right through tissue and out into the misty air over the sands.

But that damn .45 caught him beautifully. It took the Magnum out of his hand and left a bleeding stump with two fingers missing for the sand crabs to eat later and as he looked up at me with wild, unbelieving eyes, I lowered the hammer on the rod and laid it down beside me.

He knew I wanted him with my hands and didn't wait. He came at me with a funny gait, blood streaming down his arm. I met him head on, knowing how he'd have the knife ready, grabbed his wrist when he lunged in a thrust that was intended to disembowel me and flipped him on his back with the shiny blade spinning out into the sand.

I expected him to go all the way. He should have been indoctrinated deeply enough to make the mission worth anything at all. He had been trained well and had perfected his technique through experience, always emerging the winner. The only thing he hadn't been trained for was losing and facing it was too much for him. He broke and ran with a hoarsely mouthed yell in his mouth, going up over the dunes to the beach, legs pumping with a frenzied motion that scattered the sandpipers away from their feeding.

I brought him down with a vicious rolling block across the back of his legs that snapped him into the wet sand, lost him momentarily when I went right over him and turned just in time to grab his foot in my hands as he tried to kick my face in. He was a madman now, eyes bulging, every action one of pure reflex, slashing at me with desperation, bringing into play every trick of judo or karate he had ever mastered.

None of it was enough. I parried his jab to my throat, broke his jaw with a right cross that made him reel drunkenly, then threw another that caught him on the other side and he went face down into four inches of water that came in with a breaker.

He knew what I did. He was conscious of it a long time before he gave up and died. He felt my foot on the back of his neck, keeping his face pressed into the shallows at the edge of the tide, and he clawed futilely through a froth of blood from the remains of his fingers at the weight that was killing him.

When the last great shudder went through him I left him there and went back to the front of the house. I found Mason, bandaged the great gash along the side of his head and propped him up. He'd be a long while unconscious, but would live. He was another of the lucky ones.

CHAPTER TWELVE

BEHIND THE GLASS, heavy wire mesh had been nailed to the window frames, white metal venetian blinds drawn shut in back of that. Both front and rear doors were studded with carriage bolt heads where the interiors had been reinforced with some heavier material. It had been enough to slow down the killer who knew a forced entry could trigger the man inside into some unpredictable action and he had preferred to wait until he could gain entry at his leisure.

I took the pick out, inserted one in the keyhole of the lock and tried it. The tumblers didn't budge. I went through four of them before getting a response from the mechanism. Then, by manipulating it easily, I forced the tumblers back one at a time.

Whoever had installed the chain hadn't done it right. Enough slack was there so I was able to slip it out of position with a business card from my wallet. It swung down, clinking there as I pushed the door open. Inside a radio was playing softly, crackling with static as the storm moved between it and the station broadcasting.

The .45 was in my hand again, ready. I stepped in, closed the door and let my eyes become adjusted to the gray dusk in the room, picking out pieces of furniture, searching for the one I wanted so badly.

From the corner where the radio played was the barely perceptible glow of a dial, its circular face bisected by the back of a chair that faced the ocean. The crook of an elbow jutted out over the arm as the motionless figure there sat watching the sea through the partially opened slats of the blinds.

He never heard me. I had kicked off my shoes and sidled around to the side, each step calculated to take me into position for a clean winging shot if I had to.

And then I could see him, the odd box in his lap that had a pair of minute glowing red lights set in its side. He never turned his head, simply sitting there with the cigarette-sized control in his left hand, his thumb poised over one of the two buttons in its top.

I aimed the .45 at his hand and said softly, "Louis . . ."

There was no reaction . . . no movement at all.

I took a step closer, ready for the slightest motion of his finger before I took his whole hand off. Only the slightest pressure now on the trigger would do it.

Sweat trickled down the center of my spine. Outside was the world. Here was its destruction.

"Louis Agrounsky," I said again. I was almost on top of him by now. I could see his eyes, wide open, the weird smile on his face as if he were watching the greatest show of his life.

I could see something else too.

He was dead.

The syringe was lying beside him, the needle jabbed into the cushion. The rest of his kit was on the table beside the radio, the three empty capsules, the spoon with the bent handle and the stub of a candle on a saucer. Louis Agrounsky had made a decision, all right. He finally had reached it. He had been ready to carry it out, whatever it was, and mainlined himself for the event and mainlined himself right into the big black with an overdose of the heroin he had craved so badly.

I didn't touch anything. That would be handled by the experts. I left him as he was, shoved the .45 back in the holster, the crazy relief turning my legs weak a second. I looked at my watch, saw the time and swore into the darkness.

The phone was on a side table and alive. I gave the operator the number of the apartment in New York and waited while it rang twice, then Rondine said simply, "Yes?"

"Tiger, kitten."

Her voice echoed the relief I had felt moments ago, then came back with the fright real and imperative. "Tiger . . . Oh! But . . . where are you?"

"I found him, baby. You can wrap the world up again. It's safe for a little while longer. You can come off it now."

"No! No, Tiger . . . listen. I found it . . . the letter Doug Hamilton mailed. He sent it to an old address of his deliberately, knowing it would be rerouted through all of his other forwarding addresses before it was returned to him. He wrote it all down and . . ."

"But it's finished, kid."

"Tiger . . . it's Camille Hunt!"

It was like having the wind blow out of the north and chill you to the bone.

"Camille?" I repeated tonelessly.

Her voice crackled in the phone. "This Henri Frank came to Belt-Aire supposedly to get a job, but what he was doing was making contact with Camille Hunt to tell her about Louis Agrounsky. Hamilton checked him out and found out he was an active Communist. Later he accidentally saw Camille and this Frank person together and suspected something, so he followed her to where she made contact with a man he described in detail . . . it was Vito Salvi. The address was right there. He mentioned he was going to investigate Salvi further to see what the connection was."

My voice sounded cold and far away. "Did he back it up with any evidence?"

"Henri Frank was from the Eau Gallie area and she made several trips there. He had photostats of the tickets enclosed in the letter."

It all wrapped up beautifully. Wait until Martin Grady found out he had personally recommended a Soviet agent and planted her in his own critical organization. What had been her background? The publications field—a great spot where a trained

operative could twist the printed word to meet the demands of
the slave state. And she was invited into a supersensitive industry
where she could be held in abeyance until the proper time came.
The only things that stymied the effectiveness of more direct
moves were the double checks put on everybody's activities by
government directive.

She'd have to be high in the organization, a liaison operative
who could call into operation the full forces lying in wait if the
grand moment came. And that it did. One man fell out of line
with a momentous scheme to crush the world his tortured mind
wouldn't let him accept any longer, and she was ready. She had
the cover identity of Helen Lewis prepared in advance as she
would have several others in key places, ready for immediate use.
She made sure of Agrounsky's aberration with personal contact.
She was trained to read people, analyze and judge them. It
wouldn't take much to alter her appearance . . . make-up on a
woman could make her almost anybody. When she was sure, the
trap was built. Total narcotics addiction for Agrounsky, curtailing
his supply, directing him to sources leading to New York where
they could buy his will and his knowledge with heroin and pick
his brains piece by piece.

"Camille Hunt," I murmured absently.

I never heard Rondine's reply because the voice behind me
said, "That's right, Tiger. I'm surprised you guessed. Put the
phone up, please." Her voice had a hoarse, nasal quality to it and
I stopped seeing her in the soft red glow of the heater, her flesh
white and lovely. Now it fitted the personality that was truly hers
—the spider in the web, poised and deadly, one appetite sated, another about to be satisfied.

Slowly I dropped the receiver back and turned around, knowing she'd have the gun in her hand, an efficient Belgium Brown-
ing hammerless automatic, and the hole in the muzzle was staring
directly into my eyes.

"You amaze me, Tiger. Where is . . . the other one?"

"I drowned him."

It didn't seem to shock her at all. "I see. He was warned."

"And he was ready. Just not ready enough."

"Not as ready as I am."

I nodded once. "How did you get here, Camille?"

"Money is something we find valuable too. There was a helicopter and a man willing to fly it here. If you're interested, it wasn't much of a task locating the right Leesville. It was only a matter of elimination and remembering a few things he mentioned. The ocean, for instance."

"Your luck's running high."

"This time. There was a break in the clouds. We . . . landed not far from here." She smiled at me, but there was no humor in the twist of her mouth at all. "Your friendly aircraft cooperated nicely with all their noise."

"The pilot?" I asked her.

She shrugged indifferently.

"He went like Doug Hamilton," I suggested.

"Fortunately for him, much quicker."

"Why Doug at all?"

She glared at me then, her eyes partially bloodshot and filled with hate. "That one knew too much. But he talked. Vito Salvi made sure he talked." She stopped and frowned. "But he may have been lying. He said there was a report on me in his personal file. Oh, there was one, but simply a routine check."

"He had another," I said. "It turned up."

"It doesn't really matter now."

I went to ask her something else but she shook her head. Quickly, her eyes roved through the room, caught sight of the figure in the chair and didn't have to be given any explanations. "No, Tiger, talk is needless. I don't want to be distracted by anything from doing . . . this." The gun made a small up and down motion, never leaving a vital area of my body.

One way or another I was going to have to take her. I'd never make it . . . the distance was too great between us. She'd get that single shot in and it would be enough, but I was going to have to make the try. It would have to be a fast draw from a bad position, the only chance I had.

Camille read my mind and said, "There's a lamp on the table beside you. Light it. Only your hand moves and very, very slowly."

So I lit the scene for my own death. Very, very slowly.

"Now your gun, Tiger. Just pick it out with your fingers and drop it. It means a few seconds more you can live and think."

I felt for the gun, half turning, then realized that it was no use at all. The hole in my side from Hoppes' .22 Magnum had numbed half my body and any motion at all sent a violent shiver of blinding pain right into my brain. I let the gun hit the floor and stay there.

"Now empty your pockets. Everything. Turn them inside out so I can see them. I've heard of the devices you have used, Tiger. They are methods we use ourselves and I don't want any used against me."

One by one I turned my pockets out and dumped their contents on the table top. She was going to be disappointed. A wallet, spare clips, change, a ring of picklocks, and a gimmick that was totally useless now, the Bezex inhaler that had been designed for Niger Hoppes.

Her eyes went up in mock astonishment.

I said, "Why delay, Camille?"

She smiled again, her watery eyes even more like a spider's than ever behind the cold that had her in its grip. "I told you once. I enjoy studying people. I'm interested in their reactions. The dossier the committee has on you is so thick, the record of your actions so impressive that I want to see what you are like when you know you are the one dying."

"I've faced it before."

"Ah, but this time *you can be sure!*" she rasped at me. "Move back, one step at a time. Stay in the middle of the room."

I did as she told me to. If I went near anything I could throw she wouldn't wait. I'd die on the spot, and as she said, each moment was one for living and thinking.

She reached the table where I had been, the gun telling me to stop where I was. From there she had a clear view of the body of Louis Agrounsky, confirming all she thought. She could see the red dots of the control unit and knew it was operative. Later her own technicians could examine it and make use of its deadly potential.

"Why didn't you move in on him faster, Camille?"

She coughed quietly and blinked, then said candidly, "Simply because we didn't know the secret of the by-pass control. He had it well hidden. Perhaps even booby trapped. We needed the whole unit. We had hoped to get Agrounsky too, but I doubt if he'll be missed now. Our engineers will know what to do, I assure you."

"We'll all be dead. You know that, don't you?"

She shook her head, still smiling. "Only you for now. The rest we will control nicely. They will learn how to serve the state and there will be very little protest. After all, we've had a great deal of experience with what you people like to term 'captive nations.' This country will be no different."

Camille held the gun in her left hand, the other idly toying with the things I had dumped on the table. I had to force myself to keep my eyes steady where they were, just looking at her and not about to plead or beg. She would have liked that. It would have made what she was planning even more enjoyable. She would have gloried in the spider role even more than ever.

She frowned, eyes squinting, wrinkling her nose against a sneeze, and fought it back. In a way it was even funny. "I've suffered because of you, Tiger, but it helped me weave a stronger web than ever."

"Tough."

"You thought it couldn't be done. I was right in the first place . . . you are a fly. A typical fly lured into a web and dying at the greatest moment of pleasure, isn't that so?"

"Is it?"

She frowned again and breathed in hard, the air making a small whistling sound in her nostrils and her eyes showed the annoyance she felt. Only for a second did she look away, then picked up the inhaler and unscrewed the cap. She held it with a derisive gesture and said, "Thank you, fly . . . before you die, my thanks."

And she breathed in to clear her head, one side first, then moved to the other and her hand stopped midway and for one long second her eyes seemed to clear and widen as the deadly cyanide gas she had activated by the simple motion of removing the cap flooded her lungs, and she knew she had lost it because she pulled the trigger of the automatic, only by then it was pointed at the floor and she went down to join the one outside in the great lonely cave of death.

She was dead when I reached her and she never heard me say, "I told you I was the mud-dauber type, spider."

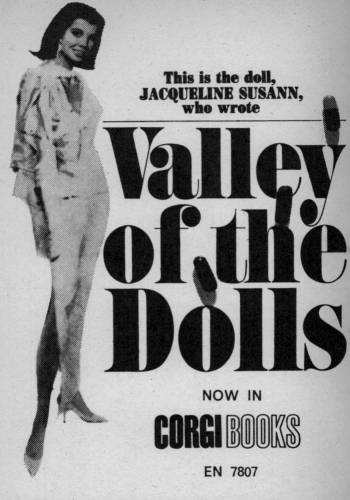

This is the doll,
JACQUELINE SUSANN,
who wrote

Valley of the Dolls

NOW IN

CORGI BOOKS

EN 7807

**THE-WORLD'S-FASTEST-BIGGEST-SELLING-PAPERBACK
OVER 7,000,000 COPIES SOLD.**

A SELECTION OF FINE READING AVAILABLE IN CORGI BOOKS

NOVELS

☐	FN7763	ANOTHER COUNTRY	*James Baldwin*	5/–
☐	FN7637	NINA'S BOOK	*Eugene Burdick*	5/–
☐	FN7317	THE CHINESE ROOM	*Vivian Connell*	5/–
☐	FN7777	THE WAR BABIES	*Gwen Davies*	5/–
☐	FN1278	THE GINGER MAN	*J. P. Donleavy*	5/–
☐	EN7488	BOYS AND GIRLS TOGETHER	*William Goldman*	7/6
☐	FN1500	CATCH-22	*Joseph Heller*	5/–
☐	FN7656	PINKTOES	*Chester Himes*	5/–
☐	EN7193	MOTHERS AND DAUGHTERS	*Evan Hunter*	7/6
☐	GN7774	THE MOGUL MEN	*Peter Leslie*	3/6
☐	FN7824	BLESS THIS HOUSE	*Norah Lofts*	5/–
☐	FN7779	THE DEER PARK	*Norman Mailer*	5/–
☐	FN7301	WEEP NOT, MY WANTON	*Nan Maynard*	5/–
☐	DN7594	HAWAII (colour illus.)	*James A. Michener*	10/6
☐	CN7500	THE SOURCE	*James A. Michener*	12/6
☐	FN7748	TALES OF THE SOUTH PACIFIC	*James A. Michener*	5/–
☐	GN7727	THAT COLD DAY IN THE PARK	*Richard Miles*	3/6
☐	FN7322	UNTAMED	*Helga Moray*	5/–
☐	EN7823	THOMAS	*Shelley Mydans*	7/6
☐	FN1066	LOLITA	*Vladimir Nabokov*	5/–
☐	FN7684	ELIZABETH APPLETON	*John O'Hara*	5/–
☐	FN7766	APPOINTMENT IN SAMARRA	*John O'Hara*	5/–
☐	FN1162	A STONE FOR DANNY FISHER	*Harold Robbins*	5/–
☐	EN7655	THE HONEY BADGER	*Robert Ruark*	7/6
☐	FN7670	HOW I WON THE WAR	*Patrick Ryan*	5/–
☐	EN7578	THE DEVIL IN BUCK'S COUNTY	*Edmund Schiddel*	7/6
☐	EN7567	THE DEVIL'S SUMMER	*Edmund Schiddel*	7/6
☐	FN7808	MOUNTAIN OF WINTER	*Shirley Schoonover*	5/–
☐	GN7810	THE PASTURES OF HEAVEN	*John Steinbeck*	3/6
☐	GN7600	THE RUNNING FOXES	*Joyce Stranger*	3/6
☐	EN7807	VALLEY OF THE DOLLS	*Jacqueline Susann*	7/6
☐	FN1133	THE CARETAKERS	*Dariel Telfer*	5/–
☐	EN7352	EXODUS	*Leon Uris*	7/6
☐	FN7116	FOREVER AMBER Vol. I	*Kathleen Winsor*	5/–
☐	FN7117	FOREVER AMBER Vol. II	*Kathleen Winsor*	5/–
☐	EN7790	THE BEFORE MIDNIGHT SCHOLAR	*Li Yu*	7/6

WAR

☐	FB7813	THE VALLEY OF HANOI	*Irwin R. Blacker*	5/–
☐	EB7829	THE WAR LOVER	*John Hersey*	7/6
☐	FB7735	THE PAINTED BIRD	*Jerzy Kosinski*	5/–
☐	FB7795	I SHALL FEAR NO EVIL	*R. J. Minney*	5/–
☐	FB7782	TO HELL AND BACK	*Audie Murphy*	5/–
☐	EN7726	THE DIRTY DOZEN	*E. M. Nathanson*	7/6
☐	FB7476	THE SCOURGE OF THE SWASTIKA (illustrated)	*Lord Russell of Liverpool*	5/–
☐	FB7477	THE KNIGHTS OF BUSHIDO (illus.)	*Lord Russell of Liverpool*	5/–
☐	FB7703	THE DEATHMAKERS	*Glen Sire*	5/–
☐	GB7830	THE ANGRY HILLS	*Leon Uris*	3/6
☐	FB7752	THE ENEMY	*Wirt Williams*	5/–

ROMANCE

☐	GR7835	A FEW DAYS IN ENDEL	*Diana Gordon*	3/6
☐	GR7802	A NOURISHING LIFE	*Kate Norway*	3/6
☐	GR7817	THE LOOM OF TANCRED	*Diane Pearson*	3/6
☐	GR7818	THERE BUT FOR FORTUNE	*Alex Stuart*	3/6

SCIENCE FICTION

☐	GS7742	THE HALO HIGHWAY (The Invaders)	*Rafe Bernard*	3/6
☐	GS7654	FAHRENHEIT 451	*Ray Bradbury*	3/6
☐	GS7803	NEW WRITINGS IN S.F.11	*John Carnell*	3/6
☐	GS7819	THE LOST PERCEPTION	*Daniel F. Galouye*	3/6
☐	GS7788	THE DARK SIDE	*Damon Knight*	3/6
☐	GS7836	THE METEOR MEN	*Anthony LeBaron*	3/6
☐	ES7682	THE SHAPE OF THINGS TO COME	*H. G. Wells*	7/6

GENERAL

☐	FG7704	THE VIRILITY DIET	*Dr. George Belham*	5/–
☐	LG7566	SEXUAL LIFE IN ENGLAND	*Dr. Ivan Bloch*	9/6
☐	GC7382	THE BRIDAL BED	*Joseph Braddock*	3/6
☐	GG7296	KNOW YOURSELF	*Dr. Eustace Chesser*	3/6
☐	FG7593	UNMARRIED LOVE	*Dr. Eustace Chesser*	5/–
☐	KG7633	THE NEW LONDON SPY	*edited by Hunter Davies*	10/–
☐	6000	BARBARELLA (illustrated)	*Jean Claude Forest*	30/–
☐	EG7804	THE BIRTH CONTROLLERS	*Peter Fryer*	7/6
☐	CG7400	MY LIFE AND LOVES	*Frank Harris*	12/6
☐	HG7745	COWBOY KATE (illustrated)	*Sam Haskins*	21/–
☐	FG1541	MAN AND SEX	*Kaufman and Borgeson*	5/–
☐	FG7652	CHAPTERS OF LIFE (illustrated)	*T. Lobsang Rampa*	5/–
☐	FG7760	THE PASSOVER PLOT	*Hugh J. Schonfield*	5/–

WESTERNS

☐	GW7834	TORTURE TRAIL	*Max Brand*	3/6
☐	GW7801	THE SEVEN OF DIAMONDS	*Max Brand*	3/6
☐	GW7756	SUDDEN – TROUBLESHOOTER	*Frederick H. Christian*	3/6
☐	GW7840	THE REBEL SPY	*J. T. Edson*	3/6
☐	GW7841	THE BAD BUNCH	*J. T. Edson*	3/6
☐	GW7800	CAPTIVES OF THE DESERT	*Zane Grey*	3/6
☐	GW7816	STAIRS OF SAND	*Zane Grey*	3/6
☐	FW7746	THE WAY WEST	*A. B. Guthrie*	5/–
☐	GW7653	MACKENNA'S GOLD	*Will Henry*	3/6
☐	FW7757	THE GATES OF THE MOUNTAIN	*Will Henry*	5/–
☐	GW7815	MATAGORDA	*Louis L'Amour*	3/6
☐	GW7739	BONANZA: ONE MAN WITH COURAGE	*Thomas Thompson*	3/6

CRIME

☐	FC7786	THE MEANING OF MURDER	*John Brophy*	5/–
☐	GC7797	DEAD SILENCE	*Jean Bruce*	3/6
☐	GC7833	DOUBLE TAKE	*Jean Bruce*	3/6
☐	GC7623	DEADFALL	*Desmond Cory*	3/6
☐	GC7755	A TASTE OF TREASURE	*John Creasey*	3/6
☐	GC7798	TERROR BY DAY	*John Creasey*	3/6
☐	GC7832	AN AXE TO GRIND	*A. A. Fair*	3/6
☐	GC7716	AMBER NINE	*John Gardner*	3/6
☐	GC7224	THE LIQUIDATOR	*John Gardner*	3/6
☐	GC7677	DIE RICH, DIE HAPPY	*James Munro*	3/6
☐	GC7814	THE TRAIL OF FU MANCHU	*Sax Rohmer*	3/6
☐	GC7753	THE TWISTED THING	*Mickey Spillane*	3/6
☐	GC7831	THE BY-PASS CONTROL	*Mickey Spillane*	3/6

*All these great books are available at your local bookshop or newsagent;
or can be ordered direct from the publisher. Just tick the titles you want
and fill in the form below.*

CORGI BOOKS, Cash Sales Dept., Bashley Road, London, N.W.10.
Please send cheque or postal order. No currency, PLEASE. Allow 6d.
per book to cover the cost of postage on orders of less than 6 books.

NAME ....

ADDRESS ....

(FEB.68) ....